DARK REFLECTIONS

DARK REFLECTIONS

The Phantom Series Book 2

LAURA C. REDEN

CONTENTS

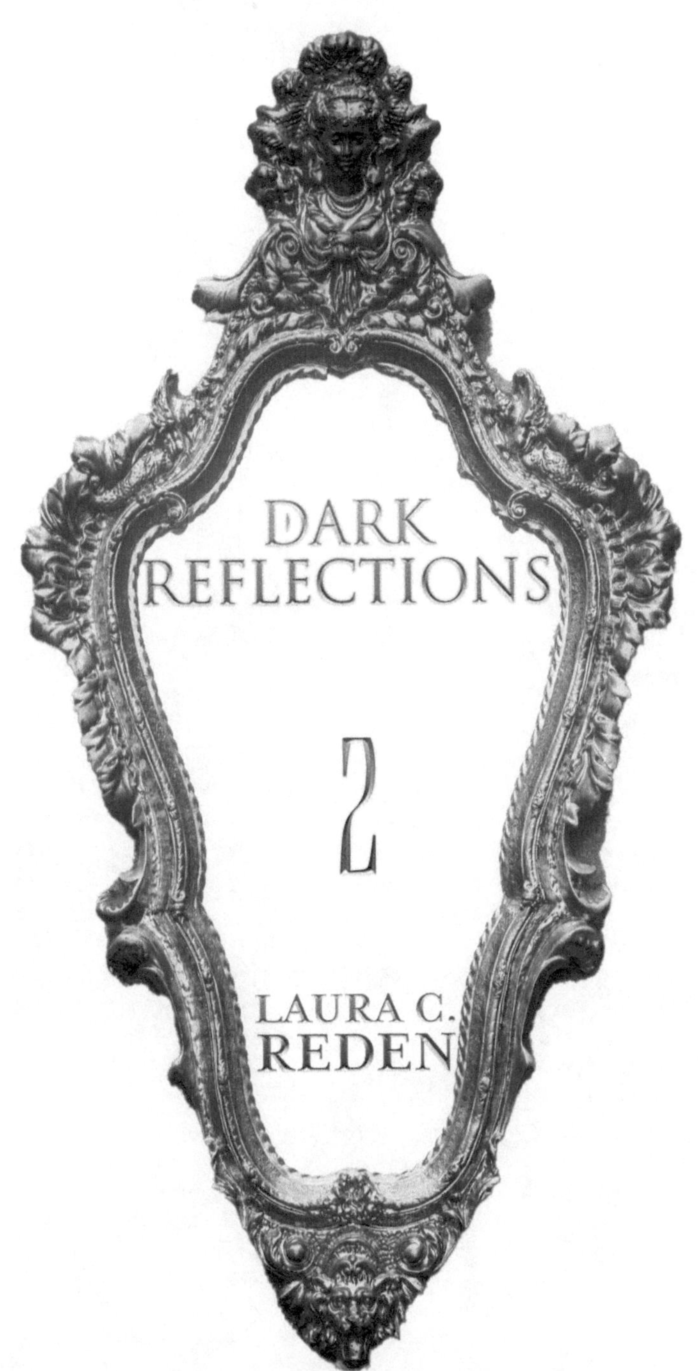
DARK
REFLECTIONS

2

LAURA C.
REDEN

We stared out the broken wall of the tower, listening to the Water's Edge Concert, watching the spotlights rotate in the otherwise black sky, and trying to understand this world we found ourselves in. When the night chill rolled in, I didn't feel it.

"I'm . . . I've—" My mouth moved, but the thoughts were too tiny and scattered to come together and form a sentence. I rotated Layla's old silver compact in my hand.

"You're like me," Walker said. His golden gaze had dimmed to black under the night sky.

"Dead?" I asked.

Walker scanned my face and then nodded.

As I watched the searching spotlights of the concert, I recalled the plane crash. The light from the explosion of impact. The heat funneled up the cabin of the plane, disintegrating everyone on board. Including me. I never should have gotten on that plane . . .

"I remember. It was terrifying—" I stared unblinking at the pine trees, my eyes drying out and then overcompensating by watering. Walker listened to me patiently while I told him my story.

"I was upset with myself. I wanted to get off the plane. And the more I thought about being an awful friend . . . letting my gran down . . . Lainey and Emma . . . you . . ." I stole a glimpse of the compact, turning it over in my hands. Did I dare face my reflection? I wasn't sure what I looked like dead. "The more disappointed I got with myself, the more the turbulence shook the plane. And when I got angry, that's when the lightning struck." The country music faded away, and I blinked several times to keep the tears from pooling.

"I did this. I ran right into the hands of death. And I brought all those passengers down with me . . ." The tears streamed silently down my cheeks, and my heart constricted so tightly, I could no longer talk.

"Think . . . think back. To an earlier time," Walker said wearily. I looked at him, not understanding. His brows pulled together, pained, and his now black eyes shone with the moonlight.

"What?" I could barely hear him. The voice in my head was much too loud.

Walker sighed. "You didn't die in the plane crash."

I froze still. His quiet voice now piercing. My eyes darted around, searching for clues. "Well—then . . . when?" Was it when the thing chased me in the woods?

"The night we met," Walker said, his voice a whisper and his head tilted. He continued to speak, but this time, his voice faded just like the music in the distance had. A high-pitched tone rang in my ears, and I grew faint. Weak in the knees. I dared to open the compact but couldn't bring myself to look within.

I don't remember Walker taking me home that night, and I don't remember when the concert ended. I had been swallowed whole and caught in the throat of the night. I hadn't existed this entire summer . . .

I sat on the back patio as dawn broke. I had no answers, and I knew it would take a lot more than just one sleepless night to wrap my head around this reality. *My* reality. I watched as the sky lightened from deep hues of navy to lilac. My favorite was when the warmth of the orange broke through, illuminating the fog-covered lake below. I listened to the loons calling into the mist, and I wondered if they were haunting me or if it was the other way around.

My friends lay sleeping in the cabin behind me. Had I been haunting them all summer?

When my grandma had died, I had nothing but sadness for her. For me. I had worried about what my life would be like without her, but never once had I imagined what it would be like for her. To be a ghost.

And yet, here I was. Living the dead life. This wasn't how it was supposed to be. This was supposed to be the best summer ever. And now, I wasn't even alive for it.

I had just tagged alongside the living, unaware that I was in a separate realm. Thinking I'd been alive for the past several weeks. It was a strange deception. One I was sure that I'd never fully understand.

I felt many things about being dead, but being lonely wasn't one of them. I had Walker, and he understood far more than I ever did. Although, being trapped in the afterlife with the most beautiful guy I'd ever known and not being able to penetrate his heart seemed like some sort of personal hell. I was kind of okay with it. Maybe I wouldn't be in the future, but for right now, I was taking what I could get. And if that meant just friendship, I was all right with that. And oddly enough, I still had all my friends too. Apart from Trinity, that is. Did they know that I was different?

Even though loneliness wasn't an issue here, it didn't mean I wasn't disappointed. I had thought my afterlife would be filled with bright, shiny things. Glorious warmth, wings, and the potential to fly. Maybe I'd be able to eat as much chocolate and ice cream as I wanted and never gain a single ounce, or I could bounce from place to place at the snap of my fingers. At the very least, I expected there to be *available* guys. Needless to say, this wasn't how I imagined I'd spend eternity. Harboring a secret as outrageous as this one seemed impossible. I didn't know how Walker did it, but I would have to ask . . . Learn. I had a lot to learn.

The lake scintillated as the fog burned up and the sun rose into the sky. I was partially hypnotized by the sparkling water that held the secrets I desperately needed to uncover, but something was drawing my attention to my neighbor's yard. Mrs. Vandal had been gardening since it was dark out. And even though I had a lot more pressing issues hurtling through my mind, I couldn't help but wonder what was so pressing in her garden that she needed to tend to before daybreak. Every now and then, I'd watch and wait, but I'd always see the same old thing. A woman who couldn't sleep and spent her time gardening. Maybe she was running from something. A bad marriage, perhaps? I knew her husband could be a little weird. Even more so since I had died. Maybe he could tell. Maybe they all could, and nobody wanted to tell me. Walker certainly hadn't.

I'd been staring out at the horizon all night. I watched it even when I couldn't see through the black sky. Yet, I still knew it was there, just beyond the shadows. It reminded me of the ghost of my gran and all the times I'd known she was there, even though I couldn't see her. My eyes were dry and weary, my soul anything but content. I jumped when the door opened behind me and Gunner rushed to my side. I jumped forward, hands spread in the air.

"You're up early," Lainey said in a groggy morning

voice, careful not to wake the others. She was already dressed, ready for a hike. The leash dangled from her hand, and Gunner knew. He pranced like he was on hot coals.

"Yeah, I couldn't sleep last night." I pulled my hoodie closed and mindlessly ran a hand through my hair. She was looking right at me. How could she not know?

"Have you been up all night?" she asked, coming to my side.

I shrugged apologetically.

"Oh wow! You look like death!"

A brick dropped in my stomach, landing with a thud. I winced. *Death? So, she knew?* "I do?" I asked, leaning forward, an arm wrapped around my waist.

"Yeah! You've got the worst bags under your eyes right now!" Lainey's eyes were bright, and she worked to hide the smile bunching in her cheeks.

Bags? I could deal with bags. As long as she couldn't see deeper. Past the sleepless skin that I wore so well. As long as she couldn't see that I was an outsider, that I was pretending to have a heartbeat, I could deal with that. I was used to looking like hell anyway—just not living in it.

"I'm sure I do," I said, rubbing at my eyes.

"Do you want to take Gunner on a hike with me?" she asked.

"Can I take a rain check? I'm really not feeling up to it."

"Sure, no problem. Is everything okay?" Lainey asked while leaning against the deck's banister.

How was I supposed to answer that? Lainey was one of my best friends, and I wasn't used to keeping secrets from her. But this was more than a secret. This was a way of life. Or more like . . . a way of death. I wasn't sure she would handle it well if I told her that I'd died nearly a month ago. Emma? Maybe. But Lainey? Lainey was of a holistic nature. Loved anything plants, animals, and nature. But I wasn't sure she could handle the supernatural. And that's what I was, right?

"I'm fine. Just have a lot on my mind, I guess." It wasn't a complete lie. I *did* have a lot on my mind. An unbearable amount.

"Is it your gran?" she asked. Lainey's head tilted to the side and her brows creased with empathy.

"Yeah . . ." I shrugged. My gran *was* part of it. She'd been visiting me in my afterlife. Maybe that's why I could see her and hear her. We were on the same plane.

"I know it's hard, but one day, you'll see her again. She's probably up there now, smiling down at you. She's probably so proud of you, going to college and everything."

I felt like a terrible person for drowning Lainey out. She meant well; she really did. But hearing about how my gran was *up there* . . . Up where? She was right here. And I was too. And nothing had changed. Except for the random glitches in reality. The stuff that didn't make sense but should have. No, my gran wasn't dressed in white, adorned with angel wings, and sipping champagne. She was reading fairy tales and murder mysteries. She was sitting by a fire that failed to heat the frigid air. And she was haunting my afterlife to no avail.

Mrs. Vandal had finished bagging her clippings and started the long haul to the trashcan in her front yard. Only her clippings looked abnormally heavy and oddly shaped. I strained my back, trying to get a better view.

"Do you see that?" I asked Lainey. Lainey whipped her head to the neighbor's house, and she straightened her back to get a better look. Her brows rose, and her face shifted from curiosity to bewilderment in the blink of an eye.

"If I didn't know any better, I'd say she was dragging a body to the trash," Lainey said from the side of her mouth. That's exactly what it looked like. It looked like a body in that bag. Long and slender, bulbous at one end, and sharp at the other.

"Right . . ." I watched Mrs. Vandal throw all of her weight into dragging the bag ever so slowly crossed her lawn.

"What are you guys staring at? Oh shit! Did they kill somebody?" Mason laughed.

"It sure looks like it," Lainey said. And then, as if it were nothing, Mason, Kai, and Levi, joined us on the back patio, making jokes about the neighbor.

"Guess her husband couldn't get it up last night," Levi said.

"It's all fun and games until you're taken out with the trash," Mason replied.

"Well, this has been fun, but Gunner has waited long enough. Are you sure you don't want to come?" Lainey asked, giving me a look that said, *anything is better than hanging out with these fools.* Gunner jumped to all fours, his tail slapping me in the shins.

"I'm going to skip this time, but thank you."

"I'll go with you?" Levi said.

"What! You can't go hiking! We have to sign up for the fishing tournament!" Mason said.

"Can't you just write my name down?" Levi asked. Lainey waited for the guys to decide while Gunner spun in circles.

"Whatever! It's going to be bad luck if you don't sign yourself up. You better bring your fishing game for that tournament!" Mason said.

"Don't worry about that! There's no way those three are going to beat us in the tournament. Asher has never even been fishing a day in his life," Levi said.

"So, you guys are entering the Baylor Bass Tournament?" I asked Mason.

"Oh yeah! Levi, Kai, and I are gonna whoop their asses. Asher, Noah, and Ethan don't stand a chance."

"Just so you know, I've fished with Noah before, and

he's pretty good. Luck kind of just follows him on the water," I said, still wrapped tightly in my hoodie from my pensive night. *Do they think I'm alive?*

"Noah? What? He doesn't fish. You think we need to worry about him?" Kai said, laughing. The boys took it upon themselves to throw Noah under the bus. And if I hadn't been dead, maybe I would have been amused.

"Was Noah lucky when Sherry Miller spilled her hot chocolate on him right before senior pictures?" Kai asked.

"Or when he was the only one benched for ditching?" Mason said, backhanding Kai's chest.

"They just had to make an example out of somebody . . ." I said, but it fell on deaf ears as they dug into Noah's luck with the ladies. Things I didn't want to think about and certainly didn't want to picture in my mind. It was my cue to leave. I took a deep breath before prying my bones off the chair I'd been glued to for the whole mind-numbing night. My back ached, and I had to work hard to stand up straight as the pain crawled down my spine. *Why did I still feel pain?*

"What's wrong, Wilde? Too much for you?" Mason called out. I waved my hand over my shoulder, too tired to chime in. It didn't matter anyway. None of it did.

I passed the others making breakfast in the kitchen, but I didn't pay them any attention. They looked at me with alarmed eyes and I knew it was because I looked like . . . death. I could feel where my eyes had sunken in, and I didn't know if it was because I'd stayed up all night or if the worry had finally taken its toll on me, but I was pretty sure that I looked on the outside how I felt on the inside. Without bothering to brush my teeth, I crawled straight into bed. I pulled the blankets over my head, but my eyes refused to give up their fight.

I must have lain there in a catatonic state for several hours before Lainey and Emma came bounding into the bedroom, loud and boisterous.

"Hey, Kins! Oh—is she sleeping?"

I threw the blanket off my head, tearing out of the self-made cocoon. "No," I groaned.

"No, she's not," Emma echoed as she sat on the edge of the bed.

"Well, not anymore," Lainey said as she took a seat. They looked at me, and an uncomfortable silence spread throughout the room as their eyes scanned my face. "You really need some sleep. We can come back?" Lainey asked.

"You look like shit!" Emma said.

I threw my arms up in the air. "I can't sleep! I'm having an existential crisis, you guys!" My eyes burned as tears began to form. If my friends had looked uncomfortable at seeing the shadows under my eyes, they were even more uncomfortable now.

"It's okay. It's okay. What's the matter?" Emma asked, her mouth gaping open.

"I don't even know where to start . . ." How could I?

"Just start from the beginning," Lainey said.

So simple.

I looked at them in all seriousness, and I said it. "I think I'm dead." And then, I gazed into the two sets of empty eyes, waiting for their response. Maybe it was so far-fetched that they never comprehended it. Or perhaps they never heard me. But all they could do was look at me with giant black pupils that threatened to swallow me whole. "Did you hear me?" I asked, my voice rising.

"I feel that way too sometimes." Emma nodded.

"You're just in a funk. I've got an idea to snap you out of it, though," Lainey said.

Snap me out of it? Were they going to snap me back to life? This was unbelievable. Walker would never say that to me. He understood. He was of like mind, and it was clear that these two were not. My confession had traveled right over their heads. I sighed. It was probably best if they didn't know the truth. Not like I had a choice in the matter. They clearly didn't want to accept what I told them anyway. I played along. A slow, painful dance between the three of us.

"And what's that?" I asked through tight lips.

"Well, you know how every year I volunteer to work on the Fourth of July floats in Decord City?" Lainey asked. It was true; she volunteered every year. She'd been doing it since she was a little girl. Lainey loved everything botanical. She was a nature-loving creature, and she adored everything from plants to animals. If it was under Mother Nature's umbrella, Lainey was in love. Getting to glue live flowers to a float was like her dream come true. She was able to volunteer, but in all honesty, she would've paid to do it.

"Yeah, I remember."

"I just found out that I can volunteer here for the Fourth of July Baylor Parade!" Lainey said with a big, toothy grin.

"That's great, Lainey. I'm sure you were worried about missing that this summer." I could barely look at her. My mental state had been snuffed like a candle. And now we were talking about flowers . . .

"And that's not all! I signed you guys up to help too. We can get coffees, volunteer, and make a whole day out of it! There's no way it won't cure this little funk you're in. I promise," Lainey said.

I tried to smile, but I knew my eyes didn't twinkle the same as Lainey's had. I agreed, and Emma did too. But there was something in Emma's expression that also lacked luster. If I had to guess, I'd almost say she looked worried. Was she worried about spending her precious summer behind a glue gun? Or had she heard me when I said I died? *Really* heard me?

CHAPTER 2

It was early the next morning when Gunner's barking had become so excessive that I could no longer lie in bed pretending to sleep. But no sooner than I was dressed and rushing down the stairs to find the spritely dog, there was a knock at the front door. I glanced around the cabin, wondering how I was the only person awakened by the non-stop barking. Not even Lainey had woken up to tend to her own dog.

I opened the door to find a man dressed in khakis and a polo shirt with a patch that resembled a police badge. "Hello, I'm looking for a Miss Kinsley Wilde," he said. I folded my arms across my chest. It was too early to be in trouble.

"Who's asking?"

"My name is Carl Stevens. I'm with Baylor Animal Control. I had a call about your dog this morning by an unnamed neighbor of yours—" Carl stopped himself right there. His eyes rolled back in his head before shutting them all together. I only had one neighbor. The Vandals' cabin was the only cabin in Rock Creek Cove apart from ours. I couldn't understand why she wouldn't have just called me before calling Animal Control. It seemed uncharacteristic of her, but then again, they'd always been on the odd side.

"I'm Kinsley. What's the problem?" I asked.

"Well, it seems your dog has been barking non-stop since . . . since 5:23 a.m.," Carl said, flipping through his miniature notepad.

A creak on the stairs told me that Lainey had finally woken. "Lain—" I began. But it was only Emma. "Emma, can you get Lainey for me?" I asked.

"She's not upstairs. I figured she was with Gunner. Why is he barking so much?" Emma asked. I sighed. That was the question.

"Look, Carl, I'm sorry you got called out here. I'll talk to the *anonymous* neighbor and apologize. Honestly, I don't know what's gotten into the dog. He's not mine; he belongs to my friend. But the longer I stand here talking to you, the longer the dog will continue to bark. So, if you'll excuse me, I'm going to tend to the barking now," I said, passing by Carl and his notepad and shutting the door behind me.

I ignored the officer's grumbling disapproval as I ventured out the front and around the back of the cabin in search of Gunner. I found him easily by following the constant barking, which bounced throughout the clearing in the cove. He stood rigid, facing the dock, his bark as consistent as a leaky faucet. Drip by drip, he called out. It was so unlike him, and it was so unlike Lainey not to have shown up. The closer I got to the dog, the more I wondered where she was.

"Gunner? Gunner?" I patted my legs as I called his name. His ears perked but nothing more. He wouldn't pry his eyes off the dark water. I approached him slowly for fear of his uncharacteristic behavior.

Gunner wasn't just a good dog; he was an exceptional dog. Lainey had always had trouble with anxiety, and her mother had gotten Gunner for her as a kind of service dog. He served as her emotional support dog, and Lainey took him everywhere. But Lainey's mother was far more anxious than Lainey had ever been, and sometimes I wondered if the dog was really to help keep her anxiety at bay rather than Lainey's. Either way, when her mother said she could only come to the cabin for the summer if she brought the dog, we were more than thrilled to have the extra mouth to feed. We all loved Gunner, and I felt I knew him well, but at this moment, as we stood on the edge of the dock, I felt like I didn't know him at all.

The hair on his back stood rigid, and his bark had begun to turn hoarse. With every step I took closer to him, I found myself less afraid of him biting me and more fearful of what I might find in the water. What was he trying to tell me? For a moment, a reflection of a girl staring back at me with fearful eyes startled me. It was my face, of course, as I looked into the water. But my heart galloped in my chest at the thought of seeing one of the Baylor Butcher's victims seeking help from the depths below. I rested my heavy hand on Gunner's back and he snapped out of his methodical barking. He turned to me with a wagging tail and a whimper.

"What are you doing out here, boy?" I asked, scratching behind his ear. I turned to see Carl with his hand on his hip. He slowly picked up his notepad and jotted down something before turning away. My eyes wandered across the way to the Vandals' house, and I thought I saw a window shade ripple in one of the back bedrooms.

After securing Gunner inside the cabin, I conducted a thorough search for Lainey. But she was nowhere inside. I called her cell phone, but she never picked up. "Did she answer you?" I asked Emma as she typed away on her own phone.

"No, nothing," she said.

"I bet she took Gunner for a hike this morning, and he got loose. She's probably out there now, looking for him." I shook my head as I turned away, searching for my shoes.

"Are you going to go look for her?" Emma asked.

"Yeah, do you want to come? She'll be out there all day if she can't find him." I stomped my heel into my shoe.

"Yeah, I'll come. Just give me one sec."

It didn't take long for me and Emma to hit the trail. The sun was still rising, and it was quite cold in the shadows. I didn't expect it when Emma brought up my comment from the other day. And my sudden burst of regret surprised me.

"So, you said something the other day that caught my attention. You said you had died . . . but . . . what did you mean by that?" she asked. I felt a sickening twist in my stomach. I never should've said anything. It was so ridiculous, the thought of talking about it made me even more unsure of myself. If I could just look for Lainey. If I could only have one focus, then maybe I could do this. But to look for Lainey and look for Layla Barns and not disappoint my grandmother and worry about my existence all at the same time was far too much.

"I didn't mean it. Not like that. I just meant, I *felt* dead inside." I felt the stress knit my brows together, and I looked away so Emma could no longer see my face as I lied to her.

"That's fine. You can blame it on depression or whatever you want. But just so you know . . . I know what you really meant." Emma's voice was small and quiet but was never mistaken for weakness.

My mouth ran dry, and I didn't know why, but I felt

like crying. I wanted to ignore it. Suppress it until I forgot about it. Allow my mind to erase it from my memory. The plane crash. The ghosts. The haunting conversations with Walker. And the nebulous Ferris wheel and red door I'd seen right before I'd drowned. I'd thought if I could just focus on what was right in front of me, everything else that threatened my reality would slip away. But I couldn't control it the way I hoped. And a tiny piece of me was thankful to have a friend like Emma to open up to.

But opening up to anyone other than Walker was going to have its own bag of hardships. Walker was dead! His spirit caught in this realm and unable to move on. Nobody could understand it like he did. And Emma? Emma was very much alive. And the fact that I was walking alongside her was almost too much for me to comprehend. I couldn't bear to think how she would wrap her head around it.

I didn't want to see her eyes when she looked at me and realized that I was a figment of her imagination. That I was no more than a hoax or apparition. Because if I didn't exist for her this summer, then what about Lainey, who was wandering the woods in search of her pointer? What about Layla Barns? And the Baylor parade? Would it all go on without me? Probably.

"You know, I never told you this, but when I was thirteen, I was playing with my aunt's Ouija board . . . and it moved. All on its own. There was a woman there from the 1800s. I swear it. So, I believe you," Emma said confidently. It took everything I had not to burst into laughter. What I was dealing with wasn't in the realm of a preteen board game. People were dying. And worse was yet to come. Still, I was relieved that my sense of humor was still intact. "Emma, it's not the same thing," I began, but stopped when tears filled her eyes. This wasn't about me any longer. Something had been going on that I had missed. "What's wrong?" I asked.

"You don't believe me. Nobody believes me. But it happened. And I've been watching you this summer, and I can tell that something's up. I just wish you would talk to me the same way you talk to Lainey." Emma's face was pink. Her voice stern.

"I do! I do talk to you the same. And I believe you about the Ouija board or whatever. I didn't want to say anything because it makes me feel awkward, but it has nothing to do with you. I promise." I no longer knew what to say. Our steps were the only sounds that passed between us for some time. At some point, I gave in. "I haven't told anybody this, but I'm going to tell you now. But don't freak out, okay?" I asked. Emma's face lit up, and she nodded fiercely in agreement.

"Promise!"

"God, I don't even know where to start. Remember when I tried to go home?" I asked.

"When you tried to go home?" The crease in Emma's brows told me this was going to be a much more difficult conversation than I had originally expected. She didn't remember.

"Remember when I hitchhiked to the airport? We texted the whole night?" The frown on Emma's face grew deeper. "It was the night the cops came after we found Trinity," I said.

But Emma didn't know what I was talking about. She looked at me like I was sprouting a second head. "No . . ." She shook her head slowly from side to side. Her eyes slanting.

"You honestly don't remember? It was just the other day!" My voice raised as I felt the heat creep into my cheeks. I pulled my blatant stare from Emma, and I scanned the woods. Was this real? Any of it?

Ultimately, it was her lack of memory that would keep me from spilling the truth. Whatever I was going through, I had to do it alone. Well, not completely alone. I had Walker.

Emma was waiting for the secret. I had to tell her something. "I had a dream I died. There was a terrible plane crash." I picked up my pace on the trail, and Emma was quick to keep up.

"It was so real. I felt the terror, the heat from the explosion. And when I woke up from the nightmare, I was convinced that I no longer existed. It was slower than I'd like to admit, but I realized it was no more than a night terror. So, sorry for the fuss. I just wasn't acting like myself,

I guess," I said. I let my eyes wander through the pines in search of Lainey, but there was no living soul in sight. The lie made me feel sad and lonely. Like I could no longer connect.

Emma nodded her head, accepting my story. Or so I thought. "But what if it wasn't a dream?" she asked.

"What do you mean?" slowing my pace once again.

"I mean, what if you did die, and this is your afterlife?" she asked. I let out a very-much-forced laugh.

"I'm serious!" said Emma, as she grabbed my arm, pulling me to a full stop. "What if this is your afterlife?" Her eyes were round and bright as suns.

"Okay. I'll play along. Say it is. Say I'm dead. Then, what does that make you? And why can you see me? Don't you think it's a little misleading that the entire cabin can still . . . I don't know, talk to me?" I laughed a harsh, gritty laugh.

"Well, they all think you've been a little . . ." Emma rolled her eyes.

"What?"

"A little . . . off," she said.

I frowned, letting her know I saw straight through her lie. But I didn't need to know what they really thought of me. I'd probably already thought much worse of myself.

"Look. I believe it. The weirder, the better," she said.

I thrust my hand on my hip, coming to a complete stop

in the middle of the trail. This dreadful summer wasn't meant for Emma's entertainment.

"I'm sorry. Not like that. I'm just saying, I'm here for you." She reached out and placed her hand on my shoulder. A thoughtful gesture that I couldn't feel.

"Emma, this isn't one of your sci-fi, fantasy, paranormal . . . sex books!" I fumbled over my words. The truth was, I didn't know what she read, and I never really cared, but I recalled seeing oil-slick abs grace the covers of her books. And more often than not, they had some sort of glowing globe of universal power or a sharp crystal that always looked phallic to me. Either way, Emma was meant for a world much more interesting than ours. And given the chance, she was ready to make whatever it was that I was going through her personal dream come true.

"I know that!" she said, looking off to the side. Guilt washed over me. Who was I to crush a bookworm's dream?

"Look—" I started.

"But what if? What if!?" she pressed, palms up and eyes wide. She wasn't going to leave this alone, and part of me loved her for it.

It was the straw that broke the camel's back. The truth spilled from me like hot lava.

"I know! I swear, Emma, I died in that plane crash!" I ran my hands through my hair frantically and began pacing back and forth on the trail. I'd died in the lake, I'd died on the plane . . . how many more times would it happen? And how? I didn't want to know. "And you wouldn't believe it. You wouldn't believe it, Emma . . ."

"What?" she hissed.

"Walker! He said it!" I threw my hands up in the air.

"He said what?" Emma's voice grew.

"He said, 'You know you're dead, too, right?'" I crammed the heels of my hands into my eyes.

It took a moment for her to respond, but when she did, all she could say was, "Too?"

I stopped in my tracks and spun around to face her. It was the one thing I'd promised myself I wouldn't say. It just slipped out. "Emma, you can't tell anyone! It's a secret. I shouldn't have said anything!" I cupped my mouth and watched her, praying she'd abide.

"No. I won't say anything. I promise," she said. I held her gaze until I stopped, feeling like a terrible friend to Walker. I'd probably just spilled his deepest, darkest secret like it was gossip.

"Do you . . . Do you think I'm . . ." Emma whispered, her long fingers pointing to her chest, her face falling.

"No! No. *You* are happy. *You* are healthy. And you are going to live a long life. You hear me? Look, Emma, if anyone was in real danger here, it would be—"

Emma's eyes grew large, ticking up towards mine. "Lainey!" she gasped.

My stomach sank. I'd known something was off the entire morning. And there we were, talking about my problems instead of trying to find Lainey. I was a terrible friend. And I'd never forgive myself if we didn't find her.

We searched for hours. When lunch rolled around, we ventured back to the cabin to get Gunner. Emma thought he would be able to sniff her out, and I originally thought it was a good idea, too, until I remembered him barking at the edge of the dock. The pale face of the scared girl that reflected in the water passed through my memory, and acid rose in my throat. I said nothing.

I was pleased to see Walker gliding up to the dock when we got back to the cabin. I hadn't seen him since the night we killed Big Jimmy, and the secrets of our souls passed like whispers in the night. He flashed me a smile, and I could see his dimples all the way from shore.

"Emma, why don't you go see if anybody has heard anything yet. And I'll be right behind you," I said. Emma ran into the house, and I ventured down to the dock.

I couldn't help the smile that spread across my face, and there was no hiding it, either. We'd bonded in a way I'd never done with a guy before. I guess murder will do that to a couple. Well, self-defense, really. But it was less about the attack and more about the thing where he and I shared a special secret with one another. There was no other soul that I'd known that walked this earth like we did. We were living a lie. And nobody but us knew about it. And, I guess, Emma too. But something about the secret made me feel even more drawn to Walker.

"Hey, you look like you're in a good mood. What's going on?" Walker asked as I approached him.

"Oh, nothing. My friend Lainey is missing."

"And you're happy about that?" he asked.

"No!" My smile completely vanished. "No, I'm not. I just. It was you. Seeing you made me feel like I wasn't . . . I don't know. I was just happy to see you. I wasn't sure I would again." I tucked my hands into my back pockets and let my hair fall in front of my face.

"What? Are you serious? We've got big plans this summer, don't we?" Walker asked, wrapping his arms around me for a hug. I melted. I'd have him all summer.

"Yeah . . ."

"Of course we do! You and I are pals! We've got to stick together," he said, patting my back.

"Right. *Pals*," I repeated, taking in his scent as we parted. We were so much more than that, though. "Hey, do you mind if Emma comes to the library with us tomorrow?"

Walker's brow creased.

"It's just that she's really good at research, but if you don't want her to come . . ."

"No, it's all right. She can come. So, you have *another* friend missing?" Walker asked.

"It's my best friend." I looked back at the house. "It's one of them."

"Well, what happened? Do you think she was

marked?"

"I don't know. We went to bed, and she was there. We woke up, and she wasn't. I think she took Gunner out for a run or something and he came back without her. Do you think you could help us look?" I asked, tucking the loose lock of hair behind my ear.

Walker rubbed the scruff on his chin, his gaze fixed on the lake. "I've got a better idea. You run back out with your friends. I'm going to head into town. There's something I need to pick up."

I nodded.

"Don't worry, Wilde. Everything is going to be all right," he said. But it didn't feel like that. It felt like everything was getting worse and there was no end in sight.

Late in the evening, when Lainey hadn't returned and Gunner sat staring out the window, Walker showed up at the cabin. With bags in his hands, he motioned for privacy. We went into the den, where nobody had gone since Mason had eaten the lightbulbs and the room remained dark.

"Did your friend show?" he asked.

"No. And nobody seems too worried either."

"That's the lake for you." Walker rifled through the bags in the dark.

"What did you get?" I asked, peeking inside.

Walker pulled out several surveillance cameras from

an electronics store. "Trust me on this. I've got a theory." He took a wide stance, shifting his weight from side to side.

"Oh? And what's that?" I asked.

"Something's off. It always is. Kind of like we're missing bits and pieces, right? Like time is slipping away from us or something?" I knew what he meant. Since I'd drowned in the lake, so much time had vanished. And when I'd resurfaced, nobody knew I was ever gone. Could it have been a skip in time itself? I didn't know. I guess that's just what happens when you pass.

"So, what's with the cameras, then?" I asked, looking up at him.

"Well, we're going to set them up tonight when everyone goes to sleep. And after a few days, we're just going to see what we find. But I have a feeling . . . we're going to find some answers in these recordings," he said, finally stilling.

I wasn't as hopeful as Walker, but who could deny that smile? I knew I couldn't. And it's not like I had any other options. So, that's what we did. We hid in the den until everyone fell asleep. My head rested on his shoulder while we waited in the dark. We'd been kicked out of the game. We were outcasts. But we had found one another, and it was the glue that held us together. We spent the night wiring three cameras inconspicuously about the cabin. All I had to do now was wait for the answers to come to me. But waiting wouldn't be easy.

CHAPTER 3

Emma, Walker, and I stood on the corner of Charleston and Grand, the heat beating down on our backs as we stared at what used to be the town library. Only, Baylor had swallowed it in the night. It wasn't there. Not now, not ever. Emma stole several quick glances at Walker, and I knew she was curious about him. About us. But she held it inside and I appreciated that. I looked down the empty streets for the tenth time.

"Are you sure it was on this street?" Emma asked.

"Absolutely positive. It's been on this corner ever since I've been coming to Baylor. It's the cutest vintage library I've ever seen. I can't believe they tore it down," I said, triple-checking the street signs.

"It doesn't look like anything was torn down. I'm pretty sure this liquor store has been here for as long as time,"

Emma said, her brows furrowed as she peeked into the window.

I scratched my head and craned my neck. Only Walker could understand an entire library going missing overnight, and he remained calm and patient while Emma and I struggled to understand. "I guess we need to ask somebody," I said with a shrug.

"Excuse me, sir?" Emma called out at the first sight of mankind. An older gentleman with kind eyes and a fragile body hunched over a cane continued to walk without so much as a glance in our direction. "Excuse me?" she called, louder this time. The man reluctantly hobbled to a stop and craned his neck toward us. "Do you know where the library is?"

"It's . . . It's . . . One block down," he said. Ever so slowly, he turned his focus to Walker and frowned before dismissing us altogether.

"Nice fella," Walker said.

There was nothing left to do but accept the impossible relocation of a historical library—there one trip and gone the next. We began walking.

I glanced at Walker, and he gave me a small nod, reminding me of the twisted way the Baylor phenomenon could make one feel as if they were losing their marbles. As we passed the old ornate pillars of Charleston, I began to pick up on missing person flyers taped to street posts and on storefront windows. At first, they were just text, and I figured that more people had gone missing than Trinity. But as soon as I saw Big Jimmy's mugshot plastered across a full page, sweat began to gather at the small of my back.

I hadn't realized that anybody would miss him. Not that it made it any more acceptable, but more like maybe it hadn't happened at all? If Emma couldn't remember the night I tried to fly home, then had Jim really died? I liked to think that he hadn't, even though the big guy had tried to kill us. Still, I hadn't wanted to see anybody get hurt.

When the body beside the tower had vanished the following day, it was easy to think of his death as make-believe. Stuff like this didn't happen in real life. Real life was cops, and real life was . . . missing person flyers.

I grabbed Walker's arm and dug my fingernails into his skin. His eyes flicked to mine, and I nodded toward the ornate pillars. I saw his face the moment he looked into Jimmy's pixilated eyes. It was enough to tell me he, too, had considered the entire event a figment of our imagination. His eyes only grew slightly wider, but I could see the panic. I lifted my finger and pointed. Flyers were on every corner, every window, and covering the bulletin board. I worked hard to swallow the lump rising in my throat. This wasn't something we could sweep under the rug. This was a man. And just because I didn't know where his body lay now, didn't mean I hadn't known where he had fallen. My chest tightened, the guilt like a tether wrapped tightly around me.

It was as simple as that. Responsibility. It didn't matter if things were unexplainable in Baylor; the responsibility I felt was still the same. It was within me to be a good person —whatever that meant these days. No matter my mental state, or my reflection in the mirror, I still strived to be the best that I could be—dead or alive. My mind tinkered with the possibilities of sitting through a trial and going to jail . . . or simply letting the guilt eat away at my conscious soul for all of eternity. There were no good options. That was, unless Walker had thought of something that I hadn't.

I peered up at him, and the crevice between his brows was so deep it reminded me of the great Baker Canyon. It also confirmed what I feared most—there was no way out. We were going to have to deal with this one way or another. And as far as I could see, it wasn't going to be a positive path for Walker and me.

We continued down Charleston, Walker and I both sweating buckets, partially due to the heat but mostly due to our impending doom. When we arrived at the library, it was the same old historical building that I had always remembered it to be. The only thing that had changed was the corner on which it sat. Emma walked in immediately, and I stood on the sidewalk, hesitating as I took in the street's location, the flyers catching my eye every now and again. Walker gave me the time I needed to wrap my head around the relocation of an entire historical building as he held the door open, eyebrows raised. I sighed, shaking my head before striding forward. As I walked past him, I took in his cologne and wished that I was back in the canoe wrapped in his flannel. And that there had never been anyone lying at the base of the transient tower.

I wished there wasn't a care in the world—only a boy and a girl and what could be. But that wasn't the case as things stood today. Today, there was one boy and two girls. There was one missing person and two dead people. Three —if I counted myself. It wasn't the summer I'd hoped it would be. And it certainly wasn't the running start into independence I had imagined. Somehow, somewhere along the way, my adulthood had ended before it even began.

I let my eyes wander across the books on the bookshelves. Not one new release. Everything was old and well-read. The books were dingy and outdated, and yet, the stories were still as rich as the day they had been written—the fantasies forever young and the infinite possibilities as fine as aged wine.

"I'm going to hop on one of these computers and see if I can locate any old newspapers relating to the accident," Emma said. Walker and I nodded. And as soon as she left, Walker grabbed my elbow and yanked me down an empty aisle. The books towered well over our heads.

"They're looking for him, but he's nowhere to be found," he whispered.

"I didn't realize that people were going to be looking

for him. I thought he went missing because of the Baylor phenomenon. What are we going to do?" I broke down right there, nestled between the rows of books. My heart rate was picking up speed, and my eyes had gone shifty.

Walker ran his hands through his hair and paced the aisle. "We have to keep it quiet," he said, pinching his bottom lip in thought.

"What? We can't do that!" I hissed.

"The hell we can't!" Walker's eyes fixed on mine momentarily before he started pacing once again.

"I'm not going to spend eternity rotting in my own guilty conscience!" I said.

"I'm not going to spend eternity behind bars!" Walker said, his golden eyes ablaze.

For a moment, I was lost—not just in the amber flame behind his eyes but behind my moral compass. I was already dead. Hadn't I suffered enough? Was I supposed to spend an infinite lifetime behind bars as well? It probably wouldn't even work. I'd wake up the next morning in the master bedroom of the cabin on Rock Creek Cove. *Incarcerate me? Impossible . . .*

"You're right. That's not going to work for us." My gaze blurred before me. Walker was finally still, stance wide and hand on his hip. It was my turn to pace the aisle. Every time I passed him, I fought the urge to wrap my arms around him and beg for all of it to disappear. I wanted to be in this library with him, but I wanted my mind to be free. I wanted his heart to be available. And most importantly, I just wanted to be an eighteen-year-old worrying about which bikini I was going to wear that day. But because we can't always get what we want, I had to come up with a plan for Big Jim's disappearance.

While Emma searched records, Walker and I whispered between the old books of the historical library. "I think the best shot we have is to pretend it never happened," said Walker, shrugging as if it might be true. It had never happened. The body never flew out the window and crashed down upon the rocks. And we'd never listened to the concert from the tower, shoulder to shoulder, as he lay bloodied below.

"You're right. It probably never happened." I looked down to the ground, debating not only Jimmy's death but the existence in which Walker and I shared a bond unlike any other. If all of this never happened, then what we shared wasn't real either. He reached out and placed his hand beneath my chin. Electricity sparked where our flesh met, reminding me that some things are undeniable. Slowly, he lifted my head so that my gaze met his.

"It *did* happen. I know you feel like there's no reality because it's twisted and everything feels fake. But it happened. I'm here, and as painful as it may be—"

I sighed, the stress flaking off me and falling to the wayside. As long as I had him, I'd stay grounded.

"—it's important you realize that what happened in

that tower was real. Now, I don't know where the evidence has gone. But just like this library, it's been relocated . . . somewhere. But it's not our job to find out. And we're simply going to step away from this case. We have no ties to Big Jimmy, and nobody will be looking for us . . ."

I nodded, taking his instructions in. He dropped his hand from beneath my chin, but I held his gaze.

"As far as anybody is concerned, he fell out a window. We were never there. Do you hear me? It happened . . . but we were never there," he said. Acknowledging that we were there was only for our sanity—not for the police to know.

It was a fine line to walk—insanity and reality. The lines were not made of rich, black charcoal, but that of a nebulous gray watercolor. The transition so vaguely defined that it might as well not even be there. And when the line was so arbitrary, I found myself lost between right and wrong. It was there, between the stacks of the well-read books, that I came to realize that, just like my reality, right and wrong had ceased to exist. And if that were the case, I might as well stop worrying about it. My shoulders relaxed when I realized my responsibility as a dead girl was next to nothing. I pinched my shirt and tried to air out the sweat that had been gathering on my chest and back. My head was full of tension and ached. I wasn't cut out for this. The fine lines across Walker's forehead told me that *nobody* was.

"Kinsley?" Emma whispered a couple of aisles down.

I looked at Walker, and it was clear that our decision had been made. We wouldn't be going to jail today. I gave him a quick nod, and he seemed to confirm that our case had been closed, never to be spoken of again.

"Kinsley, look what I found!" Emma said, coming down the aisle with a newspaper folded in her hand. "Read this!" she said, pointing to an article. I took the newspaper from her hand and read the title: "Midnight Collision." I scanned the article below, and much like my reality, the words blurred together in one jumbled mess. Letters rearranged themselves and continued without any semblance of a pattern. The white spaces between were just as prominent, if not more so, than the words themselves. I did, however, pick out a name. *My* name.

Another word that caught my attention was *accident*. I didn't know what Emma had found, but I knew it was important and pertained to me. Heat radiated down my back with embarrassment, as I knew the two of them were waiting for me to read it and come to a conclusion. A lump formed in my throat as I worried that I should have been done reading the entire article by now, but the truth was, I hadn't even started. I watched the words blur like a movie in motion, and there was no decoding this mess under all the pressure of my peers watching and waiting for me to finish. I passed the newspaper to Walker, peeking at him with questioning eyes and hoping to grasp the answers through him instead of reading the article myself.

He took it, never questioning my performance, and began reading out loud. And for that, I was forever thankful. "Accident involving Kinsley Wilde . . . On her eighteenth birthday . . ." He read, and my ears deafened as my mind raced to build a timeline before me. Eighteen? My birthday? I failed to recall the details but knew that something was terribly wrong. My birthday fell well before I came to the lake and before I'd drowned by the hands of darkness.

"—Car overturned from the bridge above. Paramedics estimate the accident happened some ninety minutes earlier, as there were no witnesses . . ." Walker continued, and I struggled to pick up bits and pieces of information.

"You were in an accident?" Emma asked, her face just as contorted as mine felt. Good question. I didn't know. I had no recollection of being in an accident, but it made sense. Perhaps that's where my life had actually ended. That's why I'd drowned and crashed in a plane and yet never really died—because I was already dead to begin with.

"I . . . I don't remember," I said, the ringing in my ears returning.

Walker reached out and squeezed my shoulder. His eyes filled with pain, and I wondered if he, too, had a moment in time that he couldn't remember. A moment when his life was stolen, and his mind worked ravenously hard to cover its tracks. I sought comfort in his eyes as I let the feelings of uncertainty settle deep into my stomach. I no longer felt the watching and waiting from Emma and Walker—only the cold, distant trepidation of not knowing my own past.

We left the library, having found more than what we'd come for. Emma knew about Walker and me being less than alive, and she did a pretty good job keeping that secret. As far as Walker knew, she was only with us to help with research about the Layla Barns accident. The article she uncovered about me came as a surprise to all of us. I was vaguely aware of the delicate dance the two of them did as they tried to figure out what each other knew. I had pressing concerns of my own. I couldn't recall much from my eighteenth birthday, let alone an accident. I heard trauma could do that. Make you forget.

As we walked down Chandler Street, there was a commotion outside the liquor store that stole my attention. It appeared that somebody was being arrested, and the three of us watched curiously. The closer we got, the clearer the picture became.

"Paul Cummings, you are being arrested for the murder of Jim Saunders," a cop announced.

Walker's eyes widened in disbelief as I felt my lungs expand in a quick, ragged breath. A part of me was relieved that it was all taking care of itself. But I knew I couldn't allow this man to take the blame for something he never did. I raised my hand to flag down the police and opened my mouth out of pure instinct, ready to confess. Walker grabbed my side, pushing me away from the cop's attention. Of course, Walker's hand on my waist was just about the only thing that could have stopped me in my tracks. And it did. My voice never came.

"Did he say *murder?*" Emma whispered.

"Some guy named Jim, I guess," Walker replied, his eyes trained on me. I remembered our agreement and closed my gaping mouth. I watched the cops slam the innocent man against the car as they read him his rights. I placed my hand over my stomach as it twisted in knots. Then, I looked away. I couldn't watch the man squint, writhing in pain as he was pushed against the police car when I knew it should have been me. I secretly vowed that I would make sure he got out of this unscathed. And as I did so, I couldn't help but wonder what evidence they had on the man they called Paul Cummings.

It was dark when we got back to the cabin. Saying goodbye to Walker was bittersweet. I didn't want him to go. But at the same time, I needed time alone to decompress. I needed to sit with myself, and I needed to shake this looming feeling of existential dread that hung over me like a dark cloud. And as I sat down on the edge of my bed, I realized that it was going to get worse before it got any better.

I'd had one accident I didn't remember and two I couldn't forget. A car accident on my eighteenth birthday, a plane crash that took 147 innocent lives, and a drowning. I was responsible for the death of one friend and the recent disappearance of another. Oh, and I'd killed a man. But if all of this had happened in my afterlife, then had it ever happened at all? I didn't know.

I didn't know who I was anymore. I brought a hand to my cheek and caressed it softly. My flesh was soft and plush beneath my fingertips, my jaw sharp and chiseled. I let my fingers fall just below my chin, and they settled on my carotid artery. If I had been dead, then why did my heart still beat? Why was there blood pumping through my veins? And why on earth was I surrounded by all my friends in this cabin?

I had never seriously questioned what happened after you died. But now that I knew, I suppose the answer was that our subconscious lived on. It lived on to imagine life as it had been. Perhaps as it *should* have been. Everything I saw as I looked around the room was make-believe. It was a memory that I had from previous trips to the cabin. My friends were a combination of memory and a projected outcome I had conjured in my head throughout my entire senior year of planning this trip. This was my best guess at what would have happened if I had lived past my eighteenth birthday.

And I was living it out. I was living it out just the same as if it were real life. The only difference? It wasn't real. And it was fragile, prone to breaking down in hellish fears. Maybe I was living out the nightmares I'd had when I was alive. Fascinated by this notion, my eyes lifted to the bathroom, where a large mirror covered the vanity wall. What would my reflection show? If it was all just a guess, how much did I get right? I imagined what I looked like when I was alive. Long dark-chestnut hair. Sun-kissed skin and red lips. Chocolate-brown eyes, with one small fleck of green. I stood up and slowly walked to the mirror, my heart pounding harder the closer I came. It was the only truth this world had, and it was just inside the bathroom. I kept my gaze low as I entered, and I grabbed the white countertop as I braced myself to see my true reflection.

Seconds turned to minutes before I found the courage to look deep inside my soul. The mirror would show a murderer. Someone unlovable. Someone . . . hideous. Only, when I stood square in front of the mirror, there wasn't a heinous spirit looking back at me. There was no reflection at all.

My deepest, darkest fear was then realized. I was *nobody.*

All my heart's desires, all my greatest wishes—they'd never come to fruition. The love I had for my family and friends would never be felt. They would never be warmed by my touch. And the only reason my friends at the cabin had acknowledged me at all was that I had wanted them to. I had imagined they had.

My existence now was as real as the reflection looking back at me. It simply ceased to exist.

CHAPTER 4

As I stared into the mirror, my hollowness staring back with no eyes to question, I wondered if my lack of reflection meant that I had no soul. No heart. If I wasn't capable of true love. One thing I was sure of: I had a conscience. I had thoughts that kept me awake at night, and I had worries that drilled deep inside me, keeping this body running on anxiety and fear. If I had no soul, then how would I have feelings of guilt? And empathy? Why would I feel sick about Lainey's disappearance? Or how would I long for something more meaningful with Walker? And how would I wonder what could have been with Noah?

It must've been hours that I stared into that mirror, searching for my soul, but no passing time could bring me back.

Gone from this world yet somehow still present, I

thought about my mom. I'd spoken to her since the accident, and there had been no mention of my passing. Should there have been? Or had my mind simply not wanted there to be? Whatever the case, with my newfound perspective, I picked up the phone and dialed.

I listened to the phone ring on the receiver and felt my hands grow clammy in anticipation. "Hello?" Mom answered in the vibrant tone of the living—a tone that reflected her daughter was alive and well. Had she not known? Or had I simply not wanted to live in a reality in which she was grieving?

"Mom?" I asked.

"Oh, hey honey. I was just thinking about you. Your ears must be ringing." I closed my eyes and imagined her on the sofa in front of a fire, her reading glasses sliding down the bridge of her nose and a mug of warm tea by her side.

"Were you?"

"Always, dear. How are you? How is everything going at the cabin?" she asked. I took in a deep breath, not knowing how to respond. Do I play the game? Or do I be myself? My authentic self . . .

"Mom?" I asked, looking for answers. The line was quiet on the other end, and I decided in that moment that I had nothing left to lose. "Mom, Lainey has been missing. We can't find her. And I know deep down that something is wrong. Gunner hasn't moved from the window, and he watches and waits for her return." My throat tightened as the words squeezed up and out.

"Well, that's a hard one, dear. Sometimes in life, people we love go missing. But there are lessons to be learned here—silver linings to look for. I know you'll find what you're looking for." Mom's voice was like a beautifully misplaced melody. It would have been comforting if it fit with the context of the situation.

It was almost as if I had made up different variations of answers a mother would give during a difficult conversation. But this particular conversation was one I'd never had with my mom—a missing person, the death of a friend. Since I had never had these conversations before, I assumed my consciousness had no way of projecting what she would have said.

There was an unsettled churning in my stomach as I realized the conversation I had with my mother was as fake as my new life.

"Silver lining? And what do you think that is, Mom?" I asked, simply needing to hear her voice.

"It could be anything, dear. When one door closes, another one opens. You just have to keep your eyes open. And you'll see the new opportunities that arise."

I imagined my mom on the other line, giving me her most heartfelt attention. And it warmed my almost-heart, as if it were there, beating within my chest. I knew now the conversation was fictitious, but that didn't stop me from needing my mother's love.

"Mom? I met a boy. And I know what you're thinking. It's not Noah." A small smile tugged at the corner of my lips.

"Oh? Go on," she said, changing her emotion to fit mine. A chameleon at its best.

"He's older than I am. And I never considered dating an older guy, but when I met him, I never gave it a second thought. It's like I saw him, and he could have said he was an alien from Mars and I would've happily nodded, accepting him. To be honest, he could be anything—a butcher, an alien . . . hell, he could even be a ghost—and I'd still want to crawl inside his flannel. I don't know, Mom, there's something about him. I can't quite put my finger on it, but it's this intangible light that surrounds him and invites me in. I feel this draw and I know he was made just for me."

"You know, when I met your father, it was like that. And your Grandma Green—she always said that Grandpa was her soulmate. She described it as much deeper than one life could possibly shed light on. That her love for him went back lifetimes. And you know what? I believe in fate."

I thought about that. Fate. I didn't know the meaning of my afterlife, but I had to believe that Walker coming into it was no mistake.

"I miss you, Mom . . ."

"I miss you too, dear."

"I better go. I know you need to get your sleep, and it's getting late." I fiddled with a tassel on the pillow, wishing my mother was there to give me a hug.

"I love you, dear. Good night." Her words lingered on the line long after I'd hung up. I wondered how the conversation would have gone if it had been real and she knew that I was dead. What would she say to me then?

And then something happened. An epiphany . . . like a lightning bolt, it hit me. The conversation I'd just had with my mother was conjured because she was alive, and I wasn't. But what would happen when I called my gran? What would happen when I called somebody who was in the same realm as me? I'd seen her in my dreams, and I'd seen her apparition in the woods and on the plane, but could I call her on the phone? Had there been a direct line of communication with her this whole time? One I had never taken advantage of it?

As quickly as I could, I picked up the phone and dialed her number. An ache spread across my chest as I realized I was calling a number I'd never thought I could again. The phone rang not once, not twice, but three long miserable rings before it happened. She answered.

"Hello?"

"Gran? Is that you?" I asked, flinching back.

"Kinsley? Kinsley, are you there, dear?" Gran asked.

"It's me! I'm here!" I said.

"I wasn't expecting your call. Is everything okay?" I sensed the trepidation on the other side of the line.

I sat quietly, unsure of what to say and how much. "I know . . ." I said.

"You know what, dear?" she asked.

"That I died—"

The silence stretched between us. And I played with the pillow's tassels as I waited for her response. Had I said too much?

"Is that really you, Kinsley?" her feeble old voice wavered.

"Gran, it's me. I'm here!" I said.

"Oh, honey, I've been trying to reach you."

"You have?" I asked. It was the first thing that had felt real in a long while.

"This is against the rules, so we'll have to be quick," Gran said.

"*Rules?* What rules?"

"I've been trying to reach you this whole time. But it's difficult. I've been having a hard time contacting you. And when I do, it comes out twisted and warped. I fear I'm doing more damage than good."

"What do you mean?" I asked.

"Every time I try, my words get twisted, and your visions become a blundered mess. I can't tell if I'm helping you or hurting you. But I keep trying, dear. I keep trying . .

." Gran said, her voice pained with sorrow so deep that I could feel it on the other side of the line.

"You're not hurting me. I'm just . . . I'm just confused. Are you trying to tell me it wasn't you I saw in the forest? Or on the plane? It wasn't you sitting by the fire reading books?" My head ached with all the questions I had no answers to. Yet, there was something more. Something real in how it hurt.

"Oh, honey, it's me. But only fragments. My intention isn't coming through the other side. And I try to help, but it doesn't seem to work. You're never there." Gran seemed frazzled.

"I'm here now. And I love you. I miss you so much." It was all I could say.

"Oh, Kinsley. I miss you too. I want you to know that I'm here for you and you don't have to do this alone. You're not alone. You're so strong, darling. You're so brave."

I began to cry as her comforting words wrapped around me like a warm hug. I could tell that this conversation was different from the rest. It touched me in a way that the others hadn't. And I wondered if I could reach her again when I needed to by simply dialing her phone number.

"Gran? Come back? Can you come back?" I asked—an impossible question. And if I only had one question to ask somebody on the other side, it was this. A request that I knew couldn't be fulfilled. The words simply tumbled out of my mouth and I couldn't take them back. I wanted my grandmother. I wanted everything to go back to the way it had been before.

I felt the disappointment in her ragged breath on the other side of the line. "Kinsley? Kinsley, are you there?" she asked, her voice dripping with worry.

"Gran? I'm here. Can you hear me?" Static filled the other side of the line, and I could hear her voice far away in the distance.

"Kinsley? Oh no . . . Not again . . ."

It broke me to hear her pain. I felt my heart break and shatter like an unreplaceable vase. I hunched over and sobbed. She knew I was hurting and scared, and she was doing everything she could to reach out to me in an impossible situation. We were both dead yet unable to find each other in the vast emptiness beyond the veil—just like Walker and Layla.

"Gran! I'm here. I'm here!" I said in no more than a whisper. The tears rolled off my cheeks and fell onto the pillow I grasped tightly in my lap. Nothing could bring her back. And I was to face this eternity on my own.

My insides felt paper-thin and delicate beyond belief. Like a house of cards that could topple over with the slightest breeze. Walker and I were two lost souls. Together, we were searching for answers. A way back to our loved ones. He to Layla and me to my gran. If I could find her, then maybe we could live our afterlives together the way they were meant to be. But what about everyone else in the cabin? The ones who were still alive but only brought together by my imagination?

It was hard to feel anything other than sorrow when you ceased to exist. But still—despite the fallen tears—I found something else to latch onto. Curiosity.

It peaked when I remembered the surveillance cameras I'd set up throughout the cabin. One pointing toward the lake dock, one in the kitchen, one in the master bedroom, one in the living room, and another in the den. If my friends were a figment of my imagination, then what did the cameras reveal? Did they have reflections?

Thankful for Walker's grand scheme, I jumped out of bed and wiped my cheeks dry of tears. I hurried to the camera set up in my bedroom, and I examined it front to back, watching as the green light blinked. Nerves of anticipation spread throughout my body as my gaze lifted to my laptop. Should I look now? Would I be disappointed? The answers would be undeniable. It didn't matter if I looked now or later. It didn't matter what the tapes were to reveal; it was the truth, and it was waiting for me.

I opened my laptop and logged onto the surveillance website. There were five cameras to scour footage from, but I chose the master bedroom first. I started from the beginning and I watched as I set the camera up and then crawled into bed. But soon after, the video feed glitched and then went black. I clicked here and there, but nothing brought the video back. I skipped forward, scanning for any sort of footage. However, there was nothing but darkness.

Four more to go. I looked back to the camera in the bedroom and the green blinking light. It seemed to be working, but I was no technician. I clicked on the footage from the kitchen, and to my dismay, it was the same deal. It had taped me as I set the camera up but froze as soon as I walked out of the room.

"What the hell?" I said aloud as I opened the footage of the living room with disappointment. It was the same thing as the kitchen. Frozen footage. It's like every single security camera I set up worked for thirty seconds and then gave out. I slammed my laptop closed.

I went around to every camera and checked the wiring. Everything seemed to be in working condition, but I unplugged them all and started them over just in case. It was the extent of my technical knowledge. And oddly enough, it fixed about seventy-five percent of my problems with electronics. I could only hope that it would do the same with these cameras. I made a mental note to ask Walker to look at them next time he stopped by the cabin, but for now, this would have to do.

When I got to the camera in the den, I never plugged it back in. With all the weird happenings at the Vandals' house, I took it to the patio and hooked it up so that it faced the neighbors' property instead. I'd probably get no footage again, but it didn't stop me from trying.

I'd known there was something fishy about my neighbors even before my eighteenth birthday. The odd happenings at their house weren't because of the Baylor phenomenon or tied to my afterlife. And I feared they had something to do with Lainey's disappearance.

CHAPTER 5

I lay tossing and turning in bed at night, the thoughts of an innocent man being sentenced to life in prison racking my mind and torturing my conscience. If my mindset was all I had left, then why let it rot with guilt? I tossed and turned while forcing my eyelids to remain shut. When I heard the familiar sound of tiny stones clinking on my bedroom window, my spirits lifted. They were the pebbles thrown from Walker's hands late in the night when he couldn't sleep and knew that I couldn't either.

I popped my eyes open and hurried to my window, cranking it open and peering outside. The mist was thick with anticipation. I gave Walker a quick wave, held up a finger to signal that I'd only be a minute, then quickly slipped on pajama pants, grabbing a robe on the way out of my bedroom. I tip-toed down the stairs and passed the sleeping bags on the living room floor. Nobody was awake.

I smiled widely when I opened the door to the back patio and found Walker standing with his hands in his pockets and an apologetic look on his face. But he didn't need to apologize for waking me up, and he knew that. I guess the dead didn't sleep. Both he and I were tortured late at night as our minds struggled to grasp the boundaries of our lives.

"Hi . . ." I said softly.

"Hi. I hope I didn't wake you," Walker said, wincing.

"Not at all. Is everything okay?" I asked, pulling the robe across my chest.

"Yeah, yeah. I just . . . I couldn't sleep. I was hoping you . . . well, not hoping, but—"

"I know what you mean," I said.

"I just needed somebody to talk to, and these days, you're all I have. I hope you don't mind," Walker said as his eyes lowered to the ground. I wiggled my feet in my slippers. This revelation did weird things to my stomach, and it felt like I was in motion—namely, falling. I didn't know what to say to that. I wanted him to know how much it meant to me and how much I wanted to be that person for him. But by the time I thought of a response, the moment was gone.

"Your neighbors seem to have a habit of gardening at three o'clock in the morning." Walker scowled, looking over my shoulder. I peered over to the neighbor's yard, and sure enough, there was Mrs. Vandal digging in her planters.

"I wish I could say this was abnormal for her," I said with a sigh.

Walker raised his brows in question, and I answered with a smile and nod. It was true. I looked up to the wall where I had plugged in a surveillance camera, and I was pleased when I saw the green light blinking. It didn't mean I had captured anything, but I was still hopeful that there was a chance.

"You see that?" I asked, pointing to the camera.

"You aimed one at the neighbor's house? Good thinking," he said, and I felt proud of myself in the wake of his compliment. "Want to sit on the dock?"

"Sure," I said.

He led the way. "Do you remember what it was like to be in the car accident?" Walker asked as we headed down the grassy hill toward the lake. The cool mist planted kisses on my cheeks as I tucked my hands deep inside the pockets of my robe.

I shook my head. "I have no memory of it." My slippers were getting wet from the moisture in the grass, but I didn't care.

"Really? None at all? See, I'm envious of you. I wish I couldn't remember. But that's all I do. When I close my eyes, that's all I see. It haunts me like a nightmare, and I can never escape it." Walker hung his head and tugged at the bill of his hat. I felt the shift in his mood as it radiated off him and surrounded us. This man was hurt, and I'd like to be the one to help him. But I didn't know how. How do you erase the pain from a tragedy? It was impossible.

"Maybe . . . maybe if you talk about it? I don't know if you have anybody to talk to, but I'm here." I shrugged. "I'll listen," I said, peering up at him.

One of his dimples deepened, casting a shadow on his cheek. "I don't have anybody to listen. It would be an odd thing if I did. There aren't many like us wandering around Baylor Lake." I looked behind me on the dock as my slippers made wet footprints on top of the wooden planks. Walker's canoe was tied to the end of the dock. The corner of my mouth tugged into a small smile that I tried to hide behind a curtain of hair. I liked the way he traveled. It was romantic in its own right.

"Do you mean there are more people like us?" I asked, taking a seat. I tucked my hair behind my ear and peered up at him as he sat down next to me.

"I'm sure there are—amongst us. But it's not something you can see. It isn't detectable on their flesh. It's not a smell or sight."

"Well, what is it then? You knew that about me. How did you know?"

"It . . . It was in your eyes. Your eyes were scared and lonely. You didn't understand the world around you any longer, and that's because you were no longer in it. Not in the way you used to be," Walker said, peeking down at me. The thought of me not really being in this world was a scary one, and I imagined my eyes were doing whatever it was that had helped Walker identify the status of my soul in the first place. I looked into the black distance.

"You got all of that from my eyes?" I asked, drawing my attention back to him. And if I didn't know any better, I'd say that he blushed under the moonlight.

"Believe it or not, the eyes *are* the windows to the soul. And your eyes . . . they say a lot," he said, leaning back on the heels of his palms. His torso taut as he stretched out.

"I'm going to have to keep them in check. I wouldn't want them telling any of my secrets now," I said with a wink.

"Secrets? Secrets are for the living. What do you need to hide in your afterlife?" he asked.

It was a good question—and one I didn't have an answer to. I suppose my crush on him was the only one worth hiding away. I shrugged coyly and tucked a loose strand of hair behind my ear.

"I don't know. I was just messing around. Do you have any secrets?" I asked, wanting to know them all.

Walker stared out over the water at the moonlight glinting off the surface. The ripples danced like ballerinas, moving to a beautiful symphony.

"I do. And what a burden they are. You wouldn't

believe what a guilty conscience can do to you over a couple of *decades*."

He steepled his four fingers beneath his chin, lost in thought. The night was beautiful, but nothing compared to Walker's profile. His nose turned up slightly at the tip, and it reminded me of the innocence of a young boy. His brows were dark and thick, and his cheeks were covered in week-old stubble. Yet, even beneath the five-o'clock shadow, his dimples were clearly marked. He didn't need to smile for me to see them. They were always there. Sometimes deep, sometimes shallow. They were my favorite of his features. I even liked the scar he had through his eyebrow.

"What would you have guilt about?" I asked.

"The accident I was in. I not only killed somebody, but it was my somebody. She was my person. The one I was supposed to be with. She was the one that made it"—he waved his hand through the air—"all worth it." Walker scowled, took off his hat, and ran his hand through his hair before securing it on top of his head again. "And I . . . I couldn't return the favor for her. I robbed her of everything she had and everything she was capable of."

My stomach churned, and I could finally see why he had problems falling asleep at night.

"She was the only person I ever really loved, and I threw it all away. I don't deserve to be happy. I don't deserve to let that go—that guilt." He buried his head in his hands.

"Of course you do. It was an accident. You're a great person. Don't say you don't deserve to be happy!"

"Tell me this, Wilde, do you deserve to be happy, after you killed Big Jim?" he asked, his words like a dagger in my back. I knew Big Jim had died because he tripped over me, and I had told myself a million times over that it wasn't my fault. That it was self-defense. That he'd brought it on to himself.

Still, the answer was no. I didn't believe that I deserved happiness after what I had done. I hung my head in admission, and Walker nodded. "I didn't think so."

"So, what?" My voice was a little louder now. "We're just going to live out eternity like this?" I asked, tightness coiling inside me. I hadn't chosen this life.

"Yeah. You and me. We're stuck trudging through this hell."

I frowned, angry at the cards I'd been dealt. "At least we have each other?" It was more a hopeful question than a statement, wondering if he felt the same way. But when he burst into laughter, I didn't know what to think. I felt as white as a ghost. I began to chuckle into my cupped hand as I tried to cover my mouth. I was only laughing because he was.

"At least I've got you," he said, as if it were a punch line. He laughed some more, and I cringed inside, wondering what I had said that was so funny. But when his laughter died, and he looked at me with all seriousness and a warmth behind the windows to his soul, I knew he was happy to have me around. "Yup. At least I have you," he repeated, nothing funny about it.

When the silence crept back, the tone turned serious once again. "What happened that day?" I asked. Walker swallowed a lump in his throat, and I could tell that he'd feared I would ask that very question. But he knew as well as I did that he needed to talk about it. It was crucial to him letting go of the guilt that haunted him.

"We were getting away for the weekend. It was a long weekend, a special one. We were just getting into Baylor late at night. I was drowsy from driving all day, and the roads were slick with fresh rainfall. It must've been the early hours of the morning. I remember my eyes burning as I tried to keep them open." Walker's fist tightened and released. The memory was consuming him, and I could almost see the stress coming off him in waves.

"We were so close to the cabin when it happened. It must've been a deer. It's the only thing I can think of. There was a reflex there that jerked the steering wheel. A hard right. The car flipped. The thought of me falling asleep and waking with the jerk haunts me to this day. It's not like a deer dashing in front of the car would have been any better. The outcome would remain the same. But there's something about me doing this all on my own, versus having outside influences that would change the way I feel about . . . who I am inside—what I've done."

I reached my hand out and grabbed Walker's forearm. I felt his muscles contracting underneath his jacket and I wished he could find peace within himself. I knew that time wouldn't be soon enough.

"The car rolled several times down the embankment and landed at the base of the lake. By the time I got out, she was already gone. She died before I could even say goodbye, or . . . I'm sorry."

Walker hid his face in the palms of his hands. I moved my hand from his arm to his back, rubbing up and down slowly. I wanted nothing more than to take his pain away. But he was back there at the site of the accident on that dreadful day, and there was nothing I could do to take him away.

"She didn't even know how much I loved her. She didn't know," he said, sniffling here and there.

"I'm sure she knew. I'm sure she did."

"I was going to tell her. I had plans that weekend. I was going to tell her how she'd changed my life and brought meaning to me when I had nothing. I was going to give her this . . ." Walker said, as he fished around in his pocket. It was a velvet box small enough to contain a ring. Possibly an engagement ring.

"Is that?" I asked in a whisper.

"Yes. I was going to propose."

I knew he'd had a girlfriend, and I knew it had been serious. Enough for him to have loved her. But I'd had no idea that he was going to propose. Or that he felt she was one in a million—made for him. They were soulmates. The same way my grandpa was with my gran.

I felt my heart sink lower inside my chest. Walker's heart couldn't be stolen, and worse, it would make me a bad person for even trying. At that moment, I knew what I had to do. I had to help him find his one true love and accept that it wasn't me. It never would be. And if I connected with him as much as I thought I did, then I needed to help him find peace.

"I'm so sorry," I said in a whisper. I knew it wasn't my fault. And for that, I had nothing to be sorry for. My apology wouldn't bring Layla back into his life. Yet, I said it simply because I had nothing else to say. Because there were no words to comfort the grieving. And I regretted it the moment it slipped from my lips.

"You have nothing to be sorry for," he said.

"I know! I'm sorry!" I said, wincing when it tumbled out again. I bit the inside of my cheek, hoping to silence myself. Walker took in a deep, staggered breath, and I watched from the corner of my eye as his back rose and fell again. I let my eyes wander over the dancing moonlight on the lake surface, and eventually, he did the same. *At least we have each other*, I thought.

"I need to find her, Wilde. The only thing I'm sure of these days. I have a loyalty to her, and if she's out there—stuck in this afterlife—then I need to find her. I found you, so I can't comprehend why I can't find Layla. It doesn't make any sense," he said.

"We'll find her," I said.

"I knew you were the one to help me. I just knew that you were the one who was going to find her. Call it a gut instinct."

"You're not the only one," I said with a chuckle. The amount of pressure these people were putting on me to find a phantom was astronomical.

"Oh?" he said.

"My gran keeps telling me the same thing," I said, shaking my head.

"That's what I'm talking about! You have connections that are going to help us find her. I feel it!"

"Connections?" I asked, tilting my head.

"Yeah, you have your gran. Didn't you say that she told you about the tower?" he asked. And while it was true, she had, I wasn't positive this was an ongoing thing—her helping and all.

"I mean, she did, but . . ."

"She's looking out for us. I don't know what's behind this for you, but I know it's going to change my entire existence. Once I find Layla, I'll finally have peace. I won't rest until it happens."

Walker was restless. He kept pulling on his sleeve and scratching at his chin. This was his life's mission, and without it, I wasn't sure what he had left. Besides me, that is. Another lost soul. "Why do you think she wants me to help you find her?" I asked.

"I don't know, Wilde. Trust me, I've racked my brain. I've stayed up countless nights trying to figure that out. The connection between us. As far as I see, other than us both being in this awful state of limbo—this afterlife amongst the living—I don't know why your gran would want to help me find her. But if she said that Layla needed you, it's worth a shot, right?" His brows raised underneath his hat, and his eyes were wide with hope.

"I would help you find her, regardless. I want that for you. I want you to be happy. And well, it's too late for me, but it's not for you. You have a purpose to find her, and I want to help." It was true. If Walker would be able to rest after making sure Layla was okay, then I would rest, too.

"What? You have a purpose too!" Walker said, surely out of instinct. But as soon as it left his lips, I could see it in his eyes that he regretted it. He had no idea what my purpose was, and he knew I was right. If I had to attach myself to his purpose to give myself a goal, that's just what I would have to do. It's not like I could go home and everything would be normal.

"Yeah, you're right. There's a purpose out there for me. Even if I haven't found it yet," I said, purely to make him feel better. I placed my hands against the damp wooden planks and leaned back. It was a beautiful night on the lake. Almost serene. It made me sad to think that all this beauty was lost in the mist. It touched my lips as I tilted my head back, and I wished it would always be like this. Calm and peaceful.

"Are you getting tired yet?" I asked.

"Who, me? Nah, I don't sleep. If I go home, I lie in bed and wonder till the sun comes up." Walker leaned back like I did, his head turned toward the cabin. "Hey, did you ever get any video feed from those cameras?" he asked, his tone lifting with curiosity.

"You wouldn't believe it. They all malfunctioned."

"Damn . . . I believe it," he said with a chuckle.

It was in this lighthearted teasing that we finished the night out on the dock. Walker was content until the sun began to rise. We talked a little more about the accident and Walker's life-long purpose. I imagined the times we spent together in the early morning hours by the lake had forged bonds that would one day become unbreakable. My hopes were that these early days were the pillars to our relationship, and that someday I'd look back on them with a warm heart—even if it failed to beat.

CHAPTER 6

I went to bed early that morning after Walker and I had watched the sunrise together on the dock. I knew he said he didn't sleep, but I didn't have any trouble drifting off as soon as my head hit the pillow. But when I woke up, I wasn't cuddled safely between my bed sheets any longer. I wasn't in my bed at all.

As if transported in a state of sleep, I woke up wandering about the forest by my lonesome. Barefoot and still in my pajamas, I woke to the sound of a squirrel gnawing on a nut. My feet were cold and sensitive, treading the rough gravel and fallen pine needles. A fine mist surrounded me, making it difficult to see any distance. Goosebumps covered my arms, and I quickly tucked my hands into my armpits as I shivered, trying to understand not only where I was but how it came to be that I was out here in the middle of the night.

I was startled when an owl called out. My heart thumped as I recoiled. I took a step back and bumped into some bushes. It sent me lunging forward with a shriek. Eventually, I recognized that my attacker had been no more than a blackberry bush. I placed my hand across my heart and I took in several deep breaths. How it came to be night wasn't important now. I only needed to know how to get back to the cabin, and to do that, I needed to know where I was. But in the dead of the night, every tree looked identical to one another.

I heard a snap, and my deep breathing did nothing to calm me. I whipped my head back and forth, searching deep in the dark forest. Blackness to my left and blackness to my right. Little critters running over dried leaves and brushing up against the bushes grew louder as they ventured closer. That was until I heard a voice. A familiar voice. And all else dropped dead quiet.

"Kinsley? Can you hear me, dear?" It was no more than a whisper through the branches, but it was enough.

"Gran? Gran, is that you?" I asked, hoping that it was her come to save me. I searched all around, but the voice had come from every direction all at once.

"Kinsley?" she whispered again. It was no closer this time, and I looked up frantically to see a small clearing of a moonlit sky through the tall pine trees.

"Gran! Gran!" I took several steps forward and then retraced my steps. When the blackberry bush nipped at my bare calves, I lunged again, only to stop when I saw a small gray light in the distance. I stood still, my eyes laser-focused on the only light in the forest. I took one small step toward it, and it began to grow bigger and brighter.

"Gran?" I asked of the darkness. But there was no answer. The light flickered between the trees, and I could tell that there was movement there. It was coming closer to me. Winding in and out of the pines. I was both afraid and comforted by the unknown presence. I hoped it was my grandmother in rare form.

The light grew bright. The lumens were high as it became almost unbearable to look at. I squinted for as long as I could until I had to shield my eyes with the crook of my elbow. And as soon as I took my eyes off the mystical light in the forest, it went out again. Only this time, I could hear that it had closed the distance between us with a whisper-quiet breath. I pulled my arm down to the bridge of my nose and was surprised to see my gran standing before me. She wasn't of blood and flesh but of smoke or mist. Translucent. The bright light turned to a soft warm glow around her . . . and through her.

I said nothing. I let my eyes take in the beauty of my late grandmother. I'd never seen such a sight like this. She was a spirit, an apparition, but her eyes . . . her eyes were of incredible detail. Full of love and happiness, her eyes were as clear and vibrant as a warm summer's day. Almost clearer than my vision was capable of seeing. Though she stood several feet away, I could get lost in the crystals surrounding her pale green, emerald eyes.

"So beautiful . . ." I whispered. She floated through the mist like a slow waltz in the night.

"Kinsley?" she said with a shudder.

I smiled, and a single tear rolled down my cheek. For a moment, it looked like she was going to cry too, but instead, she reached her hand forward, cupping my cheek. She swiped her thumb over the tear, and her hand felt just like the cold mist—only more concentrated. It sent a shiver down my spine, and she smiled at my reaction.

"Oh, how I've missed you," she said.

"Was it you I spoke to on the phone?" I asked.

"Yes," she said, overjoyed that we had found grounds to communicate.

I couldn't take the excitement any longer. I lunged forward, putting my arms around her. I'd needed a hug more than I ever had in my entire life. And disappointment crashed down upon me when I fell forward and nobody was there to catch me.

I opened my eyes and my arms to find nothing but darkness before me. I spun around, my heart stopping. She was several feet away, her back to me. I circled back around her, and her head hung with disappointment.

"I'm so sorry, dear. We're not the same. I wish for nothing more than to give you a hug, but it's not in the cards today."

"It's okay, Gran. I'm just happy you're here." I rubbed my arms, chilly in the shadows of the night. I looked around and spotted an owl whose eyes were bright and yellow. "Did you summon me or something? The last thing I remember, I was lying in bed. I'm not sure how I got here. And as you can see, I'm not dressed for a midnight walk in the woods." I wiggled my toes across the gravel, and Gran peeked down.

"Honey, it's not nighttime," she said, looking around.

"What do you mean?" I asked, my eyes searching the depth of the dark and misty forest.

"I'm sorry, dear, did you say the woods?" Gran tilted her head.

"Yes . . ." I said in a leery tone. "What's going on, Gran?" I looked around sharply. Was I not seeing correctly?

"I'm so sorry, dear. I've been trying to make this visually appealing for you. I know the void can be quite a scary place if it's not decorated well. But I'm new at this, you see. I haven't lived here long. I didn't realize I had brought us to the woods, and to be honest with you, I'm seeing something entirely different," she said, looking around. She held her hand out with a small smile and I followed her eyes as they lowered to the tips of her fingers, as if a tiny bird or butterfly had just landed on one. But all I could see was the forest with its haunting shadows and secrets.

I'm not sure why, but I began to cry. There was only so much I could take. Only so many questions without answers. They bubbled up until the stress boiled over and poured out in streams of frustration. I didn't want to spend my time with Gran complaining. I knew my time with her was limited. But I couldn't help myself from the mental breakdown that had been threatening to burst forth for weeks on end.

"I can't do this anymore! I can't be blind to this! Nothing makes sense. Nothing! How are you there in my dreams and the next day we're out in the woods? How could I talk to you on the phone and now you're a spirit? How in the world do you not see the woods? They're surrounding us! They're everywhere!" I yelled with my arms outstretched. I spun around, pointing to all the trees. "You're telling me you don't see that one right there? Or that one next to it? What about this one over here? That blackberry bush . . . you don't see it?" My voice hitched.

"I'm sorry, dear. I'm trying to tell you what you need to know—"

"Then just tell me already! Tell me!" I yelled.

"I—" she began, but I couldn't take one more second without knowing.

"Just tell me!" I screamed with my eyes closed behind my balled fists.

Tears spilled from my eyes, and I grabbed my stomach in pain as I heaved forward. I let out loud, ugly sobs that echoed off the trees. I struggled to suck in jagged air, my diaphragm locking up. And when I thought to open my eyes, when I thought the worst was already there upon me, I found my gran far in the distance, her light dimming as she was on her way out.

"Don't go! Don't go!" I choked out, my hand reaching into the darkness. I dropped to my knees, and I felt the pine needles dig into my kneecaps.

I hunched over as my hands wrapped around my waist. My forehead dipped until it rested on top of the fallen pine needles. Tears rolled down my nose and fell into the dirt. I grabbed at my waist, the thin material of my nightshirt not enough to protect me from my fingernails as they dug into my sides. In a world that I was so unsure of, I welcomed the pain. There wasn't much that was real to me now, and if all I was sure of was this searing ache of my nails digging into my ribs, I'd take it. It was better than nothing. Better than the abyss.

I had never felt more alone than I did that night. I had thought that many times before, but each time I did, it was exceedingly worse. I had died before. And I didn't even remember it. And I didn't doubt that anybody else had remembered it either. I was nothing to anybody. And now, I was lost and lonely, half-dressed in the middle of the forest. Or what I assumed was the middle of the forest. And I could only hope that it was the woods near the cabin of Rock Creek Cove.

Even the ghost of my gran couldn't stand to be near me. I had shut her out by screaming. Demanding to know more. If I had only accepted what she'd given me. But I was too greedy with questions. I pried when I shouldn't have. And I hated myself for it. I hated myself for many things. I couldn't do anything right; I couldn't make anybody love me; I couldn't even make the conversation last. I was worthless. And why wouldn't I be? I wasn't even alive.

Truth be told, I had spent my afterlife at the cabin with all my friends and it was pathetic. I should have had somewhere to go—somewhere to be—but instead, I was following these people around like a lost puppy.

At some point, the tears ran dry. I lifted my head from the gravel and dusted off my face. And sometime later, the pity I had felt for myself went cold, allowing the fear to creep back in. That's when I knew. That's when I knew it was time to leave. When the owl started calling out and sending chills down my spine. The point where I started to look into the forest and worry about predators. That was my cue to leave. I got to my bare feet, dusted off my knees, and began walking. I didn't know what direction I was heading in, but anything was better than being stagnant.

I had a long time to rethink how I was living my afterlife. There were a few things I was sure of that came to light after my gran left. One of them being I needed to help Walker find his soulmate. I needed to release his soul so that he could be free how he deserved. It was my priority—far more important than anything I had planned for myself. The second thing I knew for sure was that I was doing this all wrong.

If I was already dead, then what was I doing, spending my time worrying about any of this? I'd come here to have the best summer of my life before I went off to college. Many of us were moving away. And if I didn't take this summer to live out what should have been . . . then I don't think I'd ever forgive myself. Perhaps I wouldn't move on at all.

There was no point in worrying about the things I could not control—the things I couldn't even understand. And the things that made little, if any, sense. There was no point in worrying about things that may not even be real. And I had no way of telling what was. For this reason, as I walked through the forest, I realized I was letting this opportunity slip by me. To be dead and yet still alive, roaming this earth with my friends . . . It was a gift to have more time with them. There must've been something that I was robbed of. Unfinished business, placing me back at the cabin for the summer.

I had to make this the best summer ever, like I'd wanted when I was a senior in high school. I had to kiss boys. Fall in love. I had to go to concerts and fairs. I had to go to the farmer's market and sunbathe out by the lake. Soak up the sunlight before it penetrated right through me.

I had to do it all because if I knew one thing, this was my last chance. And I was already on borrowed time.

It hit me like a ton of bricks. My stomach felt like I had fallen off a thirty-story building. I jolted and reached my arms out wide, surprised to discover bed sheets balled up in my fists. I shot up, my back straight as a board. I looked around the master bedroom of the cabin, and I was surprised to find myself in bed where I had thought I'd fallen asleep. The sun was bright through my window, and quite some time had passed. The room was hot, and the downstairs was loud with laughter. I must've been sleeping the entire time, but for the *life* of me, I couldn't believe it. My gran, her spirit, it had been so real. More real than anything . . . more real than life itself had ever been. I closed my eyes and shook my head, but all I could see were the crystals of her pale green, emerald eyes staring back at me.

If I ever saw her again, I made a promise to myself that I wouldn't attack her with questions. I wouldn't push her away, and above all else, I would never scream at her again. I wondered if she would ever come back to me after I'd treated her that way.

Gran had mentioned something about rules, and I imagined she had already been breaking a few by talking to me in the first place. I didn't know when or if I would see her next, but until then, I had defined some purposes, whereas before, I had none. I was going to help Walker find the girl, and I was going to have fun doing it. I was going to enjoy my friends because, like Lainey—whom I hadn't seen in days—I knew my time with them was limited. And I wanted to soak them up like the sun that was void in the dark forest.

CHAPTER 7

It was the day before the fishing tournament, and I had convinced every girl in the cabin to secretly enter the tournament against the boys. Everybody thought it was a great idea, and we couldn't wait to see their faces when our boat pulled up next to theirs on the morning of the competition.

There was a different air to the cabin, and maybe it was because I had a shift in mindset, or maybe it was just going to be a good day, but either way, I was grateful that things had finally turned around. The summer of fun was just what I needed—it's what we all needed, and I was happy to be back on track. That didn't mean that I missed Lainey any less, and she still took up a lot of my mind. I still searched for her between the pines every morning when I took Gunner out for his daily walk. And though I had lost most of my hope of finding her, I knew firsthand that the alternative wasn't so bad. Secretly, I hoped she would come back to me.

I didn't know what death looked like for my gran. She seemed to be having a different experience than I. But for me, things were pretty much the same. It was a little weird here and there. I was by far the outcast of the group, but that was normal for me. I'd always been the outcast. My dyslexia had set me apart in second grade, and I had never come back from that. I'd always been pulled out for special classes, and I had always asked the other kids for help with directions. I had never been the leader, and I had never been independent, simply because I couldn't. Not at school. But maybe, just maybe, I'd find my place here in the afterlife. Maybe being the outcast wasn't so bad.

Scarlett May, Kimber, and Emma piled into the back of the cab, and I took the front seat. We told the guys that we were going out for breakfast, and when they wanted to join us, we insisted it was girl time. Kai didn't seem to care, but when Scarlett May complained about her period, he threw his hands up in the air and backed away slowly.

A sweet mountain of a woman named Henry—after her father—gave us a ride into town. She suggested Paula's Pancake House for breakfast. All the locals did. Not just because the pancakes were delicious, but because it was the only breakfast spot in town. If you wanted more options, you would have to go to the other side of the lake, which took forever to drive. It was worth it sometimes, but not today when our focus was signing up for the fishing tournament.

We had Henry drop us off at the local fishing store where we could fill out our entry forms and pay the fees for the Baylor Bass Tournament.

The door chimed, and two sportsmen stopped in their tracks when the four of us walked in.

"Hi, we'd like to enter the Bass Tournament," I said. The two men stifled laughter, and it irritated not only me but Scarlett May. I grabbed her arm when the men turned their focus and shook my head. They retrieved the forms we needed, and I scowled at Scarlett May, hoping she wouldn't say anything too snarky.

"How many of you?" one of the men asked.

"Five of us," I said, still accounting for Lainey.

"You're going to need two boats then," he said, pointing between us. "You won't all fit in the same boat."

"Sure. Two boat entries," I said, looking between the girls. Kimber nodded positively, and Emma was busy looking at a pink worm lure. Emma and I started to fill out the paperwork, and it looked like one of the boats was going to be short a member. When I counted out on my fingers, I realized I was accounting for Lainey. Emma's eyes fluttered down to the paperwork, and without much thought, I entered Walker's name on the line instead.

No harm, no foul. If he didn't want to join, he didn't need to. When all was said and done, when the fees had been paid and we were signed up, the girls and I decided to check out the pancake house. It was just what I needed—an actual girls' trip. Only a couple of blocks away, it was a short walk. The sun was still buried behind the morning fog but working diligently to burn it off. I noticed that the flyers for Big Jim had been taken down around town. The thought of it made my palms sweat.

We got settled in at Paula's Pancake House, and after looking over the menus, we were ready to order. All of us except for Kimber ordered the special. She got an egg white omelet.

"Have any of you heard about that guy that was murdered? I think he worked at the grocery store?" Kimber asked, eyeing my butter-soaked pancakes.

My stomach dropped, and I momentarily stopped chewing to survey the girls.

"Yeah, that was Big Jimmy. He's psychotic! He probably did it to himself! Everybody knows him, and he goes off his medication and gets super weird and violent. He's the guy that attacked Kinsley in the grocery store." Scarlett May gestured toward me with her fork. I felt my cheeks heat as all the girls looked at me for confirmation.

"Yeah, it's true he did," I muttered.

"Oh my god, do you think he's tied to what happened to Lainey?" Kimber asked. All the girls fell silent, as nobody wanted to think about it.

"I bet he is, that sick son of a bitch!" Scarlett May said, her fist coming down on the table.

"Do you think he did it? I mean, not just Lainey . . . but Trinity too?" Kimber asked, her voice quiet and solemn.

All of us looked at each other anxiously, and everybody was thinking about it, but nobody wanted to say it. I was the only one who had any insight on Jimmy. He had squirreled away Trinity's jacket in the tower. It was the jacket she'd worn the night she went missing. It was strong evidence that he was her killer. And I knew he had it in him from the attack on Walker and me. But he had nothing to do with Lainey's disappearance. Because he hadn't been alive when she disappeared. I feared something else was to blame for that.

There was something else. Something in the water. There was something bigger than all of us, including Big Jimmy, that threatened our lives here in Baylor. And if I had to guess, I would say their disappearance had something to do with the Baylor phenomenon.

"I don't know. I'm still hoping that Lainey turns up," I said quietly.

"You can't be serious?" Scarlett May said. Her brows furrowed, and I couldn't quite tell, but it almost looked like she was disgusted with me.

There were two groups of girls among our friends. Subdivided by popularity. Trinity, Scarlett May, and Kimber were the popular ones. Then, held together by the guys in the group, were us: Lainey, Emma, and me. There wasn't much overlap between us. We weren't friends on our own, and I imagined Noah was the one who brought our two groups together to build one. But Trinity's group wasn't just made up of the popular ones but the *mean* ones. They didn't have a problem saying what they meant or cutting you down to size. In fact, I think they liked it. I think they enjoyed making us feel small, and I imagined it made them feel more important.

Emma, Lainey, and I were the less liked and nerdier of the group. Lainey was always into plants and nature, while Emma was the bookworm. She'd read all day if she could. And I was just the introvert. I was the introspective, insecure one. I was always physically present, but my mind would be gallivanting somewhere else. Somewhere deep, full of self-doubt and observation. I looked for the reasons and the proof that I was a wallflower. And honestly, I think I liked it. I liked knowing that I was unseen. There's a lot less responsibility for an invisible person. And now that I thought of it, being dead kind of suited me. But for whatever reason, my voice was still heard . . . my face still seen. I had to deal with Lainey's disappearance, just like everybody else.

"She's dead, Kinsley. I don't know why you haven't accepted that yet." Scarlett May snapped. She brought her fork down, stabbing her pancake and scraping it against the plate. The sound of the metal scraping the porcelain was painful to my ears. I winced from both the sound and her comment.

I looked at Kimber. She had been so busy eyeing our pancakes that I didn't think she had heard a single word. She chewed mindlessly as her eyes darted from plate to plate. I felt the tension flowing off Emma, who sat next to me. Emma, Lainey, and I were always the best of friends, but it was Lainey and I who were the closest. Emma was always the third wheel.

"You don't know that," Emma said beneath her breath. It was unlike her to stand up to Scarlett May. But this time, it struck a chord. And I was proud of her.

"Oh, yes, I do. You'll see," Scarlett May said, staring deep into Emma's eyes. The rest of our breakfast was uncomfortable. It was hard to grieve for somebody you weren't sure had lost their life. It was almost as if I was teetering on the edge of hope and despair, and it changed from one moment to the next.

I hated how cold-hearted Scarlett May could be, and she had a way of making a bad situation worse. The only difference between Scarlett May and Trinity was that Scarlett May was all bark and no bite. Trinity, on the other hand—she'd let you pet her and then bite you when you turned your back.

I was thankful when Kimber finally joined the conversation and it turned from our deceased and missing friends to more lighthearted matters—like boys. I wasn't about to forget that my best friend was out there somewhere and needed me. But I was happy to engage in a conversation that pulled on the heartstrings a little less.

"Do you think that Noah and Trinity had a secret thing going between them?" Kimber asked me. It hurt to know that he was one of the last to see her, and probably he saw quite a bit of her.

Noah and I? There wasn't much to tell. He'd been my longtime crush, but something had changed when he'd gone into that bedroom with Trinity. Some sort of loyalty had been lost. He knew it. I knew it. But a part of me still had feelings for him. It was possible I might always be curious about him and what could have been.

"I can't tell you how Noah feels, but I wasn't convinced that he liked her," I said.

"That's because you thought he liked you?" Scarlett May asked, brows raised.

"No! That's not it," I said. My fork made that awful sound on my plate.

"He did, though, or *does*, right?" Emma asked.

I scowled, looking at her. It wasn't something I wanted the other side to know. What was going on between Noah and me was a secret. It was a secret because I wasn't convinced he really liked me. Or that he wanted to be seen with me. Sure, I was good enough to be his friend, but *girlfriend*? Probably not. But now that we were out of high school, things could be different. If I hadn't died, that may have . . . Well, it would never work now.

"I've been seeing you with some local. He always comes around the docks, even when you're not here at the cabin. Who is he? He's kinda cute," Kimber said. The thought of her calling Walker cute made my blood boil. I knew I couldn't have him either, but I still wanted to keep him for myself.

I found myself stuck between Noah and Walker. I couldn't have Noah because we were partially separated by a thin, translucent veil. One side living, and the other not knowing how to move on. On the other hand, I couldn't have Walker because his heart belonged to another. Yet, somehow, I still had feelings for both of them. It's true. My feelings for Noah had been seriously dampened since the thing with Trinity—and even more so since Walker came into the picture—but I couldn't deny that there was something still lingering every time I passed him in the kitchen or hallway. The tension of what-if?

"That's just . . . he's just a friend. He's staying at a cabin across the lake. He might do the tournament with us," I said with a shrug.

"Really?" Emma asked.

"Yeah. It's no big deal."

"Because I was thinking maybe you and I could be a team, and then Kimber and Scarlett May could be a team," Emma said. I looked at the other girls across the table, and one look was clear enough that they didn't want Emma in their boat.

"That sounds great. You don't mind if he joins us, though, right?" I asked.

"There's something in the water . . ." Emma said, though it didn't line up with the movement of her lips. And the voice a fraction lower than hers.

My eyes flicked from her lips to her eyes and then across the table to Scarlett May and Kimber. Nobody had a look on their face that told me something was out of the normal, and the more I looked at them in question, the more suspicious they became. I cleared my throat.

"I'm sorry. What did you say?" I asked.

"I said I don't mind. That's great," Emma said, shaking her head.

"Okay, great," I said, nodding. I let my eyes wander over the other customers in the pancake house. None of them were close enough to have spoken the secret message, but I'd heard it loud and clear.

"Excuse me, miss, we're ready for the check," Kimber said, waving down the waitress. A cute blonde nodded and ran off to get our check. But when she came back to the table to thank us for dining with her, there was only one thing I heard.

"There's something in the water . . ." she said. Her eyes fixed on mine when she said it. Although her lips said something much different. Like a bad voice-over on an old film.

I swallowed a lump that was rising in my throat and anxiously fiddled with my clothing. This had happened to me before when I was out in the forest. I didn't like where it was going, and I worried it would get worse before it got better. I reached down to my phone and called a cab immediately. I was thankful when Henry had still been in town and she arrived quickly to give us a ride back to the cabin.

I hadn't escaped the cab ride without hearing Henry advise me about the water in some secret message only I could hear. I wanted to scream. I knew there was something in the water! I had felt it firsthand. And it wasn't something I wanted to come into contact with again. I knew I would be out on that water the next day, and it was almost enough to make me cancel the tournament. But I knew I would have Walker by my side, and I felt safe when he was in my presence.

I decided right then and there, when Henry told me there was something in the water, that I wouldn't do the tournament unless Walker agreed to do it with me. Emma would be a nice addition to our team, of course, but it was Walker that I needed. When we got back to the cabin. I called Walker immediately. I was thankful he agreed to do the tournament with us. Moreover, he seemed excited.

Emma and I spent half the night hiding in my

bedroom, trying to figure out how to spool the fishing poles. It was more complicated than it first seemed. And somehow, we continued to get knots in the line.

"So, breakfast was awkward. I wish Scarlett May wasn't such a bitch!" Emma said, her tone so out of character that it made me laugh.

"You know, don't let her get to you. She means well, but she says it in the worst possible way."

"The worst."

"Um . . ." Emma began. When she said nothing more, I glanced at her. Her lips were pressed into a thin line, and her cheeks were red.

"Yeah?"

"No. Never mind," she said quickly.

"What is it?" I asked.

"It's stupid. Never mind." She batted a hand through the air.

I put the fishing line down on the bed. "Just say it. What?"

"Well, I don't want to offend you . . ." she said.

Only slightly offended already, I pressed her to continue. "Just say it so we can both move on." I shrugged, picking up the line again, and examining a knot.

"I just want to know what it's like."

"What?"

"Um. What it's like to be a ghost?"

My stomach dropped. This life was so real, I had

almost forgotten. The reminder came crashing down on me. What was it like? It was like nothing ever changed.

"I'm sorry. You're offended," Emma said, disappointed with herself.

"No. It's not that. It's hard to put into words. It's like the same life I had before, only my future's been stripped away. All the best parts of my life are now behind me. And sometimes I think I'm losing myself. Like my mind is deteriorating the further I sink into the afterlife. I'll never have anything real again, and I'll probably never find love."

Emma's brows knitted together. "Huh. I never want to die. Does it hurt?"

"I didn't either. Part of me is glad I don't remember it. I think it would be harder that way. Um, no it doesn't hurt. But I get these headaches quite often, and I'm starting to think they have something to do with the crash. They're only temporary," I said, biting on the fishing line, trying to free a knot.

"Are you going to tell your mom?"

I rolled my eyes, temporarily giving up on the knot. "I mean, I assume she knows. I did call her, but I only heard a one-sided conversation. I think I made up the whole thing," I said.

"She's probably heartbroken," Emma said.

I nodded slightly. She probably was. The thought of it made me unbelievably homesick. Emma must have realized she'd gone too far. She sucked in a quick breath and pressed on.

"Hey, did you notice Kimber was, like, oddly obsessed with our pancakes?" Emma asked, her eyes darting from side to side. I let out a chuckle because I actually had noticed.

"I totally saw that! I don't know why she didn't just order them, she clearly wanted them."

"Do you think that maybe she's not eating enough?" Emma looked at me, her eyes scrunched, as if she shouldn't be talking about it.

I sighed. "Sometimes I wonder the same thing. I catch her staring at the mirror quite often, and it's usually from her backside. She changes her clothes all the time . . . probably because she doesn't like the way she looks in them. I don't think she knows how pretty she is," I said.

"What a shame, to have it all, but not to see it," Emma said, baring her teeth.

"That egg white omelet? That looked gross." I shook my head, narrowing my gaze on the tiny translucent knot between my fingertips.

"I thought it looked good!" Emma laughed.

"You would," I said smiling, trying to bite the knot again. I rolled my eyes, giving up on untangling the line and dug through the lures we had bought. Of course, there was the pink one. Emma just had to get that one. I left the blue one for Walker and opened a small package of gold worms that felt like they had oil covering them. I smelled my fingers and made a face. Emma laughed.

"Do you think we should talk to her about it?" she asked, as I wiped my fingers on my jeans.

"I don't know. I wouldn't know what to say," I said, hating the way that I felt helpless.

Kimber and I weren't the closest of friends, but she was my favorite out of that side of the group. Scarlett May had her times when she seemed subdued, and Trinity had a few moments where she and I actually clicked. She could be a lot of fun when she wanted to be. But Kimber? She was the nicest. The only reason she hung out with the mean girls was that she was one of the most popular girls in school. If she hadn't been, I'm sure she would've come over to our side of the group long ago. But the poor girl had such low self-esteem. I'm sure the other two steamrolled her all the time. It was hard to watch.

"Maybe we can just tell her that she looks really skinny and that she should eat more," Emma said with a shrug as she tried to tie a hook to the end of the line.

"You know, I've thought about this a bunch. Sometimes when you say something to her about her looks, it's almost like she goes backward. It doesn't seem like a compliment to her. And I doubt telling her to eat more would feel like a positive thing, either."

"But why?" Emma asked.

"Because. I don't think she really wants to be skinny. I think it's like a skipping record that plays in her head. The problem is much deeper than that. Kimber doesn't see herself the way she really is when she looks in the mirror. It's all distorted by her insecurities." I held up the fishing rod, proud of my mangled mess. I was certain that when Walker saw it, he'd laugh.

I had never gone fishing before, although I had sat in the boat while Noah fished when we were kids. Sure, I held the pole every now and then, but I had no idea how to put bait on my hook or how to spool the reel. I had several knots here and there, and I was pretty sure I had done it completely wrong. But as long as the line was in the water and the worm was on the hook, I figured I would do all right.

Emma laughed, and when she showed me hers, it was even worse than mine. We both laughed together, and I buried my head in a pillow.

"We are *so* going to win this tournament!" Emma said.

CHAPTER 8

It was early morning. Gray light, the cold mist upon my face, and the smell of the lake. Emma and I were the first to wake, and we snuck out of the house holding our fishing poles. I had a sack lunch. Emma had a huge cooler she struggled to carry but a big smile on her face, and I knew that we had done right by entering the tournament. This really could be a summer to remember. Maybe not the best—not what it should have been—but I was positive that we could find a few nuggets of joy along the way. And this tournament was going to be one of them.

We were making our way down to our boat, which was tied to the dock. A bunch of bananas was tucked under my arm. It was probably the only thing I knew about fishing. It was bad luck to have a banana on the boat. Strategically, Emma and I placed a banana in each of the guys' boats.

"Should I put one in Scarlett May's boat too? Or just

the guys?" Emma asked. I looked up at her with a wicked air, and a slow smile spread across my face.

"Hell, throw *two* bananas in their boat!" I said. Emma smiled and tossed a couple in.

"Well, aren't you the devious ones!" Walker appeared out of nowhere. The fog was so thick I never saw his canoe coming. I stifled a laugh and ran to the dock's edge to help him tie up.

"Thank you so much for joining us," I said.

"Us?" Walker asked.

"I hope you don't mind. Emma's going to join us. Scarlett May and Kimber weren't exactly welcoming," I said in a whisper.

Walker looked at Emma with his head cocked to the side and a sympathetic stare. "I don't mind. The more, the merrier. Now, who are all the bananas for?" he asked.

"Boat one consists of Asher, Noah, and Ethan. Boat two is Levi, Mason, and Kai," Emma said, pointing. "Boat three is Scarlett May and Kimber. That boat there is ours." Emma dusted her hands.

"Waking up early to destroy the competition, I knew I was on the right team!" Walker said.

I held my hand out and Walker took it as he crawled out of his canoe. He didn't need my help, of course, but I was happy to give it. It was the small moments where our hands met that made me feel alive. I looked back to the house as I remembered that nobody had let Gunner out. Nobody took care of him the way I did.

"Hey, you guys, I'm just going to run up and let Gunner out real quick. He probably needs to go to the bathroom."

"We're really early, so take your time," Emma said. They situated the tackle as I jogged down the dock and back up the hill. When I got close to the cabin, I could hear him scratching on the door and knew I had made the right decision. But as I opened the door, he lurched out, blew past my legs, and took off running. Now I feared I had made a terrible mistake and that Gunner would run away. We didn't have time for this. Not this morning. I threw my hands up in the air as I watched him barrel down the hill, wondering where he was going and why he wasn't running toward the woods. It didn't take long for him to jump into the water. All he needed was a morning swim. I shrugged and held my hands out. I could hear Walker's laughter from where I stood on the back porch before I started down the hill again.

The sky was getting lighter now; everybody would be awake soon. I wanted to get on the water before they were up to find the bananas in the boats and give us all hell about it. But I knew I couldn't leave without having Gunner locked up safely in the cabin. "He really likes the water, huh?" Walker asked.

"I guess so," I said with a shrug.

"I don't think he's going to come out on his own, Kinsley. He looks like he won't go without a fight," Emma said.

I sighed, knowing that she was right.

"Let's bring him," Walker suggested.

"Bring him? That would be a disaster," I said, shaking my head.

"No, it'll be great. I used to fish with my dog all the time. Dogs like that love the water," Walker said as he tried to lure Gunner to the boat. With a little coaxing, Gunner was in the boat, getting all the seats wet. I turned to Emma, and we shared a look of trepidation.

"See? He loves it!" Walker said as Gunner shook off the excess water, completely drenching the inside of the boat. All I could think about was my jeans soaking through, making it look like I'd peed my pants. But if it was going to make Gunner happy, it was the least I could do. If Lainey had been here, she would probably want to bring him too.

We set off just as the sun made its debut. Walker did the rowing, and Emma and I sat huddled together for warmth. Gunner ran back and forth through the tiny boat, rocking it. We didn't need a banana on the boat when we had him. With all this running back and forth, I had no doubt that I would end up in the water by the end of the tournament. And the water was no place I wanted to be.

My eyes settled on Emma's pink fishing lure. There

was no way we were going to win the Baylor Bass Tournament, and likely, we wouldn't even board a fish. But my goal here wasn't to beat the guys—as much as I'd like to. My goal in entering the tournament was to see the look on their faces when we pulled our boat up next to theirs. I knew it would be a moment to remember. And with any luck, Walker would have some skill with fishing and we could at least have one fish to dangle in front of their faces. It was about making memories, and we had already succeeded at that.

It was when the cabin was far behind us that I could hear the booming voice echoing across the lake. I didn't know for sure, but I figured it was Mason yelling over the bananas he found in the boat. It brought a warm smile to my face, and I couldn't be happier with how the morning started. Gunner hadn't settled down yet, but I was hopeful that he would.

"So, I think we're going to start off on the east side. There's a cove called Blackwell's over there, and I've been pretty lucky fishing in that spot before," Walker said, rowing in that direction.

"Yeah, yeah," Emma said.

"Whatever you think," I said and nodded.

It was a little quiet in the morning before our caffeine kicked in. I could tell that Emma was uncomfortable with Walker. Not uncomfortable because she didn't know him, or even that she knew too much about him, but more like she was uncomfortable because he was attractive. She avoided eye contact with him, and when he spoke to her, she often blushed and started to fidget. I couldn't blame her for that. If I hadn't gotten to know him, or if he hadn't saved my life, I doubt I would have felt comfortable enough around him to be myself. He was *that* attractive. Walker caught my eye and he smiled, his dimples piercing his cheeks. I looked at Emma and wrinkled my nose, laughing at how her cheeks were a rosy hue.

After catching a few bass—which apparently were small ones—we changed spots. It was beginning to get warm, and I knew that all three of the boats tied to our dock were now on the lake. I didn't need to see Scarlett May and Kimber flounder around on their boat, squealing over the bait, but I did want to see the guys. I wanted to tease them about the bad luck we gave them in the early morning. And I wanted to see their faces when we told them we already had a catch and release. But it was an enormous lake. Big enough that if we didn't know where they were going to be ahead of time, we might never meet up. Thankfully, I had listened in on Asher's conversation with Ethan last night, and they were going to fish fairly close to the cabin.

I wasn't too sure where Levi, Mason, and Kai were fishing, but if I had to guess, I'd say the two boats would stay close together. Heck, even the girls would probably stay close to the cabin. I'm sure that Kimber didn't have the strength to row the boat as far as we had. Walker's arms were broad and strong. But that's not all; he'd been commanding this canoe for some time. Twenty years maybe. He was conditioned for rowing. And I couldn't say that about anybody else in the cabin.

"Let's head back and see if anybody else caught anything," I said.

"Is anybody hungry? I made some breakfast burritos," Emma said. She took out a bag of three tinfoil-wrapped burritos from the cooler and closed the lid quickly. My mouth watered.

"That sounds fantastic. Thank you," I said, reaching out for the breakfast. Walker said the same.

"What else do you have in there?" he asked, trying to peek inside the cooler.

"You'll see. It's a secret," Emma said, bright red.

Before I knew it, we were drifting on the lake, no longer fishing or rowing, but it was the best part of the tournament. The pleasant conversation and tasty food. I'd had Emma's burritos before, and while they were always good, everything tasted better on the water. Gunner pressed his nose into my thigh, begging with a little whimper. Had he not been my best friend's companion, I wouldn't have sacrificed the butt of my breakfast burrito. But because he was, I shared, and he thanked me by nearly snapping my fingers off.

I found it funny that the best part of the fishing

tournament was the part when we weren't fishing. Nothing but quality time with Walker and Emma. The more time Emma spent with Walker, the more she loosened up, and I could tell that her personality had started to come through. She was fond of Walker, but I didn't mind. I knew he was taken. And I couldn't blame her, because I thought he was adorable. Walker seemed to enjoy Emma's company as well, and I wondered if he'd had much interaction as a ghost for the past twenty years. And then I briefly wondered what would happen when everybody left the cabin and only I remained.

The day seemed to fly by. We caught two keepers, which Walker seemed disappointed by, and the three of us got ridiculous sunburns. It wasn't until afternoon that we headed back to the cabin and spotted the other three boats. It was as glorious as I had hoped. Mason stood up, throwing his arms into the air and yelling belligerently about the bananas. It was clear that he had been drinking, and none of us could understand what he was saying. We laughed so hard, Emma pointed at him, and I wrapped my arms around my stomach. Somewhere after the laughter lightened, I caught a glimpse of Noah's face. It was a look I didn't know well on him, and if I had to imagine, I'd say it was jealousy. I wasn't proud of it, but there was a part of me that enjoyed it just a little bit.

Noah had hurt me. He knew it, I knew it, Trinity knew it. The three of us knew I had feelings for him, and the funny part was, I believed Noah felt the same toward me. Why he'd done it? I'd never know. I had given up on trying to figure that out. Things never went back to normal for me and him, and . . . well, I liked to blame that on his actions with Trinity, but I knew there was a large part of it that had to do with my feelings for Walker. Still, to see him want me the way I had wanted him for the past year . . . it was satisfying in a deep and twisted way. I wasn't perfect; I knew that. Hell, I wasn't even human. I suppose I couldn't expect too much from myself. I looked from Noah to Walker and felt the uncomfortable pull of my heart in different directions . . . toward my old life and—with greater strength and possible pain—my new life with Walker.

"Hey, Wilde, catch anything yet?" Noah yelled. I held up the two fish we'd caught with pride. And Emma ripped open the cooler and stood tall and proud, holding a large salmon.

"Read 'em and weep, suckers!" Emma yelled, the salmon slipping out of her hands and hitting the bottom of the canoe.

"What!" I burst into laughter. Walker rolled onto his side, clutching his gut, laughing.

"Yeah, we're going to win the whole tournament! Caught this little guy over in Blackwell's Cove!" Emma yelled.

"Is that a store-bought salmon?" I choked out.

"Yeah, shhh. They don't need to know that," Emma shushed me.

Walker was dying of laughter.

"Is that a salmon?" Noah called out.

"Oh yeah. Just a little one," Emma gloated.

"Do they have salmon in this lake?" Mason asked Kai.

Emma's eyes grew large, and she whipped her head back to Walker. He couldn't speak, but he shook his head.

"Salmon don't live in Baylor Lake!" Kai shouted.

"You're a cheater!" Levi yelled out, laughing.

Emma sat back down and threw the slippery salmon back into the cooler. "Thirty bucks down the drain," she mumbled.

I grabbed her shoulder, laughing, and she cracked a smile. "Oh my god—"

"I thought I had this one in the bag," she said with a chuckle.

"It's okay. We got skunked too! I wonder why?" Noah said, holding up the banana. Gunner barked and rocked the boat.

"I got one!" Mason yelled, standing up as his pole darted around frantically. Kai and Levi jumped up in excitement for their first catch of the day, and their boat rocked back and forth. I imagined them falling into the water, and I watched with excitement as I tried to keep Gunner calm.

"They're going to beat us!" Scarlett May complained.

The two of them looked like they had done little all day except float around Rock Creek Cove. Kimber pulled out her phone to take pictures and video of Mason pulling up his fish, and we all watched eagerly. Walker rowed the boat a little closer, but Emma's fishing pole suddenly bent. Our attention snapped from Mason to Emma, who started screaming with delight. It was her first bite of the day, and it wasn't even store-bought.

"You got this," I said, standing up in the boat, which continued to rock. Gunner ran back and forth in the tight space of the canoe, and I reached out, grabbing Walker's shoulder to stabilize myself.

"Oh, they've got one too! Why didn't we catch anything!?" Kimber asked.

"Come on, man! We can't let the girls beat us!" Levi said to Mason as he pulled up a small fish. The guys yelled at Mason for making a big deal out of an eight-inch perch, and I could hear their laughter booming in the background. I wanted to laugh with them, but I was so focused on Emma's fight that I couldn't pull my gaze from the water. Gunner barked, running in circles.

"Slowly pull the reel up, allowing the fish to fight. Then, you're going to start reeling as you lower the pole back down. Go slow, as we don't want the line to snap," Walker coached. He placed his hand on Emma's forearm and helped guide her pole up and down. I tried to grab Gunner's collar to make the rocking stop, but it was impossible through all the commotion. I was pretty sure that Emma would catch nothing more than seaweed and all four of us would end up in the water by the end of the tournament.

"It's really fighting hard, huh?" Emma asked.

"Yeah, I think you have a big one!" Walker said with confidence.

"It feels like a big one!" she said between breaths. I tried to get a look but didn't dare lean over the water too far.

The anticipation grew as Emma fought the giant bass. Walker was kind and patient as he taught Emma everything he could in such a short time. I held onto Gunner as tightly as I could so he wouldn't rock the boat. I let my eyes flicker to the other boats in the cove. Scarlett May and Kimber watched carefully. Meanwhile, Asher and Ethan ate slices of pizza while watching Emma.

I was surprised to find Noah's eyes on me instead of the water or Emma like everybody else. Our gazes locked for just a moment and somewhere in that space I thought jealousy had turned to pain. Regret. He hated himself for the decisions he'd made, and there was a part of me that wanted to make it all better for him. Tell him I didn't care and that I still had feelings for him. But that ship had sailed.

Emma screamed with excitement. I stood up, leaning over the boat to catch a glimpse of the Baylor Bass

Tournament's winning fish. The boat tilted close to the water's edge.

"I've got it! I've got it!" Emma yelled.

"How big is it?" Mason yelled, hands cupped around his mouth.

"It's a big one!" Emma screamed as a figure slowly rose from the depths of the water. It was a big one. *Too big.* My stomach dropped as I realized this figure was no fish. It was huge. I wasn't sure what else would be in the water—something of this magnitude. Slowly, I leaned forward, trying to get a better look, but my eyes couldn't quite pierce the glare on the water's surface.

"What is that?" Walker mumbled to himself.

"I did it!" Emma squealed, looking around at everybody.

"It's really big . . ." I said in a warning tone. Fish shouldn't be that size.

As the prize-winning fish slowly rose. The glare from the water receded and medium-length brown hair surfaced. A body . . . *her* body.

A guttural scream ripped through Emma's throat as Lainey's freckled face breached the surface of the water. Emma dropped the fishing pole and flailed backward. I could hear shouts from every boat around us just as the cold water hit my back. I plunged deep into the lake, and I could see Gunner's paws hit the water just above me in the commotion.

His four legs thrashed about as my body sank deeper and deeper. I tried to swim back to the surface, but it was no good, because I wasn't in the lake alone.

Lainey's lifeless body was anything but dead—she came to life before my very eyes. Her flesh gray, and the whites of her eyes now yellow.

Her hands grabbed me as if her life depended on it. I let out a scream and wished I hadn't. It was the breath I needed to survive, and I'd just let it go. I clamped my mouth shut; the water escaping between my teeth. Fighting the urge to breathe as I wrestled my best friend under the water.

I kicked at her desperate eyes as she became more aggressive. She was oddly strong for how weak she looked, and I knew that there was no blood coursing through her veins. She opened her mouth, hissing, as I grabbed her arm and ripped her grip off my calf.

I delivered several kicks to her chest, finally freeing myself. I was swimming to the surface when I saw Walker dive into the water—he looked so far away. He swam down toward me, and I reached my hand out, but the distance between us was too far to grab hold.

Lainey's demon grabbed my foot and yanked me back down. I felt the fight leave my body, as I needed oxygen and had none.

I'd been here before, but the thing that had tried to kill me hadn't been my best friend. Neither was this, though.

The thing that had me tight in her grasp, drowning me, wasn't the girl I had grown up with. She wasn't the girl I had shared all my secrets with. She was a monster. And that was no more than Lainey's skin that it wore, and I had no trouble kicking my feet into its face.

"Wake . . ." she hissed. I watched her mouth move, and somehow her voice was a whisper in my ear and not at all muffled by the water.

I stopped fighting for just a second as not only the fatigue set in but also the confusion. I felt Walker's powerful hands grab at my arm, and he yanked my body upward.

He was just in time because I had nothing else to give. And neither did Lainey's ghost. I watched her yellow, desperate eyes begin to disappear into the depths of the water. And one last time I heard her whisper as clear as day.

"Wake up . . ."

CHAPTER 9

None of us won the tournament. Not even close. As if it mattered anyway. Finding Lainey was like a dark wet blanket that draped over us. We headed inside the cabin, leaving all our belongings in the boats. Walker joined us, and for the first time, he was one of us. I wished it was something else that had brought him close. Anything but the death of my best friend. It stripped away all the joy I would have had from him joining the team.

After the panic had subsided, silence followed. It was hard to understand how this could happen. Not once, but twice. To our friends, nonetheless. As a collective group, we didn't know what to do. Lainey was the one who had called the cops before, and as that turned out, it had never really helped anything. Not here. Not in Baylor. They showed up at our door asking questions, and they took a lot of notes, but beyond that, I don't think they did anything. And if the cops were so quick to arrest a stranger for the murder of Big Jimmy, I didn't know what they would do with this information. Perhaps the Baylor phenomenon had affected them as well.

It was a somber evening. Everyone sat in the living room. Seats were taken on the sofa, and when there was no more room, we sat on the floor. Everybody waited. Waited for somebody to speak up, for somebody to take the lead. I wasn't sure who was going to do it. By the looks of everybody else, nobody wanted the job.

"Are you sure it was her?" Mason asked, cutting through the silence.

"I'm sure," I said.

What I hadn't told him was just how sure. She was long gone, and whatever that thing was in the water, it wasn't her. I just kept thinking about those awful yellow eyes and how they had a message for me. I wondered if anybody else would've seen it or heard it. And how it was so clear even though we were submerged underwater.

"This can't be happening again . . . I can't . . ." Kimber stuttered and began to cry. Asher put his arm around her and pulled her in close. She whimpered into his chest.

"It's going to happen to all of us. One of us is going to be next. And it's not going to be me," Scarlett May said. I nodded in agreement.

"How can you be so sure?" Levi asked.

"I'm going to get out of here. I'm going home!" she replied.

That's good, I thought. *She should go home. They all should.* Why they hadn't already, I didn't know. Independence, I suppose. The fact that we were now adults. We can't run from this. We can't run from our lives the way we used to when we were kids. But they should now.

"You should go home. You should all go home. Now, right now!" I said, standing up in the middle of the group, urging them to save themselves from this evil.

"You should too. We all should," Noah said. His eyes flickered from mine to Walker's. I hung my head, remembering the time that I tried and failed.

It was then that Kimber pulled herself together. "I think I will," she said, reaching out to grab Scarlett May's hand.

"You guys go. I'll call the cops. I'm gonna stay back for just one extra day to contact the police. But I will be out on the very next flight. I promise," I said, my eyes fixed on Walker. He gave me a slight nod, and I knew we were both on the same page. He and I were tethered to this place. But there was no reason that the rest of my friends should endure the wrath of my personal hell. Walker and I could, and should, do this alone.

Scarlett May and Kimber jumped to their feet. They held hands as they left the room to go pack their belongings. Asher jumped online to buy plane tickets, and I went to call a cab.

"It's going to keep happening. And if it's not us, it's going to be them—somebody else. Somebody else's daughter . . . somebody else's girlfriend. I say we stay. We find this son of a bitch," Mason said, his voice booming with authority. It was leadership like I'd never seen from him.

"Yeah!" Levi said, jumping to his feet. The pit sank in my stomach. This was bad. They couldn't fight whatever this was. And if there was one thing I was sure of, they should've never come here. This was my mess. I don't know why or how they got dragged into it, but I was doing everything in my power to get them out. My eyes shifted to Walker, and I could see his worry. Being the older one in the room, he stepped forward.

"Look, the police are on this. They've already arrested a guy for Big Jimmy's murder. They think it was the same guy who got Trinity. And if I had to guess, it was probably the same person who got to Lainey. For all we know, he's already taken care of. But that doesn't mean that you guys shouldn't go home. This lake's not safe—not now, not ever. Mysterious things have been happening here for the last twenty years. Go home. Get the summer you deserve. And then have a life to live afterward," Walker said, looking each of us in the eyes.

I watched Mason and Levi rethink their prior

commitment to stay and fight. Levi's eye contact dropped off as he scoured the floor. He didn't want to admit it, but I could tell he wanted to go home too. It took little to sway him.

"I don't know about you guys, but I'm going home. I'm gonna take my girlfriend home," Asher said and followed Kimber out of the room to go pack.

"I'm sorry, Kinsley. I've got to go too," Ethan said, placing his hand on my shoulder. I forced a smile and nodded. I understood it. Heck, I even wanted them to go, but there was a small part of me that felt like they were leaving me behind. Because I was pretty sure it would be the last time I ever saw them again. And when all was said and done and Walker found Layla, I'd probably cease to exist.

What would happen when they went home? Would they find out about the accident I was in? Would they know they had spent the last few weeks at the lake with a ghost? Or would the phenomenon continue, and they would simply not remember, like Walker said happened to his friends. Time would leap, and they would look back on a hot and forgettable lakeside summer.

There were no flights that night, and everybody had to wait with their bags packed for an early morning flight. I tried to help Emma pack, but she insisted on staying with Walker and me. I couldn't tell if she was brave in the face of danger or so delusional that she believed this was one of her fantasy books. Maybe a murder mystery? I wasn't sure without the ending. But I insisted she leave with the others, and she came down on me very firmly, which was unlike her. I figured if Emma Olsen had raised her voice, it better be for a good reason, and I let her stay.

The night was long, but eventually the sun rose. We had big plans for the following day. It wasn't much, but it was the only thing I could think of. We were going to plant a tree in honor of Trinity and Lainey. Walker said he would go to town and get one at the nursery. As soon as he showed up, we were going to set out, find the perfect place in the forest, and give them the kind of memorial that they deserved. Of course, it wouldn't be in a church filled with friends and family, but it was the best we had in the reality we were suspended in.

"Kinsley, I wish I could say thank you for your hospitality, but this has been a total nightmare. If you were smart, you'd leave too." With that, Scarlett May gave me a tight squeeze. She didn't know how to say goodbye or thank you without criticism, but I felt her twisted love in the hug she gave me. I glimpsed Asher's face just as he rolled his eyes. I didn't want everybody to leave, but I knew it was best, and beyond that, I may or may not have been excited to have some peace and quiet to wrap my brain around my new life.

"Just get home safe, okay?" I said to Scarlett May.

Levi came up behind her and grabbed her bags. As the

night had worn on, he had become more and more eager to leave. He packed his belongings with increasing vigor.

Kimber came up to me next. She wrapped her arms around me, and though not as tight as Scarlett May, her hug was genuine. I felt her frail body shaking, and I felt terrible for putting her in any sort of distress beyond what she could handle. "I miss her so much," Kimber said.

"I know you miss Trinity. We all do," I said.

"Why don't you come with us? It's safer at home," Kimber asked. She pulled away to look into my eyes, but I avoided eye contact. The truth was, I wanted to go home. I wanted that more than anything. But from the conversations I've had with my mom, I knew that even if I could go home, it wouldn't be the same. My life was here. My purpose was here. And I needed to complete that so I could go to wherever it was that I belonged.

"I am coming home on the next flight out. I just have one little thing I need to do."

"What are you gonna do?" she asked, playing with my hair mindlessly.

"Well, for starters, we're planting a tree in Trinity and Lainey's honor in the forest this morning," I said.

"I think that's a beautiful idea. I wish I could be there to see it," Kimber said, her eyes dampening.

"I'll send pictures." I tucked her hair behind her ear and sent her on her way.

Asher was on her heels. He came up behind her, gave

me a quick hug, and told me to be safe. I slipped my hands into my back pockets, and I watched as my friends left one by one.

"Thanks for having us at the cabin, Wilde. I'm sorry we're leaving you with such a mess. Are you sure that this Walker guy can protect you? Because I have my doubts," Ethan said, hooking a thumb over his shoulder. I remembered the time he'd kicked Walker out of my bathroom, his forehead bleeding. Ethan was the strength I needed.

"Yeah, yeah, he's a good friend," I said. And all the things I didn't say were lost behind my eyes. I forced a smile and gave him a hug goodbye.

Emma was hugging Kimber through the window while Mason started pounding the side of the cab. "Let's go!" he yelled.

Noah had been hanging back to say goodbye last. He came up to me, hands deep in his pockets and a sheepish look on his face.

"Your mom's gonna kill me for not bringing you home."

"No, it's okay," I said.

"I'm sure we can get you a seat on the flight. You can take my seat? Just come home." Noah's eyes were filled with worry. And I hated to see him like that. But he couldn't help me now. That's what he couldn't understand.

"I already have my flight booked with Emma. We're leaving tomorrow morning. It's just twenty-four hours.

We're going to plant this tree in the forest. I have a meeting with the cops, and I've got some cleaning to do. Plus, I've got to tidy up the house . . . turn off the water—that kind of thing. It's easy work, but it has to be done," I said with a shrug. All of it was a lie, of course.

From years of coming up to the cabin. I had learned there was a checklist of things I needed to do before leaving the house vacant for months on end. Noah accepted my answer and gave me a hug. He pressed his lips onto my forehead. I could feel the hot air coming from his breath, and it spurred a weird tickle in my stomach— and made me curious—but I knew this was the last time I'd ever see him. I'd never know what would have happened between me and the next-door neighbor.

Kai picked me up and spun me around. He was more lighthearted than the rest. He said his goodbyes, but unlike everybody else, he wasn't worried about me staying in the house one more night. "Call us right when you get home, and we'll all go out. We'll celebrate for Trinity and Lainey," Kai said. And it sounded nice. I wanted to do that. And I hoped they would carry on without me.

"I will," I lied.

As the cab drove away, a sense of relief washed over me. A weight off my shoulders. I was happy they were driving away to safety. I wanted nothing more than to see them flourish. Have good lives. Long lives. But the selfish part of me didn't want to be left behind. A loneliness struck the bottom of my stomach. Emma slipped her arm over my shoulder, reminding me I wasn't completely abandoned. But there was safety in numbers, and those numbers were leaving us behind.

"Are you sure you don't want to go with them? I promise I won't hold it against you, and I can probably still call them to turn around. I have no doubt you can get a seat on that plane." Emma tilted her head to the side and frowned.

"Are you trying to get rid of me?" she asked. Her tone was somber.

"Are you serious? That's the last thing I'm trying to do. I just want you to be safe. That's all."

"I *am* safe. I'm with you. Nobody knows this town better than you do, and we have Walker. He's been here longer than your family has been, right? He's a local?" she asked, her brows rising.

"Well, technically, he just comes here on vacation. Kinda like us," I said, turning around and heading back inside.

"Whatever, I'm not worried."

"I wouldn't blame you if you were," I said honestly.

"I'm not scared! Do you know how many books I've read about murder mysteries? I know exactly what's happening here, and we will *not* be the next victims. Plus, for the first time, my life is more interesting than my books," she said.

This was her wheelhouse, and I wasn't going to argue with that. I'd never read a murder mystery in my life, but I didn't doubt that it had given her some ideas that she would find useful. Maybe we all would.

"Ready to go plant the tree?" I asked.

"Yeah, I guess we should go do that. I just don't want to say goodbye . . ." she said, her optimism fading.

"I know what you mean. But we don't have to say goodbye. We're just honoring them. There's a difference."

It wasn't long before Walker showed up at the cabin with an apple tree sapling in his hand. "It's all they had. I hope the fruit-bearing tree won't take away from the memorial. I wasn't really sure what I was looking for, but this was the only choice. You should see the size of that nursery—it was like a small hut," Walker said as he stepped inside. The branches were mere twigs, and they bent easily as he walked through the doorjamb. A few leaves fluttered to the ground, catching my eye.

"That's great. I had nothing particular in mind. Thank you for getting it," I said.

The three of us walked into the forest. Gunner ran off ahead of us as we walked down the trail in silence. I didn't have to ask where we should plant the tree; I knew the exact spot Walker was heading. It was off the beaten trail, where both the tower and cemetery lay. It was the landing that was different every time I had arrived. The part of the forest that changed daily. I wasn't sure we would ever find the tree again after planting it, but that wasn't the point. The point was to give back. Let roots grow where love was lost. Honor the life that they'd had, even though it was short. And we would do that by planting the apple sapling, even if we never saw it again.

Walker dug a decent-sized hole in the ground while Emma and I stood watching, our arms interlocked and her head resting on my shoulder. Once Walker had placed the sapling and covered it with the freshly turned soil, he stood by my side with dirt-stained knees and hands.

"Do you want to do the honors?" he asked me. But I didn't. How I felt couldn't be expressed in words. It was just a feeling in my chest. A feeling of hollowness without my best friend. I knew that, no matter what came out of my mouth, it would never be enough. I didn't say anything, though; I just acknowledged my pain.

"I'll say something?" Emma offered.

I nodded, encouraging her to do what I couldn't.

"Lainey, thank you for being the best of friends. Life's not going to be the same without you. I hope that wherever you are now, you're safe and your mind can rest. I love you and miss you already," Emma whispered. I squeezed her shoulder and fought the tears from forming in my eyes. I wanted to say so much . . . But I couldn't. And I knew I was going to regret it the moment we left, but the words just wouldn't come. The feeling of loss was just too massive. It reminded me of the time after my gran had passed and my mom asked if I wanted to talk about it. I hadn't been able to then either.

"And Trinity?" Walker asked.

Emma looked to me for an answer, and I knew we needed to say something in her honor too. Only she'd never really been nice to me. Therefore, I didn't feel qualified. But I found the words where they had been lost for Lainey.

"Trinity, I'm sorry we never had time to build the friendship I know we were capable of. May you finally find peace," I said. I didn't dare lift my gaze to Emma or Walker for fear of being judged.

Silence blanketed the forest as we took a moment to honor them. My throat tightened when I remembered Lainey on the days when the sun was hot and the wind picked up her hair. The days when she laughed out loud and her smile was infectious. I locked it up tight, for I had always wanted to remember her in the fresh, sunny air . . . and not in the depths of the cold, dark water.

CHAPTER 10

The tree was planted and left in the forest to thrive on its own. I hoped it would. I hoped it would survive—grow strong and tall, and find sunshine so that its roots would grow deep and rich in soil. I hoped that one day, my friends would come back to the forest and see the tree and know that it had been planted just for Lainey. Trinity too. It was one small act, but at the moment, it felt like so much more.

"Do you want to watch a movie?" Emma asked.

The cabin was empty and quiet—if you could call it that. Almost static in its energy, the silence seemed louder than the voices ever had been. I never thought it would be as unsettling as it was. And I already missed the booming voice of Mason and the testosterone that flooded the kitchen. I even missed Scarlett May's obnoxious criticisms that filled the air with the constant flow of sarcasm. I missed it all more than I thought I would. But most of all, I missed Lainey. I missed how I felt like we were on the same page. Like whatever I was going through, I wasn't alone. She got me like nobody else did. And I always imagined that, whereas Lainey understood me, Emma thought too highly of me for that. I knew she looked up to me . . . but I didn't know why. It was a lot of pressure on me, and I felt like I needed to protect her from whatever evil was out there because she was too naïve—too whimsical. She wanted this to be her open door into a magical world because that's what she read in her books. But this wasn't Emma's calling. This was my life . . . or at least my *afterlife*. And somehow, for reasons I could never understand, she was trapped in it.

"Yeah, why don't you pick out a movie? I'm just going to get some pajamas on," I said.

The truth was, I needed a moment alone. I took my time on the stairs, my fingers trailing the banister. There was an idea on the tip of my tongue I couldn't quite extract. Something I needed to do—needed to check on. I couldn't remember though, as I looked around the cabin. But when I closed my bedroom door, I gave up on the missed thought and got ready for the movie. I wondered what she would pick and hoped that it didn't have an ounce of horror in it—my nerves couldn't take much more. That's when I saw the blinking light of the surveillance camera.

I remembered what it was I was supposed to do. I needed to check on the surveillance cameras. I glanced back at the door, afraid to look at the footage. Afraid of all the things I might find and the things I wouldn't. I opened up my laptop and logged into the security website. I didn't know what I feared most. Was it another malfunction? Or something that I had never even considered? Like seeing Lainey on these cameras or my gran. What if it picked them up? What if hauntings had been happening all throughout the cabin, day and night? What if there were messages carved into the walls? What if there was evil?

The page loaded, and all cameras had a tiny thumbnail—not a black square, but an actual feed. I clicked on the video from the kitchen and watched Emma grab a bowl of popcorn and sit down on the sofa. And then I took a deep breath and scrolled back for days. My neck flushed with heat as I found the video hadn't cut out like it had before. I watched myself set up the camera and back away like an idiot. Despite being alone, it embarrassed me, and I hoped that nobody would ever see it.

I watched Kimber sit down next to Asher when I went outside, as they thought they had a moment alone. He reached over and kissed her, and my envy surprised me. I wanted to be kissed like that. I wanted somebody to *want* me like that. Nobody ever did. Right then, the video feed froze. Serves me right for watching a private moment. I slapped the back of my laptop shut. "Come on!" I said under my breath, disappointed that the video feed still had problems.

I closed my eyes for a moment and opened my laptop again. I'd refresh the page, and when it wouldn't work, I'd check the other camera files. Just when I'd convinced myself that it was the terrible internet connection at the lake house, Asher and Kimber pulled apart. The footage came back on just in time to capture me coming through the back patio door.

I sped up the feed through all the inactivity. Surprisingly, there was a lot of it, and I stopped when I found a particular moment when the kitchen was full and everybody was making lunch. I stopped to watch for anything unusual. I checked the faces, looking for ghosts that had slipped back into the cabin when nobody was watching. Nothing out of the ordinary happened as I watched myself make a sandwich. Noah watched me intently as he loaded chips on his plate. I hadn't noticed that in person. Kimber checked herself out in the reflection of a mirror, which wasn't abnormal. Mason and Levi ate three times what any human should, but I knew they had ravenous appetites. These were football guys—big and muscular. The amount of groceries I had bought to sustain them was insurmountable.

I searched every inch of that screen for something abnormal. My gran wasn't there, and neither was Lainey or Trinity. No ghost hauntings, no flickers of screens. No spiritual beings crossing the video feed. There was absolutely nothing abnormal. And I should have felt comforted by that, but I was disappointed. I watched as I took my plate of food outside. And I remembered I'd gone and eaten alone on the dock that day.

I was just about to close my laptop when everybody seemed to slow down. Not quite like they had before, where the video seemed to stop completely, but actually slow down, as if in slow motion. I watched as my friends slowly froze until they were as still as could be. I brought the screen closer to my face, trying to see the detail. Trying to see if their eyes were still blinking. It was such a weird image that it almost looked like a setting from a wax museum. I assumed that maybe the camera had frozen again, but when I saw the seconds tick by at the bottom of the camera, my blood ran cold.

I skipped forward a minute, then two. They remained still—the time continued. I skipped forward a half an hour, and they had only moved a couple of feet. Mason's sandwich was finally to his mouth. Kimber's eyes had finally made it up the length of her body in the mirror. And I was still gone. I cocked my head to the side and placed the laptop down on my bed. I couldn't grasp what was happening. It was even weirder than the cameras failing to record.

"Kinsley? Are you coming?" Emma yelled from downstairs.

"One second!" I called back.

I almost looked away, but an image of my reflection coming onto the back porch caught my eye. And just before I opened the door, everyone sped up. Like life had been breathed back into them, they were no longer statues. Everyone carried on, just as they always had been. My stomach dropped, and I hit rewind to watch it all over again. I checked the time stamp and watched it tick at regular second intervals while my friends moved in painfully slow motion.

I raced forward to another time where we had all been together. It was last night—when I had convinced everybody that they should go home and it wasn't safe here. I watched myself talk in front of the group and convince them to go home. It was exactly how I remembered—how it should be. But when I left to help Emma pack, that was the exact moment that it happened again. Everybody slowed down. From the moment I left the room, their speed had slowly decreased until they were frozen still. A lump swelled in my throat as I watched them intermittently come back to life and then slow again.

They sat like statues in the living room until I came back downstairs. I couldn't make any sense of it, but when Emma called me down for the movie a second time, I knew I had to come back to this later. I slammed the laptop shut and shoved it under my pillow. I went downstairs and put on my best fake face. I decided it wasn't something I could tell her since she had been one of the frozen. It was then that I realized I was truly on my own. Whatever phenomenon had been happening to me, it wasn't happening to them. And I imagined all of them on the plane landing in Decord City and then heading home to Clover. I imagined them all with their families in the warm embraces they'd get from their parents. I imagined them safe in their beds and what it felt like to be alive.

And then—like an intrusive thought—I imagined none of that happening. I imagined their plane crashing like mine had. The fire they'd feel from the flames. I imagined them waking up in the cabin and cycling through the vortex that I had. I was thankful that it was only me that would suffer like that. No matter how lonely the path may be, I would never wish that upon my friends. I slipped on my pajamas and thought about what I'd tell Emma. I'd tell her my mom rang and I had to take her call—that I was sorry for taking so long. I would watch the movie and pretend to enjoy it, but really, I'd be thinking about the video feed and what it all meant. I wondered what Walker would say.

A commotion shattered the silence downstairs as I placed my hand on the door handle. My heart pounded one giant thunderous thud. Maybe the intruder had broken in again? As I heard the roaring voices and slamming of doors, I raced downstairs to Emma but was shocked to see Noah, Kai, Levi, and Mason. I stopped dead in my tracks, just like they had on the video feed.

"What happened?" Emma asked.

Noah looked at me, disappointed, and Kai shook his head, his jaw clenching shut. "You'd never believe it! We were just about to step on the plane when they said there were engine problems. They told us all to go home because the next flight out wouldn't leave until tomorrow. So we're here for another night," Mason said. He ran his hands through his hair and went to the kitchen. I listened to him bang around in the cabinets as I remained frozen on the stairs. Scarlett May and Kimber came in and they were even more disappointed—if it was possible.

"We better not get killed tonight!" Scarlett May grumbled. The blood drained from my face. *Don't say that . . .*

"That might be too much to ask," Kimber said.

My eyes grew wide. I couldn't believe what was happening.

I watched as they set their luggage in the entryway, and I was happy to have them back, but the fear was screaming in my head. There was never a chance for them to leave Baylor. They were stuck here just like I was.

Emma and I never watched the movie, but while I sat downstairs amongst all the conversation, I couldn't help but think of what I'd seen in the video feed. It was like all my friends had gone dormant. The second I left the room, they froze, and I couldn't figure out why. I excused myself early that night and went to watch the rest of the video feeds. It had been very clear that it was my absence that stopped the activity in the cabin. But it wasn't consistent. Sometimes, they would move when I was out on the docks or in the forest. I opened my phone and texted Walker. I sent him the login to check the footage online. Soon thereafter, he called me. Then, we went over the video feeds together and scoured them for answers.

"There you are," I said. I pointed at the screen when Walker walked into the cabin. Somehow, I was surprised to see him captured on the feed. But then again, I was on these tapes too. Whatever life force he and I shared, it was enough to be caught on tape. And certainly, enough to fool all my friends into believing that we were alive.

"It's so weird. It's as if they only exist in your presence. But why? Why would that happen?" Walker asked.

The phone was hot against my cheek, as we'd been talking a long time. "They only exist … when I am around . . ." I said, mostly thinking out loud.

"Maybe . . . maybe this *is* your reality. Maybe this is your afterlife, and it's what you make of it?" Walker said in an optimistic tone.

I liked the way it sounded. Of course, I'd like this to be my own personal world. Have everything and everyone revolve around me. I smiled. "That's ridiculous," I said with a laugh.

"No, no. Think about it. If you're in their presence, you're thinking about them, and that gives them life. But when you move on, and you venture off to the woods or wherever else you go, you stop thinking about them. And the only actual existence is whatever's happening around you—whatever or whoever you're interacting with. They move sometimes when you're not around, right?" he asked.

"Well, yeah, but . . ."

"Then that must mean you're thinking about them."

I lost my stomach, slightly embarrassed. They'd been moving a lot when I wasn't around. Had it all been because of Noah? Because I'd wondered what he was doing? Or how I had felt about him? But the thought of me being their only source of life was flat-out egocentric. I knew this world was a lot bigger than me and stretched far beyond my emotions. The thought of its boundaries depending solely on how I felt or what I thought was absolutely impossible.

"It can't be," I said with a shrug.

"Why not? We've seen a lot of weird things, haven't we?" Walker said. And while it was true, this was too weird.

"Because I'm not . . . I'm not that special," I said, wincing. I covered my eyes with the palm of my hand. I hated the way I sounded inferior. I wasn't a natural-born leader. A strong woman. And yet, I wasn't a child either.

"You know that's not true. You're the most special

person I've ever met. I mean it, Wilde," Walker said. The back of my throat stung, and it brought tears to my eyes. I closed off my throat, not letting a single sound escape. I feared that he would hear me whimper. I clenched my jaw and held tight, but it was the sniffle that gave it away.

"Are you? Are you crying?" he asked.

I threw myself back into the pillows. "No . . ." I said, my voice quaking. Silence ensued, and I could feel his smile through the receiver.

"You're making me blush, Wilde," he said. I couldn't help it. I burst out into laughter. *Me? I am making him blush?*

"I'm sorry, I'm just . . . that was one of the nicest things anybody has ever said to me."

"It's true. I've met many people in my life, but none of them have perplexed me the way you have. You have no idea how special you are, and to be honest, I think the best is yet to come," he said.

I listened to his breathing. I didn't know what he meant by that. And it only made me sad that I had no more time left to blossom. How could I ever grow into the woman I was supposed to be when I was already dead? There was no *best to come*. I had no more days to make someone proud. And no more years to make someone love me.

CHAPTER 11

I woke to the smell of bacon, doors closing, and heavy commotion throughout the cabin. I remembered their flight was early this morning, and I threw on a robe to wish them farewell. However, I didn't know if they'd be successful this time or if the Baylor phenomenon would suck them back to the cabin like a venomous vortex. I padded barefoot downstairs, tying the cotton string belt around my waist as Emma entered the house.

"Good morning," she said.

"Good morning." My eyes traveled down to the bag in her hands. It was evident that she had packed one last night without telling me. I was happy for her. I thought it was the right thing for her to do. She needed to go home— or at least try. And if it wasn't meant to be, she'd come back soon anyway.

"I'm sorry I didn't say anything earlier, Kins."

"No, no—don't do that. I want you to go. It's safer at home, and you should be with your family," I said, running my fingers through my morning hair.

"I just . . . When everybody came back last night because their flight got canceled, I thought it might be fate. Maybe it was the universe saying that I should have been on that flight with them too."

I gave her a tight hug, and after a moment, her shoulders dropped the tension they'd been carrying.

"Emma, seriously, I'm happy for you to go. I want you to go home. Can you do something for me?" I said, pulling away. Her eyes seemed to droop at the corners with the slant of her brows.

"Anything. What do you need?" she asked.

"Can you tell my parents I love them?" I asked. Her eyes fluttered softly down my face toward the floor, then she nodded. She said nothing, though, and I wondered if the message would get through to them. I guess I had no way of knowing. Emma took Gunner on a leash. She was taking him home to Lainey's parents. I patted his back as he passed by. I was going to miss him most of all.

"Levi, are you seriously making breakfast right now?" Scarlett May scoffed from the den.

"I'm hungry! We've got a long flight ahead of us. What am I supposed to do? Starve? Here, have some bacon. I know that's what you really want," he said. Scarlett May snatched a strip of bacon out of his hand.

"You're just making a bigger mess for Kinsley to clean up after we leave," Kimber said. She passed by, giving me an empathetic look. I shrugged it off. I was used to the mess, and I didn't mind having something to do. Something to occupy my mind.

Noah took my hand and pulled me aside. "Hey Kinsley, I know I didn't have time to say this when we left for our other flight, but I really regretted that, and I wanted to say it to you now."

I looked around nervously—nobody was listening. I pulled my hand away and tucked it into the pocket of my robe, giving him my full attention.

"I can't stop thinking about you. And I think you feel the same way. Now, I know I've messed up. The whole thing with Trinity . . . and I've apologized for that. I'm hoping that when you come home, I can take you out on a date. A proper date—without all these fools around. Maybe we can finally see if this thing between us has a chance. Would that be okay?" he asked, the lines creasing on his forehead and his denim-blue eyes burrowing into mine.

"That sounds . . . nice," I said, teeth clenched. I knew I wouldn't be coming home.

Noah smiled, but it didn't reach his eyes. He gave me a nod before continuing on his way. I crossed my arms and wondered if it would have ever worked had I still been alive.

We all stood in the driveway as several cabs arrived to drive them to the airport. Right before the last door shut, Walker showed up. I felt Noah's eyes like lasers on me. The sunlight lit one half of his face from the back seat of the cab—and the other side remained in the shadows. I knew what he was thinking. He was jealous of Walker. He had every right to be. Because I had feelings for him. And not just crush-type feelings. Deep-seated feelings, like maybe we were soul mates. Lovers in another life. None of that mattered though—because the truth was, in this life, he was already taken. And I was just some sad sapling, like the apple tree we had planted in the lush forest—it never stood a chance.

Walker and I waved goodbye as the cabs pulled out of the driveway. I watched until each of them disappeared down the road. Then, with nothing left to do, Walker and I went inside and sat on the sofa. It was truly quiet now. Only the dead remained. Was this my new life? My new existence? It seemed so empty. So still.

Without the distractions of my roommates, I noticed Walker's hint of cologne. The smell alone was alluring to me, but when I added everything else—his looks, his personality, the way he made me feel—I almost couldn't keep my hands to myself. Was I really supposed to spend eternity alone when I had this wonderful guy sitting just inches from me? My mouth salivated. I couldn't stop thinking about kissing him. What would happen if I tried? Would he reject me? My mind wandered blissfully.

"Quiet. So quiet. What should we do?" he asked, shattering my daydream. My cheeks turned hot. He knew I was fantasizing about him. It must've been written all over my face.

I jumped to my feet, guilty as could be, and stuttered. "We should. I don't know. Let's go . . . check on the tree," I said with a shrug. Check on the tree? Why not? It would be a nice goose chase for us. Sure, it wouldn't be where we left it, but checking on the sapling didn't seem like a half-bad idea. We walked out to the clearing just beyond the beaten path, and Walker told me about his family.

He'd been raised by his mother, and his father was never around. It made me sad to think about the things I'd always taken for granted. Having two parents—two loving parents—just seemed like a given. I'd never realized there were so many kids being raised so differently than I was. I wondered what kind of obstacles he'd faced without a father. I imagined it branched out further than not celebrating Father's Day. I listened intently as he talked about his family structure. How he was the man of the house, taking on a lot of responsibilities at a young age. How he tried to be a brother and a father to his younger sister, Wendy. I told him I, too, was the oldest. I thought of my little brother, Conrad, and an odd sense of tugging at my heart followed. I'd been gone for so long—I tried not to think of it. The walk was such a beautiful one that I tried not to think of my past life—it only made me homesick.

The sunlight filtered through the pine trees and danced slowly over the gravel path. Listening to Walker's voice was one of the best parts. If it was he and I for the rest of eternity, and it was like this day every day, I thought I could be happy. With all the others finally gone, the stress of trying to fit in left with them. I fit in with Walker perfectly. And I didn't even have to try. I looked up at Walker as he spoke of Wendy, and I realized he was my home now. He and I belonged together. And in this vast, vicious world of the living, it was only he and I that walked in the shadows.

The overgrown bushes scratched at my pants as I walked past the blackberry bushes. It was always cooler on this path. Like dark magic swirled around the corner. I only hoped that today wasn't a new nightmare. But as we rounded the corner and the temperature continued to drop, I was in for a big surprise. Today the cemetery rested in the clearing, and in the middle of it, amid the fog, was a fully grown, enormous apple tree. My jaw dropped. I was unable to speak, and so was Walker. I took one step at a time, unsure if we should get any closer. The tiny hairs on my arms stood up, and I knew that something was very wrong.

"It's magnificent!" Walker said, the corners of his lips tipping upward.

"Magnificent? This is some sort of witchcraft or . . . or . . . evil . . ." I didn't know what it was. I only knew that it was unnatural. And like everything else here at Baylor Lake, unnatural seemed to be a bad thing. A dangerous thing.

"It's a tree, Wilde. How can it be so terrible? You know, that's your problem," he began.

"My problem?" My eyes grew wide to match my open mouth.

"Yeah, you think that everything that's happening here is bad." Walker perched his hand on his hip.

"Well, isn't it?" I asked.

"No. It's not. I know you've seen a lot of bad things here . . ."

I sighed, rolling my eyes.

". . . But I think you need to open your eyes to all the beauty. Take, for instance, the pathetic sapling we planted for your friends . . . which grew into this substantial specimen overnight. Maybe it's Lainey's way of saying thank you. Maybe it's Trinity's life force that fed the tree so that it could grow so quickly. I mean, how can a tree be a bad thing? You've seen the most beautiful skies you'll ever see here, right?" he asked.

I remembered back to the night he'd paddled me to the secret cove—and the night he'd saved my life. There *was* something majestic about them. The stars were so bright and huge. They sparkled like none other. I put my hand on my hip, mimicking him and equally frustrated.

"I'm just saying, Wilde, not everything here is bad." With that, he moved toward the tree.

I knew he was right. I needed to start looking at the beauty. I needed to settle in and enjoy myself, and part of that was seeing the magic for what it was. I took another step toward the tree. The fog was rolling in thickly, coiling around my ankles. As I really looked at it, the fully grown tree was something to behold. It was manicured perfectly, just like in a painting.

"It's kind of . . . beautiful," I said, placing my hand on the trunk of the tree. It was warm to the touch, as if the energy within was enough to radiate outward. The sunlight hadn't penetrated this part of the forest, it was decently shady and cool. Yet the bark felt like it was alive. Like a warm life hid inside.

"Must be the magic . . ." I said, peeking over at Walker.

But Walker wasn't interested in the warm bark like I was. He was staring at a headstone underneath the tree. His face was white as a ghost. "What did you say Trinity's last name was?" he asked, his voice far away.

"I didn't. Why?" I asked.

"Trinity Myers, taken by sin," he said, sending chills down my spine. My gaze dropped to the headstone, and I came to stand by Walker. There it was, etched in the stone: "Trinity Myers. Taken by sin." My heart lurched. It was most unsettling. It didn't even look like the other headstones; it looked like her name had been scratched into the marker with claws.

"That seems awfully quick for a headstone. Don't you think?" I asked, peering up at Walker.

"Who do you think would have a headstone made and placed here in Baylor?" he asked, his brows furrowing. I'd never thought of it like that. Was this the job of her parents? And if it was, then why would they've put it here? It seems more fitting that they would put it in Clover.

It was then that another headstone caught my eye farther back in the shade of the apple tree. I sucked in a gasp when I saw Lainey's name. I slapped my hand over my mouth and turned to hide my face in Walker's chest. He wrapped his arms around me.

"Lainey Summers, taken by fear."

I knew the headstone wasn't made by Lainey's parents. The ground was dug up as if the headstones had been freshly placed in the night. The tree that we'd planted in their honor, just the day before, had moss growing over the roots as if it had been here for ages.

The tears started to fall, seeping through my fingers and landing on Walker's flannel, and he let me cry. He let me cry until the eerie forest would no longer allow it. The thick fog had almost swallowed us whole, encapsulating us in an opaque white cloud. Walker tapped me on the shoulder and gently pried me from his chest. When I looked up at his blurry face, I could see that his eyes weren't fixed on mine but on the rising mist around us. It was cold, and I could see that it was moving in fast.

"We should get out of here," he said, taking my hand and leading me away. I followed him, grateful that he was taking the lead because I was still thinking about Lainey, and I probably would have remained there until it was a total whiteout and there was no way back. When we'd gained some distance on the trail and the fog was a thing of the past, Walker held my hand for what felt like a little longer than necessary. We talked little on the way home. Both of us were deep in thought, but when he finally let go of my hand, it felt cold in its absence.

"Do you see that?" Walker asked, snapping me back to reality. I followed his gaze to the cabin nestled in Rock Creek Cove. It looked as if the door from the back patio had swung closed—or open, I couldn't tell. All I knew was there was movement there, and my heart skipped a beat because of it. Was somebody in the cabin? My thoughts fell back to the time I was alone, when Gunner had attacked the thing upstairs that never was.

"The cameras!" I said, grasping Walker's arm.

Whatever this ghost was, we were going to catch it on camera. I couldn't have been more excited to finally crack the case. Walker and I took off running toward the cabin, the curiosity driving us forward. But as we got closer, it was the rumbling sound of voices that perplexed me the most.

Walker opened the back patio door and walked in first, holding his hand out for me to stay where it was safe. But as he slowly took a step inside, he dropped his hand of warning and I followed him inside to find the entire crew standing in the kitchen. My face paled as everybody started talking over one another.

"There you are! Where the hell have you been?" Mason said with a hand in the air.

"Oh my god, Wilde. You wouldn't believe it!" Kimber said, her hand on the side of her face rubbing her temple. My eyes flashed to Noah, who was quiet and stoic. He refused to look me in the eye, and I didn't know if it was because Walker was by my side or something else.

"It was like this flash . . . A flash and then we were here," Kai said, trying to make sense of it all, his hands out before him.

"No! No, it was like heat—heat spreading all over my body. I thought I was on fire. Until we were here," Levi said, looking around with eyes of wonder.

I took one look at Walker, and it was clear that the Baylor phenomenon had taken over the entire cabin, not just me. It may have spread out like fingers, touching those I cared about the most. Maybe it was a web, ensnaring those who came too close. Maybe *I'd* secretly been the one who'd spun it?

CHAPTER 12

As the tension grew, so did my drink consumption. By early evening, everybody was plastered. Some celebrating, some in existential crisis, but we were all together, under the same roof, experiencing the same mind warp. As terrible as it all had been, I was thankful to have my friends finally get a glimpse of what I had been going through. I didn't feel as lonely as I had before.

Sure, I had Walker, but there was a safety in numbers that couldn't be denied. And I felt better knowing that my friends had experienced something otherworldly, too. It was selfish, I know, but I guess that's what it took to make me feel comfortable in my own skin. To make me feel like I was no longer an outsider looking in. And for the first time since the day we'd arrived at the cabin, we were a family of misfits again.

"It was like this glowing blue beam of light that sucked me in. I traveled through it at the speed of light. And before I knew it—before I could even think about what had happened—I was back here in this living room staring at all of you. Staring at this ugly mug," Mason said, pointing to Levi. Levi shook his head, unable to comprehend what had happened earlier. Even though many hours had gone by, everybody was still in shock.

"What if we're dead?" Levi asked, his eyes growing large.

My stomach dropped as I searched the faces of those around me, wondering if they believed that might be a very real possibility. Wondering if I had let my secret out. And wondering if maybe we had more in common than I ever realized.

"Whoa. I think I might be," Mason said, examining the back of his hand.

"We're not dead, you dumbass!" Scarlett May said, rolling her eyes.

"Oh yeah? Then how do you explain what happened?" Mason asked her.

"Maybe we are? Maybe, we're all in hell?" Asher said. I scoffed.

"Why does it have to be hell? How do you know it's not heaven?" Kimber asked. Asher looked from her to Mason to Levi.

"Because there's no way these two guys would be in *my* heaven," he said, pointing to his friends.

I smiled up at Walker. And I wondered if I was in some sort of heaven. I couldn't imagine Walker's dimples would be allowed in hell. Sure, he had some skeletons in his closet; he had a curse—and a girlfriend—and he was unattainable . . . Actually, the more I thought about it . . . Maybe this *was* my hell. To perpetually be enticed by something I couldn't have. It was pure evil. Maybe I was being punished for something. I took a swig from the bourbon and seven in my hand, and my cheeks puckered.

"What's that scowl for?" Walker asked. I stared at him. His beautiful face. His golden eyes. The scar on his brow. But I had no answer for him. He laughed and poked fun at me until there was nothing left for me to do but laugh with him. No, this wasn't hell—it couldn't be.

It didn't take long for Noah to see the connection between Walker and me, and he was quick to pull me away. "Can I talk to you about something in private?" Noah asked, his hand on the back of my arm. I glimpsed a hint of something in Walker's eyes. Jealousy? One could only hope.

"Sure," I said, following him out of the room. He pulled me into the den, where the lights had still been out. There was little light filtering in through the window. Night was upon us, and a shadow was cast across his face. My heart skipped a beat, thinking of the old me. The one who would have died for this private moment with Noah and that pensive look in his eyes. Now I was just dead.

"What's going on?" I asked him, swirling the ice around in my drink.

"I've been thinking it's so weird that we didn't get home again. I thought the first time was a sign that maybe I should be with you, but now I know. Now I know that this isn't my second chance but my third or fourth. I can't stand by any longer and watch you talk with that guy. I have feelings for you, Kinsley. I think I always have. Don't keep doing this to me. Don't keep me waiting," he said, his words slurring.

Had he been sober, this might have meant something different to me. Had I been sober . . . I might've felt something different.

"What is it?" he asked. He reached out and grabbed my hand, squeezing it tight. When I didn't answer, he took a step closer and leaned in for a kiss.

It was all I had wanted. I wished for it on my eighteenth birthday. It felt like a lifetime ago. I came to this cabin for the best summer of my life, and a big part of that was Noah. His lips grazed mine with a featherlight touch, and I jerked back. The heat from his mouth left mine, and all I could think about was Walker. How something inside of me wanted him more. Maybe just a little bit, maybe a lot, but it was more complicated than my feelings for these two guys.

Noah symbolized everything I was—everything I used to be. He was the symbol of love, happiness, family, and warmth. He was sun shining down on me—the girl I used to be when I was alive. But if Noah was the sun, then Walker was the moon. Being with him was like living a life in the shadow of the night. An afterlife of darkness. With Walker, I was a ghost—scared, lonely, and cold.

Should I really leave the thing I had always wanted for the one thing I could never have? The one guy I could never get. Should I leave the daylight for a life in the shadows?

"I just . . . I just need a moment," I said, dropping his hand and running out of the dark den.

I went in search of Walker. I sifted through my dwindling group of friends as they came up with belligerent theories on what had happened to them. I heard everything from time travel to time warps to black holes and death. "Excuse me," I said, gently pushing on Kai's back.

I found Walker out on the back porch, all by his lonesome. I tripped over the doorjamb and stumbled out onto the porch, making my cheeks heat. He raised his brows, and I could see him silently judging me. "I swear . . . I swear, I didn't drink that much," I said.

He chuckled to himself, and I grabbed hold of the banister for support, my lips pursed in a thin straight line.

I needed to know right then and there if I was ever

going to have a chance with him or if this was only a wild goose chase. Because I'd spend my eternity chasing Walker in the dark if I thought I had a chance at catching him. I needed a sign.

"Your friends are really creative in there. They're coming up with all sorts of theories. But none of them know about the Baylor phenomenon," Walker said.

"Yeah, they don't know what hit them." I looked out at the placid lake. The sky was a hazy dark lavender as dusk blanketed the water. And then I asked the question I wasn't sure I wanted the answer to. "You don't think they're like us, do you?" Walker came to my side, and I took my gaze from the calm waters to his rough hand, which rested beside mine on the banister. Our pinkies almost touching. Almost.

"Like us?" he asked.

"Passed. In their afterlife?" I asked, inching my hand closer to his until my skin rested against his.

"I don't think anybody's like us. I think we're two peas in a pod," he said with warm eyes and a kind smile trained on me. Goosebumps ran down my arms. *That*. That was my sign. I had a chance.

"Are you cold?" he asked.

I shook my head and then slipped my hand over his. Slowly, I lifted my gaze from our interlocking hands to find his face pensive and pained. In a gentlemanly fashion, he picked my hand up and placed it down on the banister. He tucked his hands into his pockets.

That . . . was my sign. Denied. He was absolutely, unequivocally, unattainable. And it didn't matter if we were the last two people on this earth—two peas in a pod—he would never have feelings for me. I would never measure up to his sweet Layla Barns. I nodded my head in understanding, the tears pricking my eyes, the sting in the back of my throat. I wasn't enough now, and I never would be.

"Wilde—" he began.

I turned back to the cabin. Back to my sure thing. My sunlight. At least Noah wanted me. "I'm sorry, I think . . . I think somebody's waiting on me," I said, fumbling to open the door. He let me go.

Walker didn't even try to stop me. I guess it was a good thing, because I couldn't take being denied twice. I opened the door and shut it on Walker, leaving him in the darkness.

"Because . . . What if we never go home? What if I never see my dog again? He probably thinks I abandoned him," Kimber cried, her face red on Asher's shoulder. It was the exact conversation I was avoiding. I didn't need to get sucked into the what-ifs and the whatnots. I had too many of them in my head as it was. What I needed was to find Noah. Find the person who saw my value. I licked my lips as I squeezed by Ethan and Kai. This kiss was going to be everything I'd always hoped it to be.

I peeked my head into the now dark den, and it was almost black inside, but I could see well enough to know that Noah wasn't there. I turned back to Kai and Ethan. "Have you seen Noah?" I asked.

"Yeah, he's right there," Ethan nodded his head, brow furrowed. I followed his gaze to find Noah passed out on the sofa. I sighed heavily. Denied not once but twice in one night. I walked over to him, his limp, lifeless body, and considered kicking his foot to make him wake and kiss me. But he was out. And I wasn't worth waiting for.

IT WAS THE FOLLOWING DAY, BUT WALKER'S rejection still stung. My head ached, and I had the sour taste of defeat (and bourbon) in my mouth, but everybody else seemed well. Slightly hungover, of course, but in good spirits. Kai was still trying to get home, and he'd taken a cab into town to rent a car and drive. Nobody had gone with him. Kai wasn't easily dissuaded. I couldn't tell if he really wanted to get home or if he was more interested in the phenomenon that brought him back. If I had to guess, I would've assumed it was the latter. Kai was a smart guy, into physics and science. He probably had all sorts of theories buzzing around in his head, and if I had to guess, he couldn't wait to teleport again.

The day was warmer than normal, even for summer. It was so hot that everybody wanted to go swimming. Probably to wash off the stench of the hangover. Scarlett May had spoken of the tree swing deep in the woods, and without question, everybody wanted to go. I'd never jumped off it before, but that wasn't because I didn't want to. I did. I was afraid, though. There were three giant boulders that you had to climb just to get to the swing, and they were tall. I didn't know how tall, but I knew it was enough to keep me from climbing. I knew my fear of heights would set in about halfway up the first boulder. And I would never get myself to climb all three, let alone jump off and swing from the rope. Had I made it that far, I doubted I'd ever let go.

But everybody else wanted to try, and I didn't blame them. We packed lunches. I scoured the kitchen and gathered all the scraps of food we had left. It was going to be a sparse lunch, half a bag of chips, three sandwiches, four yogurts, and a bunch of grapes. Nobody cared. They were just happy to be alive.

I was surprised to see Walker show up at the cabin as we were heading out to the swing. I thought it was clear now that I thought of him as more than a friend, and it put us in an awkward state. The pinkness in his cheeks and lack of eye contact were obvious to me.

Noah was no better. From the lackluster glaze in his eyes to the downward stares. He was embarrassed but didn't know what for. He probably didn't even remember talking to me or that he'd tried to kiss me. He did, however, know that something had happened, because he wouldn't address me in the slightest. He reminded me of a dog cowering in the corner, his tail tucked between his legs.

As for me, my mind was still a little cloudy, but I knew enough to know that heading back to Noah after my rejection with Walker had been a grave mistake. I shouldn't settle, even if it was for a guy I'd always dreamed of.

I walked with Emma in the back of our group. Walker talked to Mason in the middle of the pack, and Noah stayed as far away from me as possible. He was up front with Scarlett May. The tension bounced from person to person like a pinball, and being in the back of the pack made me the gutter. I let Emma speak of fate as I tried to sort through my feelings for the two guys I'd never have. And no matter how I looked at it, there was only one true answer—*This must be hell.*

I watched my feet fall on the path as I tried to stuff down the rising thought that something was wrong. It shouldn't be like this. This afterlife was my burden to carry and mine alone. I looked at the back of Kimber's head and then at Asher's. They shouldn't be here.

It wasn't until we had reached the rope swing and set out a large blanket and unpacked the lunch that Walker approached me. My palms grew sweaty, and I was hot. So unbearably hot.

I gave Walker an awkward smile, and he returned it just the same. "You're not going on the swing?" he asked.

"Me? Hell no."

He laughed, breaking the tension between us. Everybody lined up behind the boulder for the rope swing.

"Yeah, I'm not going either. The last time I was on that swing, I jumped tandem with Layla. And, I don't think I want to overwrite that memory," he said, picking up pebbles and flicking them away. I watched them land and tumble in the dirt. I wasn't sure if he'd brought her up to remind me the reason why he would never choose me or if he was simply stating the truth—but it felt like it was his explanation for the other night where he pulled his hand away from mine. It wasn't easy to accept, but I respected it. I respected his loyalty. He was such a good guy. It only made me want him more.

"I don't want to fall—jump. I mean, it's so high," I stammered.

"I didn't know you were afraid of heights." Walker blushed.

"So . . . so afraid," I said, shaking my head. It was true.

I'd died, and yet falling for Walker was the scariest thing I'd ever experienced.

We watched as Ethan scaled the boulders. He was the first to jump, and everybody crowded around the base of the first rock to watch him drop into the water. It seemed so wrong—everybody having fun. They weren't even supposed to be here. This was my afterlife, and somehow, they were stuck inside of it. I held my breath as Ethan swung. He flew through the air, and he seemed to let go just a second too late. He fell rather ungracefully and belly-flopped into the lake. Everyone laughed, including Walker and me.

"That's gotta hurt!" he said, wincing.

I snickered, empathizing with the slap of the water against the softest part of the body. I remembered what it was like as a kid to hit the swimming pool like a solid surface before the water parted and took you under. I remembered that moment of pain spreading across your skin, but you couldn't yell because you were submerged under cold water. I saw myself as a kid screaming—the bubbles escaping my mouth and clinging to the corners of my eyes. And then it was Lainey's double as she pulled me down to the darkest part of the lake—the part where you can't come back from. I scowled and refocused my eyes.

Mason climbed the boulders like a monkey and it surprised me he wasn't the first to go in. Kimber tugged on her suit, readjusting the sides against her hipbone. As

Mason took the rope swing in his hand, something pinged the depths of my stomach and I knew this wasn't right. This wasn't the way it was supposed to be.

Ethan hadn't surfaced yet. I arched my back, my eyes scouring the water. But there wasn't as much as a single bubble popping at the surface. "What's going on?" I said as I jumped to my feet. "Wait!" I yelled.

Mason looked back at me, and I ran to the water's edge. I searched the lake. Walker came up behind me, doing the same. "He hasn't come up yet!" I said, breathless.

"What the hell?" Noah said, running into the water. Seconds later, it was Walker, Asher, and Mason all diving in, one after the other.

I watched their heads pop up out of the water. I held my breath each time they plunged back under. I moved in close to Emma, and we held hands as we waited for one of them to rescue Ethan and carry his lifeless body ashore . . . but it never happened. Ten minutes had passed, maybe more, and there was nothing to show for it.

"How could he just disappear like that?" Kimber whispered. It was the question we had all been silently asking ourselves. I feared that whatever had taken the lives of Trinity and Lainey had now taken the life of Ethan Patrick—swallowed him whole in the black water.

It was ages before the guys gave up the search—but the water was murky, and their lips were blue. The rescue was a lost cause, and once they'd pushed their bodies to the point of exhaustion, it was time to call it.

I couldn't help but feel like it was my fault. I looked around at the dwindling numbers, our little family of misfits. Who was next? Who would be the next victim to get stuck in my web?

CHAPTER 13

The tension rose on the way back to the lake house. It was a long walk, but that did nothing to calm everybody's emotions. We were one friend short, and the sense of defeat was insurmountable. We were fighting an invisible monster with our hands tied behind our backs—it was impossible. The fear grew as the heat beat down on our backs, and by the time we reached the cabin, we were nearly at each other's throats.

Walker headed home. He said he needed to find clues about Layla's whereabouts. He said he needed answers, and it wouldn't happen sitting around the cabin. I was thankful that he left to do the thing I couldn't, but as I looked back at the angry bunch before me, I didn't know how to deal with them alone.

Asher and Noah were particularly upset because Ethan was one of their best friends. Why they took their grief out on each other, I didn't know. But Asher shoved Noah as we were entering the back porch entryway. He stumbled forward, quickening his step to catch himself. I looked back to Walker climbing in his canoe and pushing off—I'd give anything to be in that canoe.

"Who was the first one in? Answer me that! I was the first one in!" Noah yelled, hammering his chest.

"Stop!" Kimber said in a helpless heap.

"Well, it didn't do you any good, did it? Did you find him? No! He's still at the bottom of the lake!" Asher yelled back, his outstretched hand nearly hitting Mason.

I took a deep breath, running my hands through my hair. I paced the length of the kitchen, searching for answers. How does this make sense? How does it fit together? I hated the fact that I hadn't figured it out yet. That my friends were dying on my watch. If I were smarter . . . if I hadn't been dyslexic . . . maybe I would have figured it out by now. My shortcomings affected not only me but everyone around me. I felt this huge amount of responsibility that I couldn't measure up to. I hadn't been able to save Ethan or Lainey; I hadn't been able to save Trinity. And I knew that for the rest of the people in this cabin, it was only a matter of time before I couldn't save them either.

I heard a gasp and spun around on my heels, just in time to see Asher's fist slam into the side of Noah's cheekbone.

"No!" I screamed. I rushed forward and then paused as the confrontation continued. Noah was hunched over, his hand to his face, when Asher jumped on his back, bringing him down to the floor. He brought fist upon fist down on his face. Blood splattered, marrying Asher's fist to Noah's nose. Noah never had a chance. From the moment he was hit, he never got a punch in, and Asher was relentless.

Scarlett May yelled belligerently. Kimber cried. Kai was still trying to get back home or break ground and discover time travel in his attempt. And Ethan was at the bottom of the lake. I flinched with every thud of Asher's wet fist meeting Noah's broken face.

Time slowed to a crawl. Mason jumped in and tackled Asher to the floor. At first, it seemed like the fight had grown. The three guys fumbled around on the ground, taking up the entire living room. Noah rolled onto his side and coughed up blood, clutching his nose. I ran over to him, swiping a dishtowel from the countertop as I passed by. Careful not to get hit, I pressed the towel up against his nose, trying to stop the bleeding—my hand trembling beneath the cloth. Mason wrestled Asher until he calmed down, but they shed no more blood.

"It's not fair! It's not fair!" Asher yelled, nearly incoherent. Streams of tears ran down Asher's red face. Noah's blood had smeared across his cheeks.

"I know, man. I know. We need to find this guy! We need to get him! But *that*," Mason said, pointing to Noah, "that's not your guy! You hear me?" Asher gave up his fight and Mason got off him, helping him up. But as soon as Asher got to his feet, his face came down on Mason's chest, and he wept.

Ethan always looked up to these guys. He'd followed them everywhere, and he was always so happy to be part of the group that he never cared about being on the bottom. He'd only wanted to be accepted, and they did that for him—they accepted him, and Ethan got to be part of the cool group. But what I hadn't realized was they actually loved him. They were actually best friends. True friends. They were friends like Lainey and I had been. My heart ached for them because I knew that pain. I would have taken it all if I could. I would have taken their grief into my eternity so that nobody else had to know it the way I did.

Noah groaned and pulled himself up to a seated position. I pressed the towel up against his nose, and he grabbed it with his bloodied hand.

"I think my nose is broken," he said beneath the towel. I didn't know a thing about broken noses. I'd never broken anything in my life, but I'd never seen a cast on a broken nose—I assumed it would heal itself. I looked over to Asher as he tried to pull himself together by wiping away his tears. In the process, he created stripes of blood across both cheeks and looked like a warrior, ready for battle. I'd heard that Asher had a temper, but I'd never seen it until now.

There was one time when Levi and Asher had come to

school with bruises under their eyes. They'd both looked terrible. When we asked them what had happened, they both replied, "You should see the other guy." They'd never told us what happened, but it was clear that they had fought each other. The funny part was they were over it by the next day at school. Guys didn't hold grudges the way girls did. And I hoped that was the case for Asher and Noah now. There was enough tension in the cabin, and we didn't need to divide into sides.

"I'm going to get you some medicine," I said to Noah as I pushed to my feet. I rummaged through the cabinets looking for the ibuprofen, and when I finally found the bottle, it was empty. I slammed the bottle down on the counter. Of course, everybody had been taking it for their hangovers. I crossed my arms, leaned against the counter, and watched as the panic continued to progress uncontrolled. It was like a stream that was slowly fed as the snow-capped mountains melted—only, today was hot, and the stream of panic filled all at once. Kimber couldn't stop crying. She had been upset by Ethan's death but even more rattled by Asher's violence.

"You promised me you wouldn't do this again!" she cried out, beating on Asher's chest.

"And then he was gone—just gone. He never came back up . . ." Scarlett May said on the phone.

Levi came back in from the back patio. He must have been out with Gunner because when he let him in,

Gunner ran through the house, excited to see everybody and wagging his tail. As if we needed more commotion. I groaned, wrapping my hands around my neck and tilting my head back. I closed my eyes and listened as everybody took their frustrations out on one another. I wanted to scream.

"If you don't like it, then just leave," Asher said to Kimber. I watched as she bashed her hands into his chest, crying maniacally. The tension was getting to us all. One by one, we were cracking. First, it was Asher and Noah, second, Asher and Kimber. I briefly thought about Kai and wondered how far he'd gotten today. And then I remembered—we needed to call him and tell him about Ethan.

"You don't want me. I'm never good enough. I'm never good enough," Kimber cried.

"I don't have time for your bullshit! I don't have time for this, Kimber! People are dying! Ethan died! And you're worried about how good you are? How pretty you are? How skinny you are? I don't have time for it! We're done!" Asher yelled before storming out of the cabin. Kimber wailed and took off running. I listened to her feet stomp all the way upstairs and heard the bathroom door in the hallway slam shut. Everybody else was quiet—even Scarlett May, as she held the phone away from her ear. Everybody was still except for Gunner, who was still looking for pets. I scratched behind his ears and he leaned into me.

Levi walked back out of the cabin, presumably after Asher. And slowly, Scarlett May continued her conversation on the phone about her horrific experience at the lake. She didn't care that Kimber was upstairs crying, and I felt bad for her because Trinity would have. I took one look at Emma, and we knew what we had to do. We headed upstairs to console Kimber.

With each stair we climbed, the sobs grew louder. Emma and I stood outside the bathroom door, my hand on the knob. I looked at Emma, concerned for what we might find. Her brows furrowed as she gave me a curt nod, signaling she was ready for battle. Slowly, I opened the bathroom door to find Kimber tucked in a ball against the bathtub. She lifted her head from her knees. Her face was beet red. She screamed through her tears, "Get out!" But it wasn't convincing.

"Get out," she whimpered, her hunched back quaking as she cried.

Emma and I slipped in, and I closed the door behind us. I looked at Emma and shrugged. I didn't know what to do. I bit the side of my lip and lowered myself to the floor. My back slid against the wall until my butt bumped against the tile floor. Emma joined me, leaning against the bathtub. I put my hand on Kimber's back and stroked it, but when it didn't seem to do anything except make her cry more, my eyes bulged, and I threw up a hand to Emma. "I don't know what to do . . ." I mouthed.

"Hey, it's okay. I'm sure he was just mad. He's just going through something. I mean, he and Ethan were really good friends. It has nothing to do with you," Emma tried. Kimber didn't respond.

After a moment, I tried my hand at it. "I know it's scary, Kimber. I'd be lying if I said I wasn't scared, too. We're all under a lot of stress right now, and I think the best thing we can do is band together. We can't have a chink in the armor. Not now. So we need you to be strong. Can you do that?" I asked.

"Strong?" Kimber asked, her words muffled as her chin was tucked to her chest. "You want me to be strong?" she rasped, her tone growing sharper, and I knew I had said something wrong.

"Well . . ." I began.

"I've lost one of my best friends! And now, I lost Asher too. We can't come back from this. We're done," she said. They'd taken breaks before, but this seemed different. We were on the cusp of change. High school had ended; college was about to start. If Asher was on the fence about their relationship, this was as good a time as any to sever their bond.

"Asher was the best thing I ever had. I don't know why he loved me the way he did. But I'll never find somebody to put up with my shit like he did. I'm just

this . . . *big*. . . nobody will ever love me," she wailed.

Big? Kimber was nothing but skin and bones. She was tiny. Borderline emaciated if I really thought about it. Emma and I shared a look of concern. I knew what she saw in the mirror wasn't grounded in reality. She was one of the most popular girls at our school, she was beautiful, and it wasn't until this moment that I realized just how disconnected her inner voice was from her outer appearance.

And then it struck me—maybe Kimber and I had that in common? Maybe my own mind had blocked me from seeing the truth within the mirror. Maybe I wasn't a nobody or invisible the same way that Kimber wasn't overweight.

I took my hand off Kimber's back and pushed off the wall. I stepped up to the vanity. I looked from Emma to the girl staring back at me in the mirror. I sucked in an uneven breath as I stared at my reflection, long dark hair, and ruby-red lips. My eyes were the dullest brown I'd ever seen. My skin was sallow. There wasn't one feature to adore. I was the plainest girl there ever was. But this time, I was visible.

Emma tried to console Kimber, but everything she said only made her cry more. I was stuck staring at my reflection in the mirror. I had always known this version of me. This girl. The one who was so plain that she might as well be invisible. I didn't know what was worse, seeing my true reflection or seeing none at all. I felt the burn in the back of my throat when Emma called my name for the second, third, or maybe even fourth time.

"Kinsley!"

I pulled myself from the dull brown eyes and looked down at Kimber. Things had escalated, and she was hyperventilating. The stress of it all made my head pound. I didn't know who to help first—her or myself. I grabbed my head as the migraine came crashing down on me and I bent at the waist. There was nothing I could do for myself, so I tried to fight through the pain. I put my hands around Kimber's waist and pulled her to her feet.

"Breathe, Kimber. Just breathe," I said, leading her to the sink.

"Let's get some water on her face," I said to Emma.

With Emma and I on either side of Kimber, we helped her get to the vanity. I turned the faucet on, but as soon as she dropped her hands from her puffy eyes and saw her reflection, she screamed wildly.

She startled me, and I staggered backward. Her cries were like sharp daggers plunging into my head. I looked in the mirror to see Kimber had shrunken to seventy pounds, maybe less. Her skin stretched thin across her bones—so thin it was nearly translucent. With her mouth open and her cries screeching, a single tooth fell out of her mouth. It clinked several times as it fell into the porcelain sink. I watched with enormous eyes as it circled the drain.

I looked at Emma, who was as white as a ghost. And it shocked me to see Kimber as her old self, fully fleshed out as she stood beside me. I whipped my head back to the mirror to see her skeleton piercing through her taut skin.

It was like a fun-house mirror—the kind you'd find at a circus or a Halloween fright night. The reflections were hideous and grotesque—our deepest fears, our truest nightmares, all before our very eyes. It was so real, it was no wonder we couldn't tell fact from fiction—why our inner voices had fed us lies our whole lives. Because as I stood there beside my two friends staring into an alternate reality, I couldn't tell where my dimension had stopped and the truth began.

"Kimber's hyperventilating turned to wheezing as she stared at her reflection until she was no longer breathing. Her face turned blue and her knees grew weak. Her double in the mirror was a stark purple, and I saw every vein straight through her skin. Her eyes were bulbous as they rolled back in her head and several more teeth fell out, clamoring against the porcelain sink. Kimber passed out, hitting the ground with a thud. Emma and I kneeled at her side, torn between the tangible life before us and the dark portal of our own inner makings seen within the mirror.

I picked Kimber's head up and cradled it in my hand. "Go get help!" I said. Emma leaped over her limp body and ran into the hall, yelling for help. My head pounded with excruciating pain. It was one of the worst migraines

I'd ever had, and my vision was starting to blur. I winced through the throbbing, agonizing pain. Lightheaded, I struggled to hold Kimber's heavy head in my hands.

Stop this!

Somehow, deep inside, I knew it was me who was orchestrating this. Like Walker had said, it was my manifestation. It was the things I didn't want to see that had a way of coming to life. I wanted to concentrate on helping Kimber, but my pain was blinding and all-consuming.

Asher burst through the door like a bolt of lightning. He took Kimber's limp body from my hands, and it was the last thing I saw before the darkness washed over me.

CHAPTER 14

My head ached and my mouth ran dry. The bedsheets were bunched up in the palms of my hands. My eyes fluttered open to find a dark room. I had no memory after Kimber's meltdown in front of the funhouse mirror, but when I saw the blinking green light of the recorder, I figured I could at least piece it together. I sat up; my head pounded. I sucked in a sharp breath and clutched my temples just as Noah walked in. It shocked me to see him, and his ease of coming into the bedroom left me with questions.

"Oh, you're up. How are you feeling?" he asked, closing the door behind him.

"What happened?" I asked, relieved to see I was fully clothed.

"You passed out. Asher and I got you into bed. He's

taking care of Kimber now and I just went downstairs to get you some ice water," he said, placing a glass on the nightstand. I turned on the bedside table lamp as Noah sat on the edge of the bed.

"Thank you. I'm sorry. I'm just a little groggy, I guess. I've never passed out before," I said, sitting up and bringing my knees to my chest.

"It's okay. I think you were just out for a little bit—maybe like five or ten minutes," he said.

"Jesus, you look like hell," I said, taking him in for the first time. His eye was swollen, a mix of yellow and blue; dried blood crusted around his nose. If he looked this bad now, I imagined in two days' time he would look like he'd been thrown in front of a bus.

Noah looked down at the ground and forced a smile. I could tell he was embarrassed about losing the fight. "Yeah, he got me good."

"I know you guys are upset about Ethan, but we shouldn't be taking it out on each other, you know?" I said.

"Trust me, I know." He inched his hand toward my feet and I wiggled my toes. It was weird having Noah in my bedroom with the door closed. I had run out of things to say to him, and the intimacy made me a little uneasy. If I was being honest with myself, I still felt the pull toward him from deep inside. But at this point, I couldn't tell if it was Noah that I wanted or if it was the girl I used to be before coming to Baylor. The girl I was when my gran was alive and school was in session. The girl who had only one problem in the world: getting noticed by Noah every day. I missed that life. That simple life.

"Do you remember that one time when I broke my arm and Joey had a birthday party? All the kids went swimming, and I couldn't get in the pool because of my cast, so you stayed back with me to watch a movie?" Noah shifted, inching closer.

"Yeah, I remember that," I said, smiling. The memory was so innocent.

"This kind of reminds me of that. Should we watch a movie?" he asked. It sounded nice. I wanted to escape this mess and leave it all behind. Get lost in a love story or comedy. Allow my mind to move past Ethan, if only for a little while. "I'd love that," I said. He leaped over me when I patted the open side of the bed. I laughed at his boyish ways as he got situated. I turned on the TV, excited to have my old friend back.

I flipped through the channels on the TV, and at first there was silence between us, maybe even a little awkwardness. But as Noah vetoed movie after movie, the tension eased. He'd come up with the most ridiculous reasons why the movies were no good.

"That one's too corny."

"That one's too romantic."

"That one's got a dog in it, and I think it gets hurt."

"I don't like that Scott Teek. He does the weird thing with his brows when he laughs."

I rolled my eyes and then realized he'd never really wanted to watch a movie. He'd just wanted to crawl into bed. I couldn't blame him for that. We all could use a friend right now, and we used to be the best of friends when we were kids.

"We used to be such good friends. What happened?" I asked in all seriousness.

"We're still good friends," he said, his tone climbing.

"I don't know. Somewhere along the way . . . maybe puberty—"

"Puberty?" he said, scrunching his face. "Ow!" Noah cupped his swollen eye.

"Oh, be careful." I paused, choosing my words wisely. "I thought you didn't want to be friends with me anymore because you thought everyone would think we were boyfriend and girlfriend or something," I said, a little embarrassed by my feelings back then. They had hurt a lot at the time, but I was used to it now.

"No . . . Maybe? I don't know. It was hard growing up, you know? I'm sorry I wasn't more mature about it, and middle school . . ."

I laughed. "More like high school," I said.

"What? Seriously? Oh my god, I've got to rethink my

whole life now." Noah smiled and then winced from the pain.

"Well, you've got a plan at least, right? I heard you got into one of your top colleges?"

"Yeah, I got into HU, and I'm moving there at the end of the summer." Noah's eyes lowered slowly. It was just another reason why we wouldn't work out.

"That's great. What are you going to do when you're done with college? Come back home and find a job here? Or stay out east?"

"I'm not sure yet. If I had a reason to come back home, then maybe I would . . ." His eyes focused on mine. It was the first time in a long time that I'd lost my stomach with Noah. I squirmed under his gaze, cleared my throat, and sat up a little straighter. And when I dared to look back at him, there was a twinkle in his eyes. He knew he'd won some minor victory. But I wasn't giving up just yet.

"Well, I'm going away to college too, so . . ." I began.

Noah slowly leaned down. The seconds ticked by in slow motion. He was going to kiss me. The room was dark except for the movie trailers that played on an endless loop on the TV. This was everything I dreamed of—my one birthday wish. His battered face warmed my cheeks as he came closer. His lips touched mine gently for a kiss as I sucked in a quick breath. I stilled briefly, and he parted his mouth, kissing me deeper. My head swirled as I kissed him back.

It *was* everything I'd hoped for. I opened my mouth slightly, inviting him to get lost in the longing—but longing for what? I didn't know. I wanted so desperately to only care about this kiss. To be present in this moment. But the truth was, all I could hear were Kimber's teeth striking the porcelain sink. All I could see was Ethan's belly flop into the underworld. And it wasn't what I felt but what I hadn't. I didn't feel Walker's scruff scratching my face as we kissed, and I didn't have feelings for Noah.

I did, however, realize that I was no longer the same girl I was when I came to Baylor. And as much as I wanted to be that innocent, lighthearted girl with a crush, I had to let her go, because she wasn't coming back, and there was nothing I could do about it—not even kiss Noah Hampton. My life had changed significantly in the last handful of weeks. Nearly all of it was for the worse. All of it except Walker St. James. *My* Walker St. James. I jerked away, breaking off the kiss. This was all wrong. Noah stared at me, stunned. His breath quickened.

"I'm sorry, but I can't . . . I can't," I said, throwing my legs over the side of the bed and standing to my feet.

"Kinsley, wait," he said as I hurried out the door. Once in the hallway. I closed the bedroom door behind me and rested my back against the wall. I ran my hand down my face. It was clear as day. When I'd died, so had my feelings for Noah.

I hurried downstairs because, even though I knew I

needed to tell Noah how I felt, it didn't need to be now. The cabin was pitch black and quiet. It must've been the middle of the night, and nobody was awake. Just as I got to the bottom stair, the front doorknob jiggled. I peered out the peephole and a sense of relief washed over me when I saw Kai under the glow of his cell phone light. I unlocked the door, and he rushed inside like a freight train. He scooped me up in his arms and gave me a big hug like it had been ages since we'd seen each other. Maybe it had. I didn't know why or what his reasoning was, but I hugged him back like it was the last time I'd ever see him—and it felt good. It felt good to be loved for just being me.

"You're back?" I said, trying to sound surprised. But I always knew he'd never escape this place.

"Wilde, you'll never believe it." Kai's voice was electric, and instantaneously my sorrows lifted. I closed the door behind us, and Kai spoke quickly, waving his hands in the air.

"I got the rental car, right? Then, I was driving down the highway—had been driving four hours . . . maybe three?" His eyes rolled up as he counted silently. "And then suddenly, the sky lightened! It continued to lighten until it looked like I was driving straight into a tunnel! And then, when all the windows were encapsulated in this beam of light . . . I felt like I was falling, and then guess what?" Kai's eyes were larger than I'd ever seen.

"What?" I asked.

"I was here. Not just in Baylor, but here on this doorstep. Right. Now." He pointed to his feet as if this was the very place where teleportation had been invented. Like we were upon something bigger than life itself. "Whatever it is, it's real, Kinsley. It's real. This is incredible. Do you even know what this means?" he asked.

"What does it mean, Kai?" I asked, loving how his spin on the phenomenon was incredible.

"It means we've stumbled on some sort of weird wormhole. It's like we're stuck in a time loop. Only it's not time that's passing by, it's space. It's direction. We have to test it. We have to test all the theories! Didn't you say this happened to you?" he asked.

"I was in the plane crash . . ." I said, the screams echoing in a far-off land.

"The one from the news?" he asked.

I dropped my head and he brought me in for a hug. "Yeah. That one."

"I'm so sorry. That must have been terrifying."

"It was." I tried not to think about it.

"And then what happened? You ended up here?" Kai asked, holding me at arm's length.

"Exactly. Walker says it's called the Baylor phenomenon. Maybe you can start researching it," I said, happy to have him on the team. Kai was a smart guy. If anybody was going to be on our research team, he would've been my first pick.

"The Baylor phenomenon . . ." Kai whispered as he walked past me into the kitchen. When I turned to follow, I saw Noah standing on the stairs. The heat crept across my cheeks. "Oh, um, Kai's back. He didn't get far," I said to Noah.

I was thankful that this news was big enough to take the attention off our failed kiss. Noah frowned and pointed in the kitchen's direction. He passed me as he searched for Kai. I trailed after Noah. I didn't want to, but I had to. I had to squash the awkwardness. We were living together for the summer, and I couldn't avoid him altogether. So hiding from him for one night wouldn't do me any favors.

"Wow, dude! What happened to you?" Kai asked. I sat down on the sofa, realizing how much Kai had missed in a single day. I pulled a lap blanket over my legs.

"Oh, this? That's compliments of Asher," Noah said, nodding to Asher in the sleeping bag on the floor. I hadn't realized he was sleeping downstairs, as I'd given him and Kimber a bedroom upstairs.

"Why is he sleeping down here?" Kai asked.

"After the fight, he and Kimber broke up. It was a big thing. I'm glad you weren't here for it," I said.

"Oh, shit. That's going to be weird tomorrow," Kai said.

"Yeah, awkward," Noah said. But the really awkward part wasn't the breakup or even our failed kiss—it was knowing that we had to tell Kai about Ethan drowning in the lake. My eyes flickered to Noah's, and his one good cheek turned to a pinkish hue.

"What was that?" Kai asked, smart as a whip. His eyes bounced from Noah to me.

I sighed. "It's Ethan, he—" I began, but I was thankful I didn't have to finish.

"—He jumped. He jumped into the water and never came back up. It was the last time any of us saw him." Noah looked like he had seen a ghost, and I could only imagine the movie that was playing in his head. It played in mine too, Ethan hitting the surface of the lake with a smack. Kai's expression had morphed from shock to grief to fear to empathy, all within seconds. I swallowed a lump in my throat and chewed on my lip while he gathered himself.

"Wow, I really missed a lot. How long was I gone?"

"Just today. You left this morning."

"You know, I was pretty excited about this . . . phenomenon, but now, I feel like maybe I'm just playing with fire. Maybe I shouldn't try to understand. Maybe we should run. We should all *run*. Because one of us is going to be next," Kai said in a low and eerie whisper.

He was absolutely right. We should run. But we'd tried that once, and we'd ended up right where we started. Only I knew that precisely thirteen people were going to die— that made for nine more.

"Man, I can't deal with this right now," Noah said,

bringing his elbows to his knees and hunching over till his head met his hands. I knew he had the weight of the world on his shoulders, and our kiss was just another stone to carry.

"Tell us more about your experience. It's good for all of us to hear. Maybe we can piece everything together and find a way home," I said, knowing that I'd never get the chance to go home, but that maybe they could.

We stayed up for a while. The three of us huddled on the sofa, talking about our experiences. I told them how the plane went up in a blaze and how I woke up in my bed. They both agreed they probably would've thought I was crazy if I had said anything before. And they joked about me letting them get on a plane without warning of their impending doom.

By the time I went to bed, I felt hopeful for the first time in a while. Hopeful that Kai would figure something out that I had missed. Maybe he'd get everyone home where they belonged. I hoped things wouldn't be weird between Noah and I come morning. I still had to talk with him about my feelings, but talking with him and Kai had taken some of the awkwardness between us away.

I knew I also needed to have an open talk with the remaining group—a talk like I'd had with Noah and Kai. It was time that they were all on my team. Now that they were experiencing the strange flukes that I had been, it was time that I let them in on all the secrets and clues that had been happening around us. It was time for us to band together and fight whatever this thing was as a team. An army. Because I was done doing this on my own. I simply hadn't been strong enough. Or smart enough. But together, maybe we'd have what it took to finally find Layla.

CHAPTER 15

The sunrise brought with it a friendly reunion. It was exciting for everybody to see Kai. And after losing Ethan, we were strengthened again by Kai's presence. His energy felt like renewed hope. Even Kimber was doing better. Though still thin, her teeth were intact. When she came to speak to me, I could tell that what we had seen in the mirror had weighed heavily on her insecurity by the way she rubbed her fingers across her jaw. Yet, for the first time, we were banding together. We felt like a team. That was, until Asher woke up.

He staggered to the fridge; his swollen hand covered in bruises grasped the refrigerator door. Asher wasn't the problem, though. It was his relationship. Asher and Kimber were the most popular couple in school. Kids had talked about them on the regular, and if they weren't gossiping about them, they wanted to *be* them. Everybody was in tune with the most apex relationship, and even though we were now out of school, our eyes and ears were still trained on them. And when their relationship crumbled overnight, leaving broken noses and fallen teeth in its wake, we all felt it.

As soon as Asher was up, the air in the room shifted. I looked at Emma and asked if she wanted to take Gunner for a walk. She nodded eagerly. Anything to get away from the brooding couple. I picked up Gunner's leash, and he jumped to all fours, bumping into chairs and slamming his tail into kneecaps. I grabbed a coffee on the way out and felt Noah's gaze on my back until the door closed behind me. As soon as we gained some distance from the cabin, Emma broke the silence, and I took a much-needed full breath.

"How are you feeling?" Emma asked.

With all the commotion, I almost forgot I'd passed out the night before. It was minor compared to everything else that had been happening. I shook my head. "Oh, I'm fine. But I have to tell you. Noah kissed me last night," I said, staring at her with bulbous eyes. She gasped.

"No freaking way!"

"I don't know, Emma, it was everything I had dreamed of for so long. And now? I don't know. I thought I liked it, but then I thought I would like it more if it was Walker, and then as soon as he popped into my head, I couldn't get him out. I pulled away from Noah, and I've hardly been able to look at him since," I said.

Emma looked back at the cabin as we entered the shady part of the forest. The wall of trees. "Wow, you really must like Walker. Didn't you say he has a girlfriend?" My stomach dropped because I knew I'd been lying to her. I'd been lying to everyone. But it had only isolated me. Alienated me from the group and made me feel like an outsider in my own cabin. And now . . . now that everybody was seeing things, I realized the secrets were just keeping us apart. Still, I didn't feel like Walker's past was mine to share.

"She's . . . unavailable," I said, dropping my head and feeling the defeat of just how true that overly broad statement was.

"You must really like Walker if you left Noah for him, even though he's unavailable."

"That's what I thought!" I said, and Emma giggled.

"So, I wanted to talk to you about something else that's been on my mind. You know how we talked about finding this girl? Layla?" I asked.

Emma nodded.

I hesitated. "Well, I think we should tell the group. I don't want to scare anybody—any more than they already are—but I think it's time. And I think they might be able to help us find her. Maybe we could get some answers about this place and how it all works? What do you think?" I asked.

"I don't know, Kinsley. I don't know if everyone can handle it. I mean, Kimber was nothing but a skeleton last night. You saw her. Do you really think they can deal with anything else? Especially after losing Ethan? And I read these stories all the time. I love this stuff. If it's paranormal, I'm in. Horror, I'm there. But Scarlett May? She's probably like a western romance kind of girl. And Kimber reads sci-fi—they can't handle real life ghost stories."

I reached down and let Gunner off the leash. He took off running as Emma babbled about how she judged people based on what book genres they read.

"—And you know Asher doesn't even read."

"I don't read either," I said.

"No, I know. But, I think you would, if you could—not like that. You know what I mean." I watched her fumble a little before lowering my gaze to the gravel path. I knew what she meant. It had just come out wrong. Anyway, I had bigger problems than being offended by Emma's analogy.

"Look, all I'm saying is I don't think that we should tell them about Layla Barns or the accident you were in." Emma scowled as she scratched the back of her head. "I don't even think the Baylor Butcher's connected to any of this. Maybe it's not even a *real* person—maybe it's a ghost . . . or some sort of entity, an evil one." I tried not to think about how she'd said *real* person. As if *I* were a fake. It felt that way sometimes. "And the Baylor phenomenon, isn't that just magic?"

I glowered down at the path and after a moment, nodded in agreement.

"Yeah. It's just magic that we don't know the rules to yet. I don't think any of our friends are going to believe this for one second. So, if you want to push them away, tell them. But I think this should stay between us. And Walker, of course," Emma said.

I let out a disappointed sigh. I couldn't help but feel she was wrong. I would think about what she said, but I wouldn't let it stop me from building the team I needed. Maybe I'd start to tell the group and then I would feel the room. Let it guide me. It was a slippery slope because I was harboring secrets from everyone. Once one stone came out, the whole tower would surely crumble.

We talked a little bit more about Kai coming home. I told her the things he had seen and experienced. And then I told her how Noah and I had broken the news about Ethan. I took the opportunity to persuade Emma to tell everybody the truth, because if Kai had set his mind to it, he could probably figure out the whole puzzle. And nobody could argue with that. We could've talked for days, but the words were stolen right from our mouths the moment we saw that an apple tree—*our* apple tree— had moved to the main path. It had grown even more, arching over the main pathway and now bearing fruit. An apple the size of a small melon hung right in front of my face. It wasn't just ripe; it was beautiful, red, and glossy. It could be award-winning. I reached out to touch it and the apple fell into my hand—perfectly ripened to the very second.

"I've never seen this apple tree before, have you?" Emma said, marveling under the branches filled with low-hanging fruit.

"I haven't seen it *here* before. But that's only because it was somewhere else yesterday. This was the sapling we planted." I spun the gigantic apple around in my hand. Not one imperfection was visible.

"Okay, maybe we should show the group *this*. They're never going to believe it. But this is . . . amazing." It *was* amazing. And it reminded me of something from my childhood. A book my gran used to read to me. A fairy tale filled with magic—both beautiful and poisonous.

It took me back to a time when my gran would tuck me into bed on the nights that she stayed for dinner. She'd never just kiss me on the forehead and turn out the lights; she'd sit and read me a story. My mom would always come looking for her, wondering where she'd disappeared to. She'd been right there by my side, reading bedtime stories until my eyes were heavy enough that I would drift off to sleep. Often, I'd dream of the magic. The fairy tales would whisk me off to a faraway land, and I'd fly with the monkeys, sing with the dwarfs, and ride in pumpkin carriages.

This particular apple was so perfect and lush, it reminded me of other things too—a story I couldn't quite place. My mouth watered. I brought the apple to my lips and opened wide. Emma slapped it out of my hand with surprising force. The apple flew from my hand, nearly taking my fingers with it.

"You can't eat that!" she yelled.

"What? Why not?"

"Do you know any of the classics? I mean, I know you don't read, but clearly, you've heard of the most classic fairy tales of all time, right?"

I shrugged. I had.

"Clearly, that's a poisonous apple, Kinsley!" Emma hissed with disapproval.

I scratched my head. That was it. I knew it had reminded me of something. She very well could be right. We were trapped in Baylor, after all. Surely there were poisonous apples and all sorts of things that could spin a spell so fast you could die . . . and never even know it. I shivered.

The apple had split against a rock, and a wisp of black vapor plumed from the crack. I smiled at Emma for possibly saving my life. *Afterlife?* I wasn't sure what she'd saved, but she's done well. She was a valuable member of our team.

On the way back, Emma and I discussed talking with the group. After seeing the apple tree grow without constraints and bloom in only forty-eight hours, she was convinced that we should tell the others. Show them, too. No more secrets, she said. And I agreed it was the right thing to do. But that didn't mean I wasn't scared. I felt like I was going through my own transformation. My own nightmare. And somehow, if I told everybody everything, it was like I'd be drowning them right along with me.

I nodded and agreed, but secretly I planned to hold some important details back. I thought about the first night when I'd drowned. How I'd come back into the cabin and nobody noticed I'd been gone. Nobody cared. The thought of telling them that was so mortifying, I didn't think I could. But it was the piece of the puzzle that told of the dark souls lost in the murky water. They needed to know.

As we neared the cabin, I realized there was something I needed to do. I had Layla Barns's purse tucked away in my closet. There were only a few items in there, but one of them was a mirror. And after seeing that juicy red apple— poisonous or not—I wanted to look in the mirror. I wanted to see if there was magic inside. Or, at the very least, the future. But even after the long talk Emma and I just had about not keeping secrets, that's precisely what I intended to do. Keep it secret.

Once we were back at the cabin, I headed for my room. I pulled the closet door open, halfway expecting to see the purse had been stolen, but it was there, tucked in the corner where I'd left it. My heartbeat quickened. This was a clue. I knew it. I could feel it. I was getting closer to saving my friends. The hems of my clothes touched the top of my head as I sat on the floor. I picked up Layla's purse and set it on my lap, admiring it like a wrapped gift on Christmas morning. I reached my hand inside, feeling for the compact, and I pulled it out. It was at least two decades old—probably more—and still, it was in great condition. It was gold with a round ruby button. I turned it over in my hand, examining it from top to bottom. There were only a few scratches on the side where it looked like maybe she had dropped it. I wondered if it had been scratched during the accident.

I opened the compact and was surprised when a small photograph, cut to size, fluttered into my lap. I shut the compact and placed it to my side. I picked up the picture and turned it over, instantly feeling sick to my stomach. Layla and Walker—*my* Walker. It was him in his other life. The one where he was happy and fulfilled. The one he preferred over his life with me. He was handsome, and I had never seen him smile like that before. It broke my heart thinking that I would never see him smile like that. He looked almost unchanged. As if the past twenty years hadn't aged him a day. I guess that's what happens when you die. You stop aging.

I looked at Layla in the photo. She was vibrant, full of

life. Her eyes sparkled even in the old photograph, and I could only imagine how beautiful and warm she was in person. Her hair was lush and healthy, her cheekbones lifted so that her eyes had the most perfect shape. She was smiling here in the photograph, but I imagined even on her worst days, her eyes would glisten. She was that kind of girl —a happy one. And I knew that I could never achieve that level of beauty. Not just because of what was on the outside; beauty was from within, after all. And as sad as it was to say, my insides didn't match hers. The loss of my gran and the insecurities I'd grown up with surrounding my dyslexia had dampened my energy. And that's why Walker would never love me—not because I wasn't Layla on the outside but because I was broken on the inside.

The compact cracked open as I pushed my thumb into the ruby button. The mirror reflected my ugly insides as I peered into it. I hated it. I hated how *I* was staring back at myself. This girl was dull, her skin lackluster and eyes two-dimensional. Her lips were dry and cracked; her hair brittle. And that was only on the surface. If this mirror was magic at all. It was showing me how transparent I was. I nodded, understanding it now.

Layla was never the one standing in my way of Walker. It was me. And who I was at the very core. I couldn't change that. And what I was coming to learn, I couldn't hide it, either. The mirror was proof of that. I snapped the mirror shut and tossed it back in Layla's bag, and a moment later, I threw the picture in there too. I rested my head on the back wall of the dark closet and stared up at the hanging clothes. I thought about the time I'd looked in the mirror and my reflection was vacant. Missing completely. The time I was a nobody. And then I thought about the time I saw Kimber, her skin stretched over her bones and her teeth falling into the porcelain sink. We had something in common.

Our reflections weren't that of our exterior—not our skin, eyes, and hair—but something much deeper. Kimber's eating disorder was reflected in the mirror the same way that my insecurities were reflected in mine. And at one point, I'd believed I was so insignificant that I didn't have a reflection at all. Now I knew better. I knew I had a purpose and that I held the power to get my remaining friends out of Baylor. And I supposed that was why I'd found my reflection again.

I thought about Walker's photo. He'd had the scar across his eyebrow. It was the same one he had on his eyebrow half the days I saw him. Some days it was magically gone; other days, it was a fresh wound—bleeding all over again. Could that be his reflection? Could he be so beautiful on the inside, except for that one little piece? A piece that refused to heal. I wondered what it could be. What marked his soul? What ran so deep that it showed on his surface?

If Walker had only one scar to bear on his face for all of

us to see, then I had one hundred. I had a long way to go if I ever wanted to like what I saw in that funhouse mirror. It felt impossible, and at times it felt shallow. But I knew that this was much more than a beauty contest. There were answers hidden beneath our reflections. And if I could figure out what Kimber's truth was, then maybe, just maybe, I could figure out my own.

CHAPTER 16

s I sat at the base of my closet, the darkness and clothing smothering me, I knew I had to tell the group what I'd learned about the Baylor phenomenon. It was snatching souls and destroying minds, and if they knew, they'd at least be better equipped to combat it. They'd have a better chance of fighting if they knew the manifestations began in their heads. I couldn't leave out a single detail. Because if I missed even one little thing, I knew it would inhibit us from solving this puzzle. One missing piece could bring us all down.

I didn't want to tell them about my gran, though. The nights that she had come for me, the twisted conversations I'd had with my mother over the telephone that were rehearsed and fake. It was too personal, and I didn't want them to see my weakness. But that's precisely why I *needed* to tell them. I needed to stand up for myself. Stand up to the fear that kept me caged inside. I scrambled to my feet, my face getting caught on hanging clothes. I batted them away and strode downstairs with newfound purpose. I tried not to let myself think of how terribly this could go, because then it surely would.

Kai and Noah sat making dinner plans in the living room. It sounded like an epic barbecue night, and they were making a list of items they needed at the grocery store. I didn't have to look for Kimber and Asher; I could hear them clearly from the other room. They were fighting like they had been ever since their breakup. They were tucked in the dark den; only it wasn't as private as they'd probably hoped. One look at Noah and Kai, and I could tell that everybody was annoyed with them. I sighed and headed into the kitchen to find Scarlett May and Emma washing dishes. It was nice to have the extra help.

"Do you know where Levi is?" I asked, trying to round up the troops.

"Levi and Mason are throwing a football outside," Scarlett May said, pointing a soapy finger out the window.

"What's up?" Emma asked.

"There's something important we need to talk about. I want to get the group together before dinner so we can all chat," I said, picking up a dish towel. As I started to dry the dishes, Kimber and Asher marched into the room, stealing the show.

"Don't make this about me! This is all about you and

what you're going through. But you push it off on me like it's all my fault, and it's not! You make me sound so crazy!" Kimber yelled, stomping out to the back patio and slamming the door in her wake.

"What the hell?" Asher fisted a hand in his hair and then stormed off in the opposite direction.

"I swear, if those two don't get back together, I'm going to pull my hair out strand by strand," Scarlett May said. Emma took a deep breath, visibly stressed. We all were. The relationship fighting was just the icing on the cake.

We finished the dishes, and I had high hopes of gathering the group for the speech I never wanted to give. But now, Kimber was gone, taking Gunner for a walk, and a few of the boys were off to the grocery store in search of supplies. Emma retreated to her room to do some more research, and I grew more and more anxious about delivering my speech as the minutes ticked by. What if they didn't believe me? Or worse, what if they did? What if it elicited fear and everybody went crazy? What if it made *me* crazy?

I was worried that I was missing something. Something so simple that I hadn't seen. What if I told them everything, and they knew the answers almost immediately? Was I ready to face it? Was I ready to understand what was happening? I didn't know if I could handle all the responsibilities. I was most afraid that the terrible things that had happened to my friends were my fault—I couldn't live with that.

There were already monsters in the water, magical fruit trees in the forest, and the most handsome walking dead guy I'd ever seen. If there was even one more abnormal evolution, I might fall to my knees and crumble to ash. Yet, I knew if that were to happen here in Baylor, I'd be the phoenix and rise to do it all over again. There would be no break for me. Not until the hard work was done.

When the guys got back from the store, they fired up the grill. The smoky smell of barbecue permeated the air and rose to the second story of the cabin. I was riddled with anxiety about all the ways our conversation could go, and I was stuck trying to find the courage within myself to do it anyway. I was pacing back and forth in my bedroom when I heard one of the guys call out through the window. "Dinner is served!" It sounded like Mason.

I peeked out the window and saw the football rolling down the grassy hill toward the lake, left behind by the guys as they ran for dinner. Scarlett May grabbed a plate and got in line for dinner. Her jean shorts and cowgirl boots were the perfect attire for a lakeside barbecue. I looked down at my joggers and tennis shoes and briefly thought that I should try harder. Put on some real clothes. Especially if I was going to be speaking in front of everyone tonight. So, I did just that. I rummaged through my clothes and changed into jeans and a hoodie—only slightly better. I wasn't dressed up by any means, but at least I didn't feel like I had just rolled out of bed.

I loaded up a plate with a bread roll, barbecued corn, and steak. It smelled wonderful, and I had no doubt these guys had been perfecting their barbecue game over the course of the summer. When they went back to Clover, they were going to impress their parents and future girlfriends with their skills.

"There's something I wanted to talk to you guys about before dinner," I said in a meek tone. Only a few of them heard me.

"What's that, Kinsley?" Kai asked. He had compassion that reached out beyond his senses. He heard even the weakest of voices, and he worked hard to bring them to light so that everybody could hear. "Hey, dipshits, Kinsley's trying to tell us something," he said in a booming voice. Maybe he didn't do it with grace, but he got the job done. My face heated, as I had the stage. Everybody froze, holding their plates or tongs mid dish.

"Um, I just, I wanted to talk to you guys after dinner. It's about all the weird things that are going on, and I think I might have some insight that I haven't quite shared with you all yet. There are things I know. And, um, I think it's time that we all share the little bits of information that we've gathered. I'm probably not the only one who's had strange things happen to them or seen things that seem abnormal. I think if we piece them all together, as a group, we'll be stronger. And maybe we can go on the offensive for the first time if we're a team," I said.

"Sounds like a plan," Levi said, loading up his plate.

I nodded, my face hot. Kai patted me on the back. I looked around and couldn't find Emma. My stomach sank, hoping that she hadn't been the next victim.

"I think that's a great idea, Kinsley," Kai said. And I felt validated for the split second before I ran inside and searched for the only friend I had left.

"Emma?" I called out. But I heard no answer. I ran upstairs where I had known her to be last, and when I burst through her bedroom door, I saw her sitting at a small desk with earphones in. My heart pounded against my chest, and I felt dizzy in my relief. I backed up against the wall, hand across my heart.

"Hey!" Emma lurched, catching sight of me from the corner of her eye. Her expression remained unchanged with the passing seconds. Had I interrupted something? Perhaps Emma had secrets too.

"What's going on?" I asked, catching my breath and looking around the room for signs of secrecy. I found my sign the moment that Emma reached for a book and placed it over an article on her desk.

"Nothing. You just scared me, that's all," she said, her voice higher pitched than normal. I moved toward her desk, and slowly I reached out for the book. I didn't take my eyes off her. I watched as her face wrinkled with grief.

"What is it?" It must've been something terrible if my only friend was hiding it from me when we had just discussed secrets being off-limits. It had to be something absolutely atrocious. Something that made her think it would destroy me if I saw it.

She said nothing, but her eyes turned glassy as she looked down at the article. I, too, looked down at the article. The print was tiny, and the black spaces of the font merged with the white spaces in between the letters. They danced as I watched, knowing that if I could only focus hard enough, I'd know exactly what that article said. My name popped out, bigger and bolder than the rest. Words like accident were next.

"What is it?" I asked again.

"I found a new article. I swear it wasn't there the first time we looked. It must've just come online." Emma picked up the article and watched me intently. I took a moment to decide if I wanted to hear it, and my ultimate decision was that I had no choice. I was nothing more than a victim. Everything had been happening to me at lightning speed, and I had no control over stopping it. Or slowing it down. I nodded.

"It talks about the accident you were in. It talks about how you . . . *survived*." Emma's eyes flickered up at me, checking for my reaction, but I had none. *Survived?* "It says you spent some time in the hospital recovering, but ultimately, you're a fighter." Emma paused, and my eyes turned glassy as the news soaked in.

She continued, "You were able to heal even when the doctors said you wouldn't. They're calling it a miracle." Emma's eyes drooped with sadness. My throat burned, and even though I was on the verge of crying, my mind was quiet. Thoughtless. It made little sense to me. And the fact that she was sad about it only confused me more.

"Do you believe it?" I asked. Emma's eyes floated back to the article.

"I don't know what to think," she shrugged.

"If I survived . . . Then why am I here?" The room silenced.

It was the million-dollar question. How could I be here, dead, amongst my dying friends at a cabin in the woods? How could the woods be filled with mysterious and surreal happenings? How could apples appear overnight? How could Lainey come to life under the water? How could she speak to me without ever saying a word? —If I were alive?

"Lainey . . ." I whispered, taking a seat on the edge of the bed.

"Lainey?" Emma asked.

I looked out the window. The wheels turning and grinding in my head. Gears I had never explored before.

"When I saw Lainey under the water, she told me to wake up. She said *wake up!*"

My mouth parted, and time stopped altogether.

"Oh my god, Kinsley! *You're dreaming*. It's a dream! It's nothing but a damn dream!" Emma said, coming to her feet. Her eyes searched mine.

"I'm . . . I'm dreaming? That can't be . . ." I shook my head.

"Why not?" she asked.

"Because. I don't know, you're here. And Noah's here. And everybody is here!" I felt sick to my stomach. Like my world had come crashing down on me. "It makes no sense. How are you all in *my* dream? I mean, you're real, aren't you?" I asked, and a sense of dread poured over me the moment it slipped from my lips. I couldn't do this alone. I needed her to be real.

"Of course, I'm real!" Emma said, insulted. But after a moment of silence, I watched as a new thought creased her brows and her eyes lowered to her body. Slowly, she patted her arms and gripped her shoulders. "Yeah, I'm totally real," she said quietly. I wasn't so sure. I wanted to touch her too, but I couldn't insult her like that.

"Could we all be dreaming together?" I said.

Emma snorted. "More like you've summonsed us into your dream. I think you're pulling us into it."

I was like a dark vortex. I sucked in anybody who got

close enough, and then swallowed them into the throat of the night.

Emma looked out the window, her eyes traveling the distance. When she turned back to me, she looked upset. "I don't want to be here, Kinsley. And if this is your dream, can't you send us home?" Emma nodded. "I want to go home. I don't want to die here." Tears spilled from her eyes, and I felt absolutely terrible. She cried on my shoulder when I pulled her in for a hug.

It didn't convince me I was alive yet, but somehow I had been hurting the people I loved most. Somehow, I knew this was my fault. I never put it past me to hurt the people I loved. But it was never my intention.

"Oh Emma, I would send you home if I could. But I don't think I can control this. I'm not convinced that I'm alive, let alone dreaming up this whole Baylor phenomenon. I'm just not . . . I don't know," I said, my thoughts a jumbled mess. I let go of Emma and pinched my arm. I shrugged. "I feel it. So, that means I'm real. I'm not dreaming, right?" I asked, unsure of anything at this point. I was worried that I was giving myself false hope, and I knew I couldn't survive another letdown.

"A pinch? That's all you've got? We need something bigger." Emma looked around the room, and I feared what she would do next. I watched as her eyes settled on a pencil, and I instinctively stepped backward, thinking that she'd bring it down on me, stabbing me in the back—just to test her theory.

"I feel . . . I feel! You don't need to stab me," I said, holding my hands out. Emma laughed. It had never been her intention. And I sure felt stupid for believing it.

"I thought I said *we*. I was thinking bigger. Much bigger."

"Bigger than stabbing me?"

"Hey, you know what would be really great?" Emma said, a smile broadening across her face. "If Asher and Kimber got back together and all the fighting stopped." I frowned. They were an unnecessary thorn in everybody's side, but I couldn't see how the two things were connected.

"I mean, yeah, that would be great. But—"

"—Make it happen," she said. Demanding the impossible of me.

"Make it happen?" Now it was my turn to laugh. It was so ridiculous. She acted as if I could dream up anything in the world and it would happen before our very eyes. Like a manifestation.

Manifestation . . .

Walker told me that my fears came to life here—and if that didn't sound like a dream, I didn't know what did. A weird feeling swirled in my chest, and I didn't know if I was about to like this theory or not.

"Just *try* to make it happen. Think about it. Think about what you would see if they got back together. Let's go downstairs for dinner, and I want you to feel as if they'd already gotten back together and the tension in the cabin was long gone. Go downstairs with the firm belief that everybody is getting along. Can you do that?" she asked. Who knew Emma could give motivational talks? If I had, I would've tapped into them more often.

"Okay, I think I can." And that's exactly what I did.

We went down for dinner. I'm sure my plate was already cold, as I had set it on the banister before running in to check on Emma. But as we walked down the stairs, I concentrated. I tried my hardest to feel what it would be like if everyone was happy, despite the fear, the anger, and the grief. Not just Kimber and Asher, but everybody. I imagined unity and laughter. And just the thought of it made me feel lighter, as if it had already happened. I smiled, feeling stupid, and embarrassed for believing it could work. It reminded me of the time Walker and I found the tower by way of sixth sense.

By the time we hit the bottom stair, I could see the change in Emma's face. Behind her smile and sparkling eyes, there was genuine happiness. Butterflies fluttered in my stomach as we opened the back patio door. The entire group was playing football out on the grass. Kimber ran and jumped on Asher's back as he tried to score a touchdown. She roared with laughter as the guys tried to rip the ball out of Asher's hands. A normally aggressive game of football was now child's play. And it was like walking into a scene from a movie. A scene of normalcy and happier times.

I couldn't pry my eyes off the faces out on the grass. They were happier than I had ever seen them . . . and all at the same time. The way I felt inside—I had seen it in their eyes. They felt it too. Emma grabbed my arm. And as we watched them with unhinged jaws and wide eyes, she laid her head down on my shoulder. The sun set, turning their figures into dark silhouettes in play. It was the summer I'd always wanted.

If this truly was a dream, then why had all the bad things happened? I was a good person. My soul was pure. If I was in control, then how were my best friends dead? It couldn't be. I couldn't be the only one flying this plane right now. There had to be outside factors contributing to the pain and misery we'd all experienced this summer. Because this wasn't my plan.

I rested my head on Emma's and we contentedly watched everybody play, if only for just tonight. When they caught sight of us, Kai waved us to join. Emma looked at me with a twinkle in her eye that reminded me of a child on Christmas morning. She slipped her hand out of my arm and took off running across the grass to join the team.

But if I was dreaming, then she wasn't real. And if she wasn't real, then what was she?

On her first step forward, I reached out behind her and touched her hair in curiosity. My hand touched nothing at all. It swiped through her brown locks as if they were nothing more than air—pushing little specks of particles around as they glimmered and disintegrated. Emma ran off to play football as I stood on the porch watching the pieces of her fall to the ground, sparkle, and fade into nothing.

CHAPTER 17

After a long, sleepless night, I awoke to the sound of my alarm, though it was far too early to volunteer for the Baylor Fourth of July Parade. It was Lainey's commitment, but she'd enlisted our help before she had disappeared. Back home, she did it every year without fail, and she was more excited to glue live flowers on floats here in Baylor than to watch the parade itself. I'd done it once with her before when we were a little younger, but this time was different, and I wasn't looking forward to it.

Today was going to be full of Lainey memories, and it hurt just thinking about it. Walker decided last minute to join us, and I was thankful for his distraction. However, I knew I needed to tell him about what Emma had found online—the part where I'd survived the accident. *Survived* —it sent a shiver down my back. Maybe it was good news to tell, I didn't know. But I found myself worried about how he'd take it. Walker and I had always been two peas in a pod. The only ones of our kind. And today, I was going to tell him that it was simply him. Only him. That he walked alone in the shadows.

Theoretically, it should be good news. I wasn't dead after all—assuming the article was real. I wasn't totally convinced. But if it were, I'd have a life to live outside of Baylor. I'd go on to college—maybe even have a family of my own one day. But regardless, I couldn't help the terrible feeling that swirled in my chest telling me this was a bad thing. That I was leaving Walker behind. To a world of solitude. An eternity of it.

Solitude. It was man's worst punishment. Walker didn't deserve it. He deserved to find his real love, Layla Barns. And if she had died in that crash, there was no reason we couldn't find her and set him free. I knew he didn't look at me the way I did him, but I was still heartbroken to tell him that I would not be in his eternity. I'd always thought that he would find Layla and leave me behind, but if I was alive somewhere, then I'd be the one leaving him. We had become good friends over the summer. Better than friends. We had become afterlife mates. We shared a bond like nobody else. And today . . . today was going to be the day that I broke that bond.

Walker and I walked side by side as he handed me a

hot coffee. I thanked him as we checked in for volunteering. There were several floats to be assigned to, and Emma was hoping to work on anything that originated from a book. If it had, she'd probably read and loved it at one time or another.

With that said, we were assigned to the furthest thing from a fairy tale. We were assigned to work on a beer float. An advertisement. But to me, sticking golden flowers on a cold brew was no different than placing the red flowers on a poisonous apple. It was, however, the ultimate blow to Emma. Her disappointment was obvious in her droopy gaze and pouty lips. I squeezed her shoulder.

"It's okay. I'm sure that an hour from now you can go stick flowers wherever you want." The corners of her eyes lifted, and she smiled mischievously.

The beer garden float was a long walk away. One of the farthest floats from the check-in stand. A kind old lady gave us volunteer badges and sent us on our way with a map. The place was a madhouse. It was crawling with volunteers, engineers, and even a news crew. There was a lot to see and a lot to take in. I knew as we passed each subsequent float that I wasn't enjoying the flowers to the fullest, how Lainey would have. I slowed, reaching my hand out, and my fingertips praising a freshly glued flower. I didn't even know the names of the flowers. If Lainey were here, she would have told me. She wouldn't have stopped telling me, and at some point, her words would have fallen on deaf ears. But I wanted to hear their names now.

"That white one right there—that's a carnation. The brightly colored ones in the front of the float are chrysanthemums. Mums for short. They symbolize death and grieving," I heard Lainey say in my ear. Her voice tickled, and I batted at my ear, checking behind me. I searched for Lainey and then realized it had only happened because I'd wanted it to. It brought a smile to my face, even if I'd made it up. Because it was her voice—her essence—and it lived on through my memory. And that much was real.

"You know, if Lainey were here, she would tell us all about these flowers. She wouldn't shut up about them," I said with a smile. Walker hadn't known her very well, only having had a few brief encounters with her, but I could tell that he enjoyed hearing about her.

Emma laughed. "Oh yeah. All day long. She'd tell us how they collected the flowers and have stories about each kind. She loved this stuff," Emma said.

"The bright-colored ones in the front of the float are chrysanthemums. Mums for short. They symbolize death and grieving," I said in my best impersonation of Lainey.

"Oh—how'd you know that?" Emma asked, taken aback by my comment.

I shrugged. "A little birdie told me," I said.

The smell of flowers was overwhelming, and it

reminded me of walking into a flower shop to pick the perfect bouquet when my gran died. It wasn't a good memory, and the smell was intoxicating. My heart had broken while looking at the beautiful varieties of flowers and smelling the sweet petals. It was a terrible mix. The beauty, the nature, the colors, and the smell—all laced with grief. And what never seemed to make sense to me was that flowers were for every occasion. You get them when you're in love and when it's your birthday; you can get them with a new job or a raise. And how is it supposed to make you feel when all you can remember is the smell of heartbreak, and it takes you back to that space and time? It doesn't feel like a celebration of anything, but more like torture. Torture of the mind and soul.

But today was the day that I was going to overwrite that memory. I'd never inhaled so many flowers before, and I was pretty sure I'd smell like petals for the rest of my life. I didn't think a shower was powerful enough to rid me of the rose bath I was marinating in. I held my coffee close and took in a deep, cleansing breath, the roasted bitter beans under my nose. But there was only so much coffee I could drink, and at some point in the day, I'd have to get used to smelling flowers again.

They stationed me near the top of a giant beer stein. I had a million tiny white flowers to glue to the float, which would soon become the effervescent head of the beer. It all felt so elaborate for a small-town parade. Where in the world had all these flowers come from? Walker was below me with deep amber flowers at the base. Emma was on the other side of the float, gluing greenery to make grass for the beer garden. I watched as she pointed to a book in another girl's purse. They hadn't stopped talking since.

"How's it going down there?" I asked Walker.

"Slow. How long do we have to do this for?" he asked, stopping to peer up at me.

"We've only been working for eleven minutes. We have all day."

"I see. Can we take breaks?" he asked, hopeful.

"I don't see why not. We're just volunteering." I stuck another white flower on top of the beer stein.

"Now?" Walker asked. I laughed. He made his way up to me and started picking from my flowers. He wasn't supposed to be working on the same project as I was, and it made my heart smile that he wanted to be closer to me. There were a million reasons why that could have been the case, but I settled on distance. He didn't like the distance.

"Any idea where our next clue is?" he asked, looking around. And then I realized he didn't like the distance between him and Layla.

"Actually, I think I might have a clue." I searched around for floats with seven dwarves, but I saw no such thing.

"Really? Did your grandma pay you another visit?"

"No. I haven't seen her in a little while. But, I've been

thinking . . . and you know that apple tree we planted?" I asked.

"Yeah, the gigantic one. How could I forget?"

"Well, it bloomed. It's got the most beautiful, giant, red apples you've ever seen. They're perfect. Emma said they might be poisonous."

"Poisonous?" He glared at me with one eyebrow raised —the one with the gash running through it. It was healed today and looked as if it had happened a decade ago.

"I know it sounds weird, but didn't the tower sound weird? I'm telling you, I think these fairytale books my gran used to read to me are clues. And where there's an apple . . . there must be poison." I said, picking the sticky glue off my fingertips.

"Okay, so what fairytale are we in now?" he asked, leaning in.

"I'm thinking our next clue is going to lie on one of these floats. Look for anything with apples, seven doors, a witch, or . . . a magic mirror," I said.

We made it just shy of half an hour before Walker was so restless we ditched our stations and wandered around in search of fairytale floats. We came across superheroes, big-box labels, and mythological creatures but had no such luck when it came to fairy tales.

Since Emma had stayed back chatting with her new friend and working diligently to cover the float, I decided it was time to talk to Walker. I had to tell him about the article. But the more I tried to spit it out, the more it seemed to bury itself deep down inside of me. I considered keeping it a secret and never letting it see the light of day. I'd allow Walker to think that we were two of the same kind so that he'd never have to feel alone again. But I knew that was wrong, and it would never last. The truth needed to be told, no matter how painful it would be for him to hear.

"I found something. Or rather, Emma found something. She found an article on the accident that I was supposedly in . . ." I said, tiptoeing around the facts.

"She found another article? Did it say anything new?" he asked, his attention only partially on me as he continued searching floats.

"Yeah, I learned that I'm still alive—" I said, wanting him to stop looking for Layla and see what was right in front of him. It worked too well. Walker stopped dead in his tracks. He looked back at me with his brows stitched. I couldn't quite read his expression, but I knew enough that it wasn't a positive look. I grimaced.

"I hate to tell you this, but I don't think you have that right, Wilde. I mean, you're just like me, and nobody's ever been just like me."

My heart sank. "The article said that I survived the crash. It said that I spent a long time in recovery and it was thought to be a miracle. I think it's true. I think I might be alive. And this . . . this is all just a dream . . ." I said quietly.

Walker stepped close to me. Our faces were close enough that I could feel his breath upon my lips. "You think you're in a dream?" he asked.

I swallowed hard, questioning the real possibility. If I were in a dream, he'd kiss me—and that wasn't happening. "Well—" I began.

"—I'm not dreaming. This is my real life. My *afterlife*. This can't be your dream because I've been living it since long before you drowned in that lake. I'm sorry to be the one to tell you, but I don't think you're alive, Wilde. It just can't be. What about your gran?" he asked. His voice was harsh and filled with skepticism. But I knew that whatever the answers were, we were still in this together, and he would be by my side, no matter the state of my mind and soul.

"Well, I stayed up all night thinking about that," I said, leaning in closer, our heads nearly touching, my eyes searching his. "I think that maybe it's *because* I'm in a dream state that I can talk to you and Gran. I think I've passed the veil of the living and somehow gotten closer to wherever you and she live. I think my heart and soul are traveling at a different frequency somewhere closer to yours, on the other side. I think that's what makes us so similar," I said, nodding. He pondered my best guess as his face contorted.

I knew the moment he believed it to be a possibility. His forehead softened, and his eyes appeared deeper, more distant, like he'd already begun slipping away from me. I spotted a mum—the flower of death. I plucked it from the base of a float and held it between him and me. Then, with all my concentration, I imagined it evaporating like I'd seen Emma's hair the night before. I stroked the petals between my fingers and they turned to tiny sparkles and glimmered all the way down to the ground.

Walker's eyes lifted with wonder but quickly drooped with sadness. He nodded. If I was alive, he was alone. The special bond we shared was a double-edged sword.

"One living, one not," he whispered.

But Walker was living. He was—just not the way that I was, or like anybody else back home. He wasn't even living the same as my gran. She was in another realm altogether. And if I had to guess, I'd say that it was the torture he'd put himself through that isolated him in such a way. If he'd only believe that Layla didn't blame him for her death, then maybe he'd be free. Free to get out of Baylor and follow her to their happily ever after. But instead, he believed he was cursed. It sure felt that way now.

When Walker's expression darkened, I could see the hurt in his eyes. "What's wrong?" I asked.

"This is good news. I'm happy for you. I'm happy," he said.

I knew the possibility of it was good news, but it didn't feel that way, and I could tell he had mixed feelings about it too. With my old life still ahead of me, I knew that one day we would be broken apart, and I would no longer see him. It made all the time between us even more precious. We had grown to like our peculiar arrangement. We had learned to lean on one another in times of need. Our bond had been strong from the start, but it had only strengthened each and every day this summer. It felt like a lifetime ago. Like I'd known him my whole life—or at least my soul had.

CHAPTER 18

After a long, failed attempt at locating anything remotely helpful to find Layla Barns in town, Emma, Walker, and I came home empty-handed. We had, however, honored Lainey and her love for Mother Nature by gluing countless flowers onto a giant stein of beer. She would have been proud.

But Walker wasn't ready to give up, so he headed home to do some research on the seven dwarfs. The fairytale lead was only a hunch at this point, but I recalled the bed of purple Rapunzel flowers blooming on the forest floor, long before the tower had appeared. And while we hadn't found Layla in that tower, we *had* found her purse—not to mention Trinity's killer. I'd also discovered some rather disturbing things about my existence . . . or lack thereof. But when Emma swiftly smacked the most perfect red apple away, mere inches from my mouth, I'd thought of another fairy tale. This one, in particular, would have a witch, seven dwarfs, and a mirror. I'd already found the mirror—I couldn't forget it.

Emma and I slumped down on the sofa and turned on a movie. It wasn't long before the entire cabin got sucked in and we were packed like sardines on the couch. We were sandwiched between the once-again-happy couple and Noah. Scarlett May was at our feet with Sampson. Mason and Levi were lying on the floor, and Kai was popping popcorn in the microwave. I couldn't help but look at the empty spots on the floor. There was a spot for Ethan, one for Lainey, and one for Trinity. Now and then, my eyes would wander to the empty spots and I'd imagine how they would have lain or laughed.

The movie was packed with action and kept everybody on their toes. But no matter how many explosions, fistfights, or car chases sprawled across the screen, Emma had something else working through her mind. She leaned over and whispered during a loud suspenseful crash. "I've been thinking about the dream theory," she said. I watched as two cars collided, one going up in a plume of smoke and fire. I knew nobody could hear us, so I leaned back and gave her my attention—I wasn't fully invested in the movie either.

"I want to test it again. I have an idea," she said.

"Shut up back there," said Scarlett May, swatting a hand at Emma.

I said nothing but gave her a curt nod. I was up for testing dream theory—it could be fun.

"You made it happen once. I think you could do it again," she whispered.

"Shut up!" Scarlett May hissed. Emma's face turned red, and we knew that this conversation would have to wait for another time. Emma said nothing for the next half hour, and my mind swirled with the possibilities of tests. Kimber and Asher could have been a fluke. They were bound to get back together at some point. Couples fight all the time, and they had a long-standing relationship, not to mention they were hidden away in a remote cabin for the summer. There was no way they *weren't* getting back together. The fact that I imagined it happening could very well have been a coincidence. The more I thought about it, the likelier this explanation seemed.

But the part that irked me most—the part that I couldn't get out of my head—was Emma's hair as she ran away to play ball. I questioned if she was real, and she just disintegrated. I didn't know what that told me, but when I tried it again to show Walker, there were particles of that flower that I saw disintegrate too. There wasn't much. But it was enough to get me thinking. Truth be told, I couldn't stop thinking.

The movie ended with Emma giving it one more shot. She leaned in and whispered in my ear, but this time, we'd caught Kimber's attention.

"What are you guys talking about? What could possibly be more interesting than Danny McCoy without a shirt on?" Kimber asked, her eyes glued to one of the most handsome actors ever known.

Emma shook her head, not wanting to divulge. But when the movie was over, and Emma and I snuck into the dark den to chat, little did we know that Kimber followed.

"It worked with Kimber and Asher, so I was thinking maybe you could try it again," Emma said in the shadows of the den.

I folded my arms and looked at her suspiciously. I wasn't okay toying with people's emotions, but that didn't mean I wasn't curious. "What did you have in mind?" I asked.

"Well, I was kind of thinking that maybe you could see if . . . possibly . . ." She twisted her fingers in ways they weren't meant to bend.

"Just spit it out," I said.

"Levi. I like Levi." Emma's face contorted, knowing that it was a paradoxical match. I stared at her, wondering if it could be true. Emma was smart. She was one of the smartest girls I knew, and she was sweet, too. Levi couldn't be more opposite than that.

Levi was cute—maybe that was the reason she liked him. I wasn't sure. He was built like a tree trunk, strong and stout. He had black, spiky shards of hair that were on the brink of flopping at all times. And he only smiled from one side of his mouth. There was a real bad boy air about him, and his reputation with the girls preceded him. If Emma truly did like him, she wouldn't be the first, and she wouldn't be the last.

If I could pair Emma with anybody, it would be Kai. Kai was smart, compassionate, and also attractive. But I knew that's exactly why she didn't like him. Because as much as it never made sense to me, opposites truly did attract. And Emma liking Levi was proof of that. "So, what then? You want me to make Levi like you?" Levi wasn't in it for the long game, and I didn't think he had the emotional depth to carry a relationship of any kind. He was easy to fall for, but nobody ever stayed, and nobody ever wanted him for more than a one-night stand. I knew this was a bad idea.

Emma fidgeted, tucking her hair behind her ear and looking down to her feet in the dark, even though they were buried in the shadows. "Come on . . . Just do this one thing for me. I'm asking for a favor. I've *never* . . ." My eyebrows shot up right before Kimber walked in.

"You've *never* what?" she asked. And even though the room had no light bulbs, I could see the horror written all over Emma's face.

"How long have you been there?" she asked.

"Long enough to know that you like Levi and you're asking for Wilde here to do something mysterious—maybe evil. I want in," Kimber said, folding her arms.

"No," Emma said dryly.

"I heard you did, whatever it was, to Asher and me. You did *something*. I need to know what you did." Kimber wasn't budging. And I shrugged. She had a right to know. Emma shook her head, mortified, but I saw it differently. If I was going to enlist everyone's help, it started with the truth. And I was going to tell them, eventually. Maybe not about this, but about other stuff. The dream theory included. It made sense to do some testing to make sure it had some merit before telling the others. I put my hand on Emma's shoulder and she tipped her head back, moaning exhaustively.

"It's nothing more than a little manifestation," I said, improvising.

"You . . . *manifested* Asher and I getting back together?"

I could see the hesitation in her eyes. She knew there was much more, and had it not been for Kimber's emaciated reflection in the mirror, we might have gotten away with simple manifestation. But just nights before, we'd watched her teeth fall out, one by one, and as she glared at me now, she was certain I was lying. There was something much bigger going on, and she wanted in on it. Kimber slowly tilted her head and stiffened her shoulders; she wasn't budging until I spoke the truth.

"Emma has a theory—a theory that this is just a dream. And if it's a dream, then we can basically . . . *will* what we want to happen." I strategically left out the part where this was *my* dream and mine alone. I didn't think it would go over well. I wasn't the star of the show here, and if I needed teamwork, there couldn't be a frontrunner; a single dreamer.

"And you tested this theory out on me?" Kimber asked, her head dipping and her eyes looking up at us through her lashes mischievously.

"Well, you and Asher fighting was hell for all of us. You two aren't the only people in the house, you know," Emma said, her tone higher than normal.

"Okay," Kimber said, taking the news with a grain of salt. She was used to hearing that she affected people in ways she never knew. It came along with being popular in school. She must have been sick of hearing about other people's feelings by now.

"So, we were going to try Levi and Emma next," I said, pointing a finger at Emma. I knew that this was wrong. I knew that playing matchmaker with my friends like they were marionettes was like playing with black magic. I was tapping into something mysterious and powerful, and I knew it wasn't for the right reasons. Unfortunately, my curiosity trumped my moral compass. If Emma wanted a little kiss from a guy who enjoyed kissing, then what harm was there in that?

"Did I hear that you've *never* . . ." Kimber said, her finger swirling towards Emma's pelvis in the dark.

"Stop," Emma said bluntly.

"And you want Levi to be your first?" Kimber asked. This was the other half of the bad idea that made this test one gigantic, terrible plan. It was bad enough to play with my friends' emotions, but Levi would end up hurting innocent Emma, and we all knew it. Even she did.

"I mean, he's really, really hot. You can't argue with that," Emma said, her voice jittery and her arms folded tight across her chest. I shrugged because I couldn't argue with that. Kimber took on the parental role that perhaps I should have.

"But you know he's kind of an asshole, right?" Kimber asked.

"Mmm . . ." I nodded and looked at Emma for her response.

"I know," she said, looking at the ground.

"Okay, are we going to do this? Or should we find a different test? A safer one?" I asked, wanting to test the theory any which way possible. Emma nodded her head vigorously, and Kimber rubbed her palms together like she was starting the kindling of a fire.

"Okay, that settles it. How do we do this?" Kimber asked, her eyes bouncing from one of us to the other. A swirl of excitement ambushed me, and for the first time since the naked cheetah races, I had something to look forward to.

"We . . . We just imagine it as if it were true. We imagine what it would feel like, look like, smell—"

"Eww—" Kimber grimaced.

"Not like that, no, we just kind of spread that feeling all throughout the cabin," I said. Emma nodded in agreement.

"But what feeling?" Kimber asked.

I sighed, trying to think of how best to describe it. "Think of it like this: Levi falls for Emma. Now imagine how that would change the dynamics of the group. Feel the charge of flirtation in the air like electricity—"

"—Just picture it," Emma said with wide eyes.

"Yeah. That." I shrugged.

We closed our eyes, and I imagined Levi taking notice of Emma for the first time. I imagined Levi flirting with her. Grazing his hand against hers. Smiling out of the side of his mouth. I pictured her swooning and him grabbing her for a deep and passionate kiss. I smiled when I thought of her reaction. She'd blush like she'd been swept off her feet. And then I imagined what she would do if he actually swept her off her feet. If he threw her over his shoulder and charged upstairs to the bedroom. She'd be giggling the whole way. She'd have the night of her life, and when all was said and done, she'd fall back on her pillow with flushed cheeks and fall asleep with the large goofy grin that spread from one ear to the next.

Emma squeezed my hand as she snickered. I opened my eyes to see both of them giggling at me.

"What's with that look on your face?" Kimber asked. I realized I'd been the one with a stupid grin on my face, and it faded as the embarrassment sank in. The feelings I'd felt were so real that I couldn't wait to see if it would come true.

"I was just imagining it all. You guys did it too, right?" I asked.

"Yeah, I imagined Levi ravaging Emma all right," Kimber said. Emma slapped her shoulder, and we all laughed.

"Okay, let's see if it works. Let's go," I said, heading out the door.

"Oh my god, I'm so nervous," Emma said, completely frazzled. She hung behind, and I grabbed her shoulders, shoving her out of the den. The three of us laughed as we entered the kitchen, and as soon as we did, Levi snapped to attention. He looked Emma up and down. Kimber and I stared at each other with wide eyes as Emma's gaze darted straight to the floor and her cheeks turned crimson.

"Hey Emma, catch," Levi said, holding a piece of popcorn high over his head. I'd never seen Emma so embarrassed. She opened her mouth and tilted her head back, her cheeks as red as port wine. Levi threw the piece of popcorn and it landed perfectly in her mouth, just like magic. Levi jumped and yelled, and without hesitation, he swept her off her feet. He spun her around in a circle and high-fived her.

"That was awesome!" he yelled.

Kimber and I backed up slowly and leaned against the back counter. We folded our arms and watched from the shadows. At first, they were just talking, but it didn't take long for his fingers to graze her hand. Emma wasn't as sly as she had hoped. She jerked her hands back and stuffed them into her back pockets. Her eyes continued to dart in our direction, and every time they did, we pretended not to be watching.

"Is this really working?" Kimber asked, huddled toward me.

"I think it might be . . ." I said, not believing my eyes.

"If we can make this happen, what else can we do?" Kimber asked. I glanced at her, and her blue eyes were dark as the depths of the ocean, but they sparkled with the light of intrigue.

Somehow, I knew this curiosity would get me in trouble, but it did nothing to stop me now. I waited for him to throw her over his shoulder. I bit my lip, willing it to happen, and we watched as he grabbed her waist to tickle her. He leaned in close and whispered something in her ear. Kimber and I were fascinated. The suspense was far greater than that of the movie we'd watched earlier. No gunfight, car crash, or explosion could match the intensity we felt from watching our own manifestation play out in front of us.

"*Holy shit.* It's really happening," Kimber muttered.

I couldn't believe my eyes. Whereas Kimber and Asher making amends very well could have been a fluke, this was like watching a pig sprout wings and fly over the cabin. Levi liked girls, but he only liked them for one night. I knew he'd never looked at Emma with anything other than a friendly eye. But this was different. He was looking at her like he was under a spell, and I knew I'd been the witch who'd cast it. But Emma was happy, and Levi certainly didn't mind, so that made me a good witch. At least, that's what I told myself in the moment.

"We need front-row seats for this. Come on." Kimber grabbed my arm, and I lunged forward. She ran upstairs, and I was quick to follow. Just as we reached the top, I heard Emma squealing, and I knew she'd been thrust up on Levi's shoulder.

"Come on," Kimber hissed, her hands tight around my wrist as she pulled me into Emma's room.

Levi's heavy steps were on our heels and we could hear Emma giggling the whole way up, getting closer and louder. The second that Kimber and I realized they were coming into the bedroom, she shoved me into the closet. Kimber jumped in and slammed the closet door shut. Levi barged through the bedroom door with Emma draped over his broad shoulders. I worked to slow my breathing as my eyes adjusted to the dark closet. Slowly, Kimber let go of my wrist and I could tell by her warm breath that she had moved her ear to the closet door. I stood frozen, not wanting to be discovered. I didn't have to place my ear on the door to hear everything that was going on. Neither Levi nor Emma was trying to be quiet.

"Damn, Emma, what's gotten into you?" Levi asked.

Emma giggled, unable to talk. It was quiet for a while. Nothing more than the sound of lips meeting and pulling apart.

When it was obvious Kimber and I were trapped in the closet and we would probably be in there for a while, I slowly made my way down to the floor and got comfortable. Kimber did, too, pushing some clothing on the floor that we couldn't see.

Levi moaned, and Kimber and I did our best to keep our snickering silent. "I'm glad you're hanging out with us. This wouldn't be the same without you," I whispered to Kimber in the dark. I listened for her response, as I couldn't see a single thing except for the illumination of the closet door, and it wasn't long before even that had darkened when one of them switched the lights off. I leaned my back against the closet wall and I felt Kimber do the same.

"Sampson is hanging out with Scarlett May. I didn't really have another choice, now that Trinity's gone," Kimber said. It should have burned that we weren't her first choice . . . not even her second, but her *only*. I didn't take it personally. I knew Kimber liked us well enough. And I could tell that she was having fun. I was too.

"Do you think this is what she really wants?" I whispered.

"I think it is. But I think she'll regret it one day," Kimber said. I nodded, even though she couldn't see it. I thought she was right. This is exactly what Emma wanted . . . in the moment. But I knew Levi would fall back on his ways, and soon enough, her heart would be crushed.

As the sounds continued from the bedroom, I wondered if I had accidentally imagined too much. Maybe I should've stopped with a simple kiss. I cursed myself for allowing my mind to wander. It seemed fun, but I'd probably taken it too far.

When Levi's moaning started, Kimber grasped my arm so tightly she nearly cut off my blood circulation. My hand was going numb as she tried not to snicker out loud. But as Levi's moaning began . . . and ended, shortly thereafter, the excitement in the closet had dwindled too, and I was now worried that maybe Kimber was right. That Emma would regret this one day, and it would be my fault.

I dropped my hand down, shaking out the pins and needles, and I felt a sweater that I knew to be Lainey's. It was one of her favorites. I wrapped the ribbed material between my fingers, knowing it was the blue sweater that she used to wear all the time. It was cinched around the waist, and I always admired the way it hugged her figure.

I wasn't sure why and how Lainey could've passed away, especially if this was my dream. Because never once would I have wanted that to happen. I never would have manifested that or conjured her ill departure in any way, shape, or form. And as we hid in the depths of Emma and Lainey's closet, buried in the clothes that she would never wear again, the thing I feared the most was the network of unexplored crevices in my dark mind . . . because perhaps there was no such thing as a *good* witch.

CHAPTER 19

Even though the night had ended just as I imagined it would—with Emma's face buried deep in a pillow, hiding her blush, I had gone to bed with the swirling distaste of regret. I didn't know what kind of monster I had unleashed, but I feared the capability I now possessed. I wanted Emma to be happy. She was supposed to experience a night to remember with her crush. And even though that happened, it had still been with Levi, and he wasn't the right one for her. I battled between right and wrong into the wee hours of the night when sleep finally won over.

By the next day, Kai had come up with a new plan. He was going to hitchhike until one mile before the spot where he had evaporated. The spot where he had been sucked in and spat back out, landing him here, with us. He knew the exact spot, said it was burned into his memory, and he believed there was some sort of force field holding him in. Once he got to his spot, he was going to walk, step by step, looking for signs of change. He had all sorts of math equations tucked under his armpit as he shoved a banana and three granola bars into a backpack. He planned to document it all, take pictures, and report back.

"Are you sure this is going to be safe?" I asked.

"I'll be back before you know it. After I document everything, I'll turn on my recorder and step into oblivion, and I'll be back here, probably standing on the doorstep. I'll be back in time for the party tonight, and I'll tell you guys everything," Kai said. He gave me a wink before he left the cabin. And I sighed, knowing that it wasn't the best plan. But I couldn't stop him. He was a man on a mission.

Walker had plans to meet us at the party tonight—another bonfire at Sampson's house. It was good to keep the morale up. I spent the day watching Levi and Emma flirt. Emma had no regrets, and Levi seemed to enjoy himself as well. He had already enjoyed her company one day longer than I'd imagined, and I hoped I was wrong about him hurting her.

But as I got ready to go to Sampson's house and meet Walker, I had a knot in my stomach and an awful ache in my head. The headaches were coming more and more frequently, and even though I'd had them often as a child, this felt different to me. The pain, dull but widespread, was sometimes enough to blur my vision or make my stomach queasy. I went to the party anyway, as I was looking forward to seeing Walker. He always made everything better—no matter what reality I was living in. Dead or alive.

Once we got to the party, I grabbed a drink and headed out to the bonfire. Many of the girls stayed inside the cabin, grouped in cliques. I wore a beanie to keep my ears warm, and even though it was summer, the nights had dipped into cooler temperatures quite quickly. I wanted to be prepared for a night outside in the woods, and I was hoping for more campfire stories about Layla and the Baylor Butcher. The fire was warm enough for me to slip my jacket off, but as soon as I saw Walker striding toward me, my whole body heated from the inside out. I pulled my beanie off and ruffled my hair. I hated the way my body reacted to him, making it so obvious. There was no manifestation in the world that could knock down my feelings for him. And even if I could, I wouldn't want to. Because even though I hated the way my body melted around him, I loved the torture. The inner turmoil I felt when I saw him was addicting. I wanted Walker so badly that the torture of knowing he'd never love me was also welcome in my heart. Anything that came along with him as a package I had accepted long ago, when I thought we were the only souls of our kind. Even if I was just the girl to help him find his one true love, I would show up, every damn day.

Walker smiled at me by the fire, and my nauseated

stomach swirled. I forced my gaze to the white-hot flames and made a deal with the Devil himself. I was going to make Walker fall for me. I was going to conjure up whatever I had for Levi and Emma, and I was going to see it to the end. I was going to dwarf his former epic love story with one of my own. And I'd do it, even if it made me the Wicked Witch of Baylor.

I knew it was wrong, but I wanted nothing more. And I was willing to take whatever consequences came along with it. Should I do it here? Should I do it now? What was the perfect way to make him fall for me? A slow burn? Or a tidal wave? Oh god, I wanted a tidal wave to crash down on me this very moment.

I smirked.

"If I could only read your mind," Walker said, peering over at me.

I snapped out of it, the blood draining from my face. Had he been watching me the whole time?

"Why would you say that?" I asked, my voice squeaky and wavering.

"You should see the look on your face. What were you thinking about?" he asked. Walker smirked, as if it embarrassed him to even ask.

"Is it hot? Super hot?" I asked, fanning my face. I tossed the beanie in my hands behind me with my jacket and tugged at my shirt for airflow.

Walker laughed and surveyed the crowd.

I looked at all the faces; many of them I'd seen at Sampson's house before, but there were a few new ones. I saw the girl who had been interested in Noah in the kitchen, and I picked out several of Jack Sampson's friends, whom I'd spoken to the last time I was here. But there was a tall guy with a freshly shaved mullet that I'd never seen before. And a girl with short, curly black hair and large hoop earrings who was quite flirty with Levi that I couldn't recall either. Many of the faces disappeared into the background like white noise.

Levi followed the girl around like a puppy dog, and it pissed me off. I knew Emma had been in the kitchen with some of the other girls, and I hoped she wouldn't see it. I leaned over to Walker. "So, last night was interesting," I said. He tucked his hands deep in his pockets and focused his attention on me.

"Oh yeah? Mine was uneventful. I should've stayed over. I found nothing useful about the fairy tale. Nothing relevant whatsoever."

"Emma and Levi hooked up," I said, trying to find Emma through the kitchen window. I couldn't see her.

"What? Isn't Levi kind of a . . . meathead?" Walker shrugged.

I laughed, nodding. Even Walker got it. Emma wasn't supposed to be with him. "Yeah, and now look at him," I said, pointing to a dark corner of the waterfront cabin. It was just Levi and that girl—the one with the hoop earrings.

She was taking his baseball cap and trying it on. He was pretending to want it back. Walker rolled his eyes. I could tell he felt bad for Emma. I did, too.

"Does she know yet?" he asked.

I craned my head to see through the windows again; even so, I couldn't see her. "I don't think so."

Walker blew out a long and heavy sigh. "Hey, you want to get out of here? Let's take a little walk," he said.

Naturally, I'd follow him anywhere, so I nodded. I left my jacket and beanie behind, and I was quick on his heels. We walked in silence, not far into the woods. The heat from the fire left my skin and the night air cooled my cheeks. We were still close enough to see the bonfire and the cabin's front driveway where all the cars had been parked. But we were a few rows of trees deep in the forest. Hidden from everybody else. Hidden in the shadows. Walker leaned against a tree, and I thought this was my moment. I should ravish him. I imagined what it would be like to spread my hands over his chest and lift on to my tippy toes to kiss his lips. I'd be the wave crashing down on him.

"I've been thinking about you. Your dream state. Do you really think it's true?" he asked, running a hand over his chin.

I took a moment to shake my lustful visions free. This walk wasn't alone time for us, it was to get away from the listening ears at the campfire. "You saw what happened to the flower. It was like magic, right? Either I'm a ghost and I have the power to change my surrounding outcome, or I'm trapped . . . in some sort of reverie, and I'm lucid. I think those are the only options here. And to be honest, I don't like either of them," I said, running my hands through my hair, feeling stupid for even saying it.

"Or . . . It's the Baylor phenomenon. Just like I said before. It's the manifestation of our deepest desires." The way he said *desires* slipped me into a trance, and I felt the heat in my stomach dip even lower, spreading into my thighs.

"Deepest desires?" I said breathily.

"And fears. Lots of fears," he said, his eyes ablaze. Was he saying that he was afraid of falling for me? Or had I made that up?

I took a step closer, and he looked away. It was as if the word *fear* had soaked into my subconscious, making him turn from me. From then on out, all I could do was fear his rejection. So much so that I didn't even try to kiss him.

I took a step back and turned toward the cabin. My skin crawled with rejection. Like I had actually tried to kiss him, and he flat-out denied me. It hadn't happened, but it felt just the same in my head. All the heat that churned in my stomach dissipated, and the air turned icy.

"It can't just be deep desires. I never wanted Lainey to die," I said, crossing my arms.

"But it was your fear. Don't you see? Your fears are coming true too," he said.

"No. I never feared she would die. I never even thought about it. I never imagined her body floating in that water. So how did it happen?" I pointed to the shore and raised my voice.

"It's because of that damn calendar. That's how. You have it in your mind that thirteen of your friends are going to die. Thirteen deaths, all on your hands. Whether you thought it in the forefront of your mind or if it was a seed planted deep in your subconscious, you must've imagined that Lainey was on the chopping block. Just like with the rest of us." Walker pushed off the tree and took a wide stance.

"Are you saying that I killed my best friend?" I asked, turning to him and feeling sicker than I ever had.

"No! Yes. No."

"Spit it out, Walker!" I said in my full voice.

"I think there's a chance. I think there's a chance that you're manipulating this whole thing. This is your summer for the taking. Why don't you do something useful with it?" My chest burned like he'd sunk a knife into me. It was my deepest fear—that I'd hurt them, and that I had no control over it. He thrust his hands on his hips and leaned in.

"Your friends are all along for the ride. And I . . . by chance, I met you. I'm on my own mission here. I don't know what you're doing," he said, looking away from me as if he were disgusted. And that was a genuine fear of mine —anything to do with him not liking me or wanting me. Disgust was the very worst manifestation of rejection I could imagine.

I clamped my mouth shut and sank deep into my emotion, feeling the worry swirl around me and build like a tornado, until it just dropped, and it left me with nothing more than a thud in my chest. I looked up at Walker with teary eyes. "Are you mad at me?" I asked with nothing more than a whisper.

"Why don't you do something more? Something meaningful?" Walker's voice echoed in my mind, though I could see his mouth moving to a different tone. It was then that I knew our conversation was misleading. I wasn't hearing what Walker was truly saying. My mind was playing tricks on me again. And it was up to me to figure out what the truth was.

I could see in Walker's eyes a reflection of fear. I took a deep breath and fell back on my trust—something I wasn't very good at—that he wasn't telling me that I'd killed my best friend, that I was a bad person, or that I was doing evil things. There was no blame behind his eyes. And even though those were the words I heard in my head, I trusted the feeling I felt in my gut. He was scared—nothing more.

Walker's eyes turned glassy, and he looked like a trapped soul. He wasn't being portrayed the way he wanted, and it was my worry that was preventing the truth from coming out. He stared long and deep into my eyes, and I knew that he'd been subjected to my fear—that they all had been. I knew that nobody was safe when they were with me.

When it was obvious to both of us that our communication had failed, Walker slipped an arm around my shoulder and pulled me in for a hug. I held back my tears as I squeezed him tight. I pressed my cheek against his chest and breathed in his sultry, warm scent, which reminded me of the beach, knowing that this was the only communication we needed. In that moment, we weren't just friends; we were prospective lovers. We weren't the dead and the dreaming but two souls leaning upon one another.

I kept my head on Walker's chest, there in the woods, for some time. It took a while before his voice matched with his lips again—till my insecurities dropped back down to a manageable level—and we had come full circle. Yet, I didn't let go, and Walker didn't make me. We watched the party from afar, knowing that no matter what happened between us, we'd always be two of the same kind.

I didn't lift my head until I saw Levi follow the girl with the hoops into the cab of a truck. I scanned the crowd for Emma, but she was nowhere in sight. "Damn it," I muttered. Walker and I watched as the truck heated enough to fog the windows.

Anger boiled inside of me, and this time, I didn't try to stifle it. I hated what Levi was doing to Emma. I let go of Walker and crossed my arms over my chest.

"What an asshole. I can't believe him. He was just with Emma. It might have meant nothing to him, but it was her *first* time. It's always going to be important to her. She's always going to remember how he just ditched her the very next day. He's such an ass!" I went on and on, as the window completely fogged, and the truck began to rock like a wild animal had been caged inside.

I saw Emma walking around. She could have been in search of me or Levi, but I was afraid of what she might find. "No. No. No," I said, my heartbeat skipping.

"Maybe we should intervene? Maybe you should get Emma and go back to the cabin. Tell her you're not feeling well." Walker had a soft heart, and he cared about Emma because he knew she was my friend. I considered it. I could tell her that my stomach hurt, my head ached—all of which was true.

"Yeah, let's do that. Do you want to come with?" I asked. Walker nodded, and we hurried toward the cabin. When we approached the front row of trees, just on the outskirts of the clearing, something happened. The tall, muscular guy with the mullet approached the truck. He ripped the door open and started yelling. Walker and I froze as the girl scampered off with her shoes in her hand, and Levi stepped out, buckling his pants.

The arguing had caught the attention of everybody by the campfire. Heads started to perk, and it didn't take long for people to come out of the house and around the front yard to see what was happening.

"Oh no," I said, placing my hand on Walker's chest, keeping him back in the shadows. I wasn't upset that Levi was about to take a pounding; I was upset because I saw Emma come out of the cabin. "She knows . . ." I said beneath my breath. I backed up to a tree, and I was thankful that Walker and I had been hiding in the distance. I didn't want to get any closer.

Once the crowd formed, the tank with a mullet swung, his fist making contact with Levi's jaw. It only took one hit. The crowd stepped back, and Levi spun like a top. As he fell, the gasps echoed into the trees and beyond. I couldn't quite see what happened next, but I knew enough to know that Levi was still and he wasn't getting back up.

Screams ensued, and several of the guests immediately ran for their cars. Amid the commotion, a fine dark smoke rose into the air. Emma approached Levi, and I watched in horror as she slowly stood up, staring at her trembling hands.

Not like this! I didn't mean to do this!

Emma shrilled, and everybody at the party scattered like rats in an infested restaurant on fumigation night. I wanted to take it back. Take it all back. I wasn't mad at Levi any longer! I grabbed my stomach, feeling like I might throw up, but no matter how terrible I felt, I couldn't peel my eyes away from the brewing storm.

Walker and I watched in horror as every single soul departed that party and the smoke grew denser. Several bodies piled into single cab trucks and even more into the beds. Cars peeled out over the gravel, and trucks ran over planters and knocked over trashcans. Meanwhile, Levi lay on the ground as still as could be, black poison billowing above him.

I wasn't sure what happened because we had been some distance away, but I knew he was dead. Nobody wanted any part of it. Most of them had been at my cabin when Trinity's body had washed up on shore, and several of them had stayed back and been questioned by the cops. That couldn't happen again. Not without suspicion.

I had seen the inner workings of the fear. The memories of Trinity's death. I'd seen every one of my friends fight over involving the authorities. By the time Ethan drowned, nobody even mentioned the cops. And now, none of these people wanted to be tied to cold-blooded murder, either. I understood it. I wanted to run too. I would have, except my feet were planted like tree trunks, the roots deep within the soil. Neither Walker nor I could move a single inch.

Goosebumps covered my body from head to toe, and I was forced to stay and deal with the fears instead of running from them the way I always had. The smoke grew so dark and twisted, I couldn't see Levi's remains at all. Leaves and small bits of trash lifted into the air like a vortex, circling above where he lay. Black crows cawed into the night, taking turns diving into the mist. I knew it was my rage that had taken over and stolen his life. And I knew it was my regret that rumbled like a tornado before us now. If I hadn't loved Emma so much, would Levi still be alive tonight?

If hatred was the flip side to my love . . . then there was no telling what I was capable of. If my emotions were fickle and unpredictable, if they were deep and scarred with insecurities . . . Then I had just become the most dangerous thing in Baylor.

CHAPTER 20

Walker and I stood side by side, unable to move as our feet were planted into the forest ground. Everybody was gone now except Levi, who lay in the middle of a black vortex in Sampson's driveway. My hair whipped wildly, and I squinted, turning away from the wind. It was my fault. No, I hadn't laid a hand on Levi, but I'd hated him for just a moment in time. I'd hated him for what he had done to Emma, and that's when it happened. I never thought that my anger could kill, but clearly, I knew very little about the power I possessed.

"I can't move!" I said, trying to lift a leg one at a time—they felt like they weighed a hundred pounds each. I looked over at Walker, and he was also trying and failing to move his feet.

"I can't either!" Walker yelled against the wind. He nearly lost his balance, trying to free himself.

The forest grew cold as the tornado raged. Deep in the distant woods, I heard a beeping sound. It was a long, drawn-out, high-pitched tone. At first, it was infrequent and random, but it was growing more repetitive now. Louder too.

Every now and then, I glimpsed Levi lying on the ground as the plume of smoke continued to rise above him, and I was consumed by the monster within me. I'd never thought very highly of myself, but in this moment, every worry that I'd ever had was solidified like my feet to the forest floor. I was no good. A rotten apple. Poison. I closed my eyes and let the guilt swallow me whole. Inch by inch, I sank into the ground.

"What is that!?" I asked, grabbing at my temples and whipping my head around when another beep sounded. It echoed off the forest trees and bounced back and forth until it hit us in waves. I couldn't tell how far it was, but I could tell that it was getting closer.

"What's what!?" Walker yelled, looking behind us.

"You don't hear that?" I asked.

The beep sounded loud and shrill. "That!" I said, looking all around me.

I tried to lift my feet, but the more I did, the deeper they sank. It was like quicksand, sucking me under. It was up to my ankles, but I deserved it. I deserved to be swallowed alive. Buried for the good of my friends. They were better off without me. Safer.

Soon, the cops would show up, and Walker and I would be the only ones tied to the murder of Levi. I was ready to accept my fate, rotting in the ground for the rest of eternity. If this was a dream, it was a nightmare.

The crows came in by the dozens and began diving into the pine trees. I ducked, covering my head with my hands. The birds cawed and swooped before me, causing me to reach out for Walker. I tightened my grasp around the sleeve of his flannel. The poisonous smoke had expanded, seeping into the forest and blooming high into the sky. The beep sounded sharply over the howl of the storm, as if it wasn't just behind us, but all around us. Inside us. I startled, opening my eyes against the wind and pulling Walker closer. But it shocked me to see that Walker was no longer there. I clutched his flannel in my hand as it draped to the ground.

In his place stood my gran. She was an ethereal light, drawing power from the dark of the storm. The storm I'd created. Tears pricked my eyes. She was always there when I needed her most. Even though I didn't deserve it. I whipped my head back to the deafening tornado, horrified that she would see what I had done, but Levi had vanished. The black mist had lifted to a light gray fog. And the sky was littered with hundreds of crow feathers that fluttered to the ground, but not a single bird was in sight.

In the distance, in Sampson's driveway, was a hospital bed. Doctors were running tests and checking fluids. The beeps came more frequently now as I was transported from the hell I'd created to a hell I'd never deserved. I was standing inside the hospital room. My feet were freed from the depths of the soil, my hair static from the storm as I stood at the foot of the bed, unseen.

It was so real; I could smell the antiseptic. The sterilization. It was more real than anything I'd ever felt. And in that moment of clarity, it made the rest of my life look like a dream. A memory, dancing in the wind.

The bright lights burned my eyes as I tried to refocus. I wasn't used to the sharp, defined lines or bright lights. I turned my head back to my gran, and I was somewhat surprised that she was still there by my side. I couldn't speak. I could only observe.

I looked back at the patient in the hospital bed, and I thought I saw a version of myself. The girl lying in bed was bloodied and swollen. Tubes in her nose and around her neck. She didn't look like me—especially not now—but somehow, I knew. Somehow, I felt it. That lifeless body lying in the hospital gurney—*it was me*.

There was a detachment there. Not because I couldn't recognize myself, but because I didn't remember, and I couldn't feel. After all, as far as I knew, I had been spending my summer in Baylor. I wondered if the detachment meant that there was no coming back. If I was so far removed from what lay in that hospital bed that I could never find my way home. I wasn't sure I wanted to. Could my life ever be normal with how battered I'd been?

Tears filled my eyes and pressure swelled in my throat. I wasn't exactly sure why, but it hurt to see myself like that. I ached for the girl I used to be. Not just the one that wasn't injured, but the one that hadn't hurt her friends by mistake. The one who was powerless, but safe. The wallflower. I missed her.

I watched as doctors ran various tests, and scribbled down various notes. I had no idea what they were doing, but I assumed the results were subpar. My head throbbed, and as I ran a hand over my temple, I could feel the wound that I saw on my body. It was all coming together. It was starting to make sense.

I didn't look in a mirror, and I was thankful there wasn't one around. I was afraid of what I might see. I knew my headaches were because of the accident that had brought me here to this hospital. An accident I remembered nothing about. I could not only feel the dried blood caked in my hair, but I could see it crusted on the body in the bed. It wasn't a pretty sight. And it felt even worse.

Slowly, my eyes dropped from the version of me in the bed, to my own body. The one I inhabited. I was wearing a hospital gown—a dingy white one with small blue flowers. My feet were bare and dirty as if they'd just been plucked from the forest floor. There was an IV taped to my wrist, and my hands were bruised and trembling. I turned my attention back to the girl lying in bed before us. It was easier to see her battered than me. There was no movement at all. She . . . *I* . . . was in a deep, deep coma. And I knew then that I had been dreaming of Baylor, my gran, and all my friends.

I'd been living a nightmare. A twisted lie. They were just stories I'd told myself while I tried to survive.

"Kinsley, dear, can you hear me?" Gran asked, tired, as if she'd asked the same question five times over. It took me a second, but I pried my eyes off the body and looked toward my gran. Unable to find the words, I nodded slowly.

"They're running tests on you. Looking for brain activity. Luckily, there is no shortage of that . . ." Gran looked at me with a wicked smile. She knew just how much brain activity there had been. *Way* too much.

"I'm alive. I . . . I didn't know it was a dream—"

"Yes. Very much alive, dear. I figure it's much like a normal dream. It happens every night, but people just forget about it when they wake up." Gran's eyes were glassy as she looked me over.

"Am I going to wake up?" My stomach turned with the question. It was the only question that really mattered. And yet, I didn't want to know the answer.

"Oh dear, of course you will. You're still at the

beginning of your journey. I know it's hard, but the real work will begin when you wake up. There will be a lot for you to do to get back to your old self. This accident is going to change you forever. And it has the potential to change you in negative ways. But, it's ultimately up to you how you want to live your life. If you're strong enough—which I know you are—you'll fight this. You'll come back stronger. I know you will," Gran said, with encouraging eyes.

"You said I'm still at the beginning of my journey? What does that mean?" I asked.

I didn't know how that felt on my tongue. Was it the sweet taste of reality coming my way? Or was it sour? Sour because I'd be leaving Walker behind. *My* Walker. I couldn't leave him. I didn't want to. But if I felt this way now, it would be downright impossible to leave him by the end of summer. I was already on the trajectory of getting my heart broken into a million pieces. He'd told me once that he was cursed by love. I suppose the only difference now was that I knew *how* it would end. And *why* we couldn't be together.

"The accident was recent. Your body is healing. But your mind? That part's up to you. You're going to wake up whenever you decide to. You're stubborn like that. You always have been," Gran said.

I peered down at the IV connected to my wrist. "Can I wake up now?" I asked.

Gran chuckled. "Dear, you're not ready. And you know it."

"Well, why not?"

"Have you found the girl?" Gran asked, sending an icy chill straight through my veins. She stared at me blankly, and I couldn't tell if this was part of the dream or reality. Was it still her? My sweet grandmother comforting me? Or was this my mind, twisting and bending in dreamwork, fretting over a girl I'd never met?

"What's so important about this girl?" I asked.

"Some things need an end. They need closure. It's no fluke that you and Walker met. Just like it's no fluke that you and I are here, able to talk. He needs you, dear. And as fate would have it, you're able to see him. Help the boy out. You have a lot of growth to do. And when you're good and ready, you'll come home. Hopefully . . ."

"Hopefully?" I flinched back, and she was gone. Her word, *hopefully*, was floating in the air like a soft echo in her wake. Hopefully? When I was good and ready? Did she mean that there was a choice for me to stay? Why would I ever do that? Of course, I wanted to go home. Perhaps I'd just stay here. I thought back to the storm brewing in my dream. The crows swarming like bees, in and out of the poison I had created. *No, thank you.*

I watched as the doctors finished their tests, determined to live out my recovery as a ghost at the foot of the bed. But then, my mother came in. Her eyes were red and weary as if she'd been up for days. Weeks. Or maybe even longer. Her skin was sallow. I hated myself for what I had done to her, regardless of fault. She kissed me lightly on the knuckles as she cradled my hand in between hers. I lifted my own hand, taking inventory of the bruises, and wondered why I couldn't feel her kiss.

I moved in closer.

My mom sat on the edge of my bed, and I sat beside her. I tried not to look at my old self. She was a disaster. Barely hanging on by a thread. And it was hard to imagine that I could make a full recovery. It made me sick to look, so I kept my gaze on my mother, but her heartbreak didn't make it any easier. She started to break down, her back quaking as she sucked in uneven breaths.

I reached out for her, desperate to comfort her, but as I placed my arm over her shoulder, it sank completely through her back. And worse, she never noticed. It wasn't the first time I had felt invisible, but it was by far the worst.

Seeing my mom hurt so deeply and not being able to help. Being so close and yet so far away. It was soul-crushing. I was the very reason for everybody's pain and misery. And I knew that if I wasn't strong enough to turn this cyclone around, then I would rain nothing but terror and agony upon the ones I loved most.

I'd brought my deepest fears and subconscious insecurities to life. Everything I was ever afraid of wreaked havoc on me mentally, but now, it tortured my friends and family as well. It was happening in my dreams and in my reality. But what I hadn't realized until then was that I could bring positivity in the same creative way. I didn't know how I was going to pull it off. I only knew that it was possible for me to turn it around.

It was time that I learned to control and master my destiny. If not just for me, then for Emma and Walker. For all of them. And I was positive that as soon as I could, I would find Layla Barns. If I could master my destiny, then I was sure I could figure out where that girl was hiding. She was the secret to all of this, after all. She was the key out of here.

My mother was startled when a doctor walked in. I remained seated by her side as he told her the good news. There was lots of brain activity, as I had expected, and they thought I could make a full recovery. My mom nodded, listening intently for as long as she could hold herself together, then broke down in the middle of his explanation. She simply couldn't hold it back any longer, and I didn't blame her. I wanted to cry too. And I probably would have if I hadn't felt so detached from the other me lying in the bed asleep. In my world, it was summer at Baylor Lake. Things were a little bit foggy, and more than dangerous . . . there was a handsomely rugged stranger there who needed my help.

The doctor told my mom, now that the tests were done, they were going to push some meds to help keep me sedated. I still needed time to heal, as my brain was swollen. They injected a vial of something into my IV fluid, and I felt it instantly. A weird swirl of disorientation tore through my veins like a cyclone and whirled up toward my head. I grabbed hold of the bedsheets and scrunched them between my hands, gripping onto the reality that would be lost to me. The room spun, ticking like the hands on an analog clock. The edges of my vision became dark and clouded. The central tunnel of light was getting smaller and smaller. I was drifting away.

"No!" I called out, scraping at the bedsheets. Only my mom never heard me, and the doctor never saw.

"No! Mom! Mom!" I hollered as it swept me away to the land of broken dreams.

CHAPTER 21

I came to, tangled in my bedsheets. When I opened my eyes, I realized I was back at the cabin. My prison. It was like a filter had been placed over my eyes. In comparison to the hospital, this was dingy and somewhat blurry. I saw now how I'd been living in a dream state. But just like stepping into the bright hospital lights, I knew my eyes would adjust quickly. And that soon I wouldn't be able to tell the difference between real life and the one I'd created for myself.

I let out a long breath of disappointment. Just once, I'd like to wake up back at home. I missed the smell, the way the light filtered in through my bedroom window, and I missed the quiet. I even missed my little brother, Conrad. It all seemed so far away now. Sanity was just out of my reach.

I could hear the rumbling downstairs of voices trying to

trump one another. Mason. Scarlett May. They were the loudest. I grabbed my phone and checked the time. It surprised me to see that it was afternoon—though time mattered very little to me now. I drew the covers over my head. What's the point in any of this? The sheets fluttered down to my face, kissing my nose. Walker St. James. He was the reason this mattered.

If I didn't help him find Layla, he'd be lost in the afterlife for eternity. I would go back to my family, and I'd always wonder about him. I'd probably feel guilty, and I'd miss him far too much. Even though I wanted to be with him, I knew that him being with Layla was the next best thing. I'd worry about him less, knowing that he was happy.

Play the game. That's all this was. A mental game. I wasn't any good at those, but this time, I had an advantage. Nobody else knew what I did. I had the power to manipulate this realm any way I saw fit—if only I could figure out how. To build that control like a muscle would mean that I'd be the Sorcerer of Baylor. Then, I'd have Layla eating out of the palm of my hand. Hell, maybe Walker too?

I jumped to my feet, fully clothed, and walked downstairs, reminding myself this was only a game. I didn't want to know what they were fighting about this time. It all seemed so petty while I was out there fighting for my life. It was difficult wrapping my head around the idea that the body I possessed was an astral projection—an avatar in the silo of my mind. I had very little interest in parenting the rest of the group.

As my hand slid down the banister, I looked at the polished wood beneath my hands. *It wasn't real.* The voices I heard wafting through the air? *They weren't real.* And for the life of me, I couldn't figure out why I would imagine an argument at a time like this. It wasn't what I wanted. And if this was truly my dream, and that was really my body in the hospital, then why wasn't I dreaming of Walker alone? My literal dream man. Why wasn't I dreaming of the best summer ever? Was this the best I could do?

I came upon the group in the living room. They'd been in a circle, huddled over something, and their voices were sharp and cutting. "But there's five. Five! Not four but five!" Kimber exclaimed.

"Who is the fifth?" Noah demanded.

"There are seven of us here. Kinsley's missing," Asher said.

"She's just sleeping—as always," Emma said. And I felt the sting of the only friend I had left talking behind my back.

The temperature dropped as soon as they noticed I'd entered the room. Everybody froze, glancing at one another, but nobody wanted to speak. It was an uncomfortable moment of silence, which told me that they most certainly had been talking about me. And not just where I'd been or how much I slept these days—which, by now, I knew was erratic.

"What's going on?" I asked, genuinely curious, my eyes locking onto Kai's. He'd returned from his trip sometime in the night.

"Do you want to tell us what this is?" Scarlett May asked.

"What?" The group parted as I stepped closer, and I found a calendar in between them, sprawled on the coffee table. It was a thirteen-day calendar like the one I'd been seeing everywhere. In the tower. In the void. And by the looks on their faces, they knew I had something to do with it. I didn't want to be blamed for anybody's death. Or any negative notion that happened this summer. It was my biggest fear because deep down inside, I knew I was responsible. And I didn't know how to make it stop. They were all afraid. I was, most of all. The only difference was, I was afraid of myself. And all the dark places in my mind.

"I . . . I don't know . . ." I said, scratching my head. It wasn't a complete lie. I didn't know where the thirteen-day calendar had originated. I only knew that I'd started seeing it early on this summer.

"Why are there only thirteen days, Kinsley?" Noah asked. It was clear this was bad when even Noah—who had feelings for me—had turned on me. *Really bad.*

"I . . . I," my eyes flicked from the calendar to Noah and then to everybody surrounding him.

They weren't real. But I couldn't help from getting sucked back in. They were all staring at me, demanding answers. And my eyes were quickly adjusting to the dark filter. I felt my reality slipping away.

"Why are there five crossed off?" he asked, his face deadpanned. I looked back down to the calendar and five days had been slashed through with the red marker.

Trinity. Big Jimmy. Lainey. Ethan. Levi. I couldn't say it. I didn't want to. How could I?

"You know why. It's us. It's the ones who have died," Emma said, her voice meek but still present. I felt the dagger slide into my back. I could understand why she was turning on me, but she was all I had left. She was someone I'd always imagined would be with me till the end.

"No! There's only four of us who have died. There are five on the calendar. Who is the fifth, then?" Scarlett May bickered with Emma.

"It's us! I told you. *She* told me," Emma said, lifting her eyes to meet mine. The room grew quiet and the shame heavy.

"There's Levi, Ethan, Lainey, and Trinity. That's four," Scarlett May said.

I choked back the tears and stuffed them down deep. I couldn't cry. Not while I was on trial.

"Who's the fifth, Kinsley? Who's the fifth!?" Noah demanded.

I took a deep breath, my foot starting to bounce. Part of me wanted to run out of the room. Out of the cabin and into the woods. But I knew I needed to face this. I knew there was no running from my mind. This was my guilt. It would follow me anywhere, and if I didn't learn to deal with it, it would eat me alive. Just like the crows did Levi.

"Big Jimmy," I said.

"Grocery store Jim? The crazy one?" Scarlett May asked. Her jaw hung as she looked around the group. I bit my lip and waited for their response to rain down on me.

"Why is he on this list with our friends?" Kai asked. It was a good question. But the answer was simple.

"Because he died," I said. My mouth ran dry.

"Is he the thirteenth person?" Asher asked.

I looked around the room and said what I knew to be true but never wanted to admit. "No. It's me. I'm the thirteenth person." I tried to swallow, but my tongue stuck to the roof of my mouth. Everybody looked at one another.

"So none of us will survive?" Scarlett May asked. Mason counted on his fingers over and over.

"But, if Big Jimmy was one, then maybe it doesn't have to be us," Kimber said, checking everyone's expression.

The chatter climbed until one question rose above the rest.

"Who's next?" Asher asked. It's what they all wanted to know. I took a step back, fighting my instinct to flee.

All I could do was stutter. "I don't . . . I don't know . . . I don't. I don't."

"Kimber told us. She told us this was a dream. She said you guys were somehow manipulating it. What else have you done? What are you doing now?" Noah asked.

"I'm not doing anything!" I said, taking another step backward.

"Did you or did you not get Kimber and Asher back together?" Noah asked. My eyes flicked to Emma's, and hers darted to the ground. Her face was red, and she almost looked sick to her stomach. I looked to Kimber, but she stared back at me with a deadpan expression, head cocked and waiting for the truth to spill.

I wanted to ask Noah why he was doing this. Why he was turning them against me. But I knew the answer—I'd hurt him. I'd rejected him. And somehow, hurting me back was making him feel better. Either that or I deserved it, and this was fate taking its revenge on me. I deserved more. I had killed a man. Come to think of it, I'd killed five people. Many more if I counted the plane crash. Tears streamed down my face, though I told myself I would not shatter. I held my breath as much as I could so that my back wouldn't quake. I locked my jaw so that the cries would not seep out.

These were my friends, and they were turning on me.

It was time to face the facts. It was all there in the open, and there was no hiding it anymore. I was doing bad things to good people, whether I wanted to or not. And I had been the reason everybody was in danger. By the next time I looked at myself in the mirror, I'd be a monster.

"And you set Levi up because you were mad at him. Isn't that true?" Asher accused me. Kimber nodded. There had been a talk while I lay sleeping, and for the first time, I wished they had gone dormant.

If I could, I'd make it stop. All of it. Especially this interrogation. But, for whatever reason, I couldn't. I didn't know how. So, I stood there in the middle of the room, my head hanging and their accusations flying.

"Why is this only her dream?"

"Maybe it's all of ours?"

"It's not a dream. It's a nightmare!"

"Who else would have wanted Levi to die?"

"What about Lainey, though?"

It was that last question that lingered in my mind, lashing at me like a whip, slicing into my innermost memories. It stung. And it was lasting.

While it was true, I'd wished ill will upon Levi and possibly Trinity, I'd never wanted anything bad to happen to Ethan or Lainey. And Big Jim was just . . . it was self-defense, really.

While the comments flew like air darts, I thought about Lainey. I thought about why she'd gone missing. All

I could think of was that I needed her. I needed her friendship when I was scared. And I was afraid to be alone in this. It must have been as simple as that. And Ethan? I didn't want him to drown. But I recalled the way I felt that day. It was an uncomfortable feeling. Something was off, and I knew it. I was looking for reasons, and as soon as Ethan jumped into that water—which I knew was haunted —the worry took over. I worried he would be the reason that the air was stiff and suffocating. And when he never resurfaced, my fears were solidified.

I didn't have to direct ill will at somebody for something bad to happen. That was the scariest part of all. All that was required to change the destiny of this summer was a simple thought. A simple worry. Insecurity. Something that would fester and grow, and as soon as the seed was planted, inevitably bloom into disaster.

I had never felt more exposed than I did standing in front of those seven friends. Seven parts of my brain telling me I was no good. It felt like elementary school all over again. Worksheet after worksheet, when everybody could read, and I harbored a secret—I wasn't good enough.

I knew I had to look everybody in the eyes and tell them the truth because they were already in my head, and there was no hiding now. There was no way for us to unite into one strong team if I ever wanted to wake up. And I wanted desperately to wake up. I needed all the help I could get.

I started with the death of my gran. That's when Noah's eyes dropped to the ground. I could see the guilt on his face for accusing me of all the harm I've done. Because he and his family knew just how much pain we had gone through recently. I told them how I started seeing her here at the lake. Even though she'd passed away. I told them how I thought I was crazy. That's when it turned around because several of them empathized with that.

A couple of them even had stories of their own. Stories I'd never heard before. Where *they'd* thought *they* were going crazy. Weird things were happening to all of us, not just me. But the one thing we shared in common was that none of us were comfortable enough to talk about it. It was the fear of judgment that had kept us silent and kept us tortured in solitude.

I was starting to feel like maybe we could be a team. I talked with them about the Baylor Butcher and my search for Layla Barns. The only thing I didn't tell them was that Walker St. James had been the phantom of the lake. I didn't tell them because he'd been isolated enough, and I didn't want them to pull out their pitchforks the way they had on me. And while he'd been the ghost in the story that haunted the lake for years and years, he wasn't a killer. That was merely a story changed by the hands of time. A scary campfire story is all. And if I knew Walker like I thought I did, he wouldn't harm a fly. He had a heart of gold, and he was just as broken as the rest of us.

I told them all how Layla Barns held the secrets to unlock the dreamwork that we had all been summoned into. I told them I knew because my gran had told me so. I told them how Big Jim had been determined to keep people like me from finding out. How he'd attacked us in the tower. Naturally, they wanted to see the tower, and I had to tell them I couldn't find it again. It lost me some credit, but I continued.

I told them all about my latest dream. Which hadn't been a dream at all. Quite the opposite. I told them about my glimpse of reality. How I was pulled back for a moment in time to a place unlike this one. To a place we all knew and feared—where death was final.

I told them how we were our own worst enemies in life and how we were out to get ourselves. That's when I saw the recognition in their eyes. Each one of them had a monster hidden within. They had tormented themselves in ways I couldn't possibly imagine. Kimber folded her arms across the tiny waist of her thin, frail body. Her demons were easy to see, but what about the rest of them? What torture had they put themselves through that was potentially going to come out at Baylor Lake? These were the questions that we all needed to ask ourselves. And as a group, we had a lot of work to do.

I wasn't out of the fire yet, but I tried my best to salvage the friendships I had left. I knew they needed to deliberate, so I stepped outside to the back patio for some fresh air and vitamin D. I watched the birds flock over the placid lake, and I let my memory lapse back to my mom's capsized frame as she cried on the edge of the hospital bed. As their voices grew louder and louder inside the cabin, I closed my eyes and tilted my head to soak up the sun.

They were fighting about whether or not to trust me. Whether I was their friend or foe. And the worst part was that Noah and Emma were inside, and I didn't know if they were fighting for or against me. The patio was my waiting chamber as the jury deliberated inside. I didn't know what the days and weeks ahead had in store for me, and I didn't know if I would ever return home, but I knew this: I knew we were stronger together. We were smarter together. And I knew I needed their help. In fact, I was desperate for it.

CHAPTER 22

I t was a long afternoon of deliberation inside the cabin. Voices rose and fell like the ebb and flow of the ocean washing over the sand. My emotions were no different. They changed like the tide, optimistic for change one second and riddled with angst the next. I contemplated leaving. Running away. Maybe I could seek a safe haven with Walker across the lake. After all, my friends would just go dormant, and as long as I didn't think about them, they'd be safe—as far as I knew.

But as the loons flew overhead and the sun set over the scintillating waters, I realized I couldn't run from this. I'd be running from . . . myself, and that was impossible. The only way out was the opposite of running. I had to dive in deeper, find the scariest place in my mind, and with the help of my friends, conquer it. I'd been so afraid this entire summer, but now I was just afraid of losing my friends. I needed to be the opposite of what I'd been. I needed to be a leader, the one they drew strength from. I just didn't know how to get there. I wasn't born a leader. I needed to find something inside of me that I never knew existed. And I had to be strong enough to pull it out to see the light of day. Then, I'd ride the power all the way home. Home to my mom, dad, and little brother.

I'd been hypnotized by the sunset—the bright oranges and neon yellows—but snapped back when the cabin door opened.

"Have you seen Gunner?" Scarlett May asked. I couldn't recall the last time I'd seen him. I glanced around to see if he was lying at my feet, but he had been nowhere on the porch.

"I haven't. Is he missing?" I asked. Scarlett May said nothing. Her brows furrowed, and she slammed the cabin door and disappeared inside. I listened to the voices rise again, but all I could think about was Lainey's dog. Where had he gone? And how long had he been missing? A few minutes later, Noah came outside, followed by Kai and Mason.

"You haven't seen Gunner?" Mason asked. His tone was accusatory, and I couldn't understand why this was now the primary focus.

"No, I haven't seen him. Is he missing?" I asked again.

"If you are the one making this all happen, then you are the one that caused the dog to go missing. Why did you cause your *best friend's* dog to go missing? Why would you do that?" Noah asked. His hands waving about in the air. I felt the dread drip down my neck and scatter across my back. I stretched my neck, uncomfortable in my own skin.

He was right. I'd been worried that something else would happen, something would tip the group over the edge and all hell would break loose. That I would get blamed for things beyond my control. And here it was: the dog. I shook my head. I should've known. But it was impossible for me to control all of my thoughts, feelings, and fears. They flowed freely, whizzing and whirling in circles all day long.

The accusations flew like darts, and I dodged them with agility, running into the cabin and up the stairs. The fighting stopped, and I felt their eyes heavy on my back. I wasn't hiding upstairs—though I wanted to—I was looking for evidence. Evidence to clear my name. I opened my laptop and went straight to the security website. I scanned all the video feeds until I landed on one with Gunner sauntering towards the neighbor's house.

It was late in the evening as he meandered into their backyard. It was hard to see. He was only a little black dot on the screen, but I zoomed in and watched him move around their yard until he ceased to exist. The dot disappeared before my very eyes. I watched it repeatedly until I was convinced that the Vandals had taken him. And then I marched downstairs with my laptop, eager to clear my name.

"Look at this. I set up surveillance cameras all around the cabin—"

"You what?" Scarlett May asked. I froze. Her mouth hung open like it offended her that her personal space had been invaded.

"I set up surveillance cameras."

"Why would you do that?" Asher asked.

"That's not the point, guys. Things are getting weird around here. I thought if I could catch something on video, then I would have a better understanding of what's going on. And it's helped; I know where the dog is," I said, pleading.

"She's right, guys. It's a good idea. We could use all the help we can get," Kai said. Finally, something had gone my way, and I appreciated Kai's kind words more than he knew.

"The dog went over to the neighbor's house last night. See the little dot?" I pointed to the screen. Everybody watched in silence as he disappeared into their backyard.

"What happened to him?" Emma asked.

"I don't know. I think they have him." To be honest, I wasn't sure if they did or not. But I was desperate to clear my name.

The tactic worked better than I had imagined. Within

minutes, the guys were ready to break into the Vandals' cabin. They grabbed anything they could; a baseball bat, a meat cleaver, flashlights, and then they were ready to raid the place. This wasn't about the dog; this wasn't even about Lainey; this was about fighting back for the first time this summer. It was about taking what was ours and not living in fear anymore. This was about control. Every one of us had a reason to fight for that. And what better place to make a stand than at the Vandals'? They had been weird all summer long. And I knew they were hiding something.

Emma, Scarlett May, Kimber, and I crouched down inside the den, peering out the locked window. It faced the Vandals' house, and we had a good view of the guys as they crept across the yard. Mason, Asher, Noah, and Kai fell into step, making for a stealthy mission. They moved quickly across the lawn and only slowed once they reached the neighbor's house. We watched as two split off around the front, and the other two went around the back. I couldn't tell if I was watching a natural and incredibly talented sting operation or if it had simply been the inner child in these guys playing army. But either way, my eyes were fixated, and it was better than any action movie I'd ever seen.

"Where did they go? I can't see them," Kimber said, her nose on the windowsill.

"I can't see them either," Emma said, lifting her head.

"Open the window so we can hear them," Scarlett May

said. I unlatched the window and slid it open. The four of us listened in silence. There wasn't much to hear, but we waited anyway.

"Is it supposed to be taking this long?" Kimber asked.

"No. We probably just lost all of our men." Scarlett May glared at me through the moonlit room.

"No. Don't say that!" I hissed.

The only thing we needed for that to come true was a seed planted in my mind, and her sarcasm was just that. I felt the panic rise inside me, as I couldn't stop my mind from exploring the option of the guys never returning and us four girls having to deal with this murderous summer all by ourselves. The thought of losing four in one night was too much to bear. And I wanted to rain down on her for even bringing the thought to light. If it came true, this was her fault. Not mine.

We watched, crouched on the floor, our fingertips gripping the windowsill as the Vandals' house lit up. A light in the front room illuminated the windows, and subsequently, it traveled back into what I had imagined was their kitchen.

"Why are they turning the lights on?" Emma asked.

"They're dead for sure," Scarlett May said.

All I could do was shove her. I did it with enough force for her to tip over on her knees and fall to her butt. "Shut up!" I said.

"Jesus! What's your problem? You're the one doing all of this!"

"That's not true. None of it's true. This is all happening because we're afraid of it happening. It's happening because people like you are planting the seed of them never coming home. And then we all think about it." I pointed to Kimber. "Haven't you thought about it?" I asked. Even in the dark. I could see her eyes lower to the ground.

"That's right. Now that she said it, we're all thinking about it. And our thoughts, here in Baylor . . . they come true. So, unless you never want to see them again, stop thinking that way!" I said in my full voice.

I stormed out of the room. Unable to stay for the aftermath. Afraid of what else Scarlett May might say and what might come to fruition. As I left the den, I heard whispers behind me. I went upstairs and crawled into bed with my laptop. I watched the surveillance camera, which had the same view as the window downstairs, but with night vision.

Although I was alone, I was in better company. I tried to make sure I did everything to bring those guys home safe. I took deep breaths and concentrated deeply. I imagined them coming back, that nobody got hurt, and that we were reunited as a team. I wanted so desperately for us to be the family of misfits that we were in the beginning of summer. I watched the video feed, as grainy as it was, and waited. I waited until I saw four tiny dots emerge from the neighbor's cabin.

Four dots became five, and the loud, boisterous voices of the guys echoed throughout the clearing. I slammed my laptop shut and ran downstairs with a smile on my face. Gunner was barking with excitement, and everybody was cheering. It had been a successful mission. The first of many. And we were a team celebrating our first victory.

"Hi, boy! Hi, boy! You're such a good boy! Yes, you are!" Emma chirped, scratching behind Gunner's ears. He barked and barked, his tail bashing the legs of everyone around him.

"So, they took him?" I asked, looking between the four boys.

"No. It looks like Gunner somehow got inside and was trapped. The neighbors weren't even home," Noah said, his head tilted apologetically.

"Those neighbors haven't been home for a long time," Kai said.

"What do you mean? I see them over there every day."

"Yeah, Kinsley and I see them do weird stuff in their garden," Emma said, agreeing with me. She'd been shy to speak up, but this was how she showed her support. She inched closer to my side. I gave her a small smile and nodded to Kai.

"I don't know what to tell you guys. That house was covered in boxes and dust. It looks like they started to pack and then just vanished. There are white sheets draped over the furniture. It looks like an abandoned house for sure," Asher said.

I scratched my head, wondering how that could be true. I glanced at Emma and my confusion reflected in her face. Her brows furrowed, and her mouth slightly parted. I suppose it wasn't the strangest thing that happened in Baylor, and it wouldn't be the last. For now, we were all just excited that Gunner had returned home. Our success at the Vandals' house had taken the spotlight that night, and it seemed that maybe I'd been let off the hook. After all, I couldn't be the only one responsible for all the terror brought to Baylor . . .

I didn't know when I started calling Gunner ours, but now that Lainey was gone, he felt like a team mascot. When he'd gone missing, like so many others had, it had felt like a turning point for us to get him back. Nobody had ever come back before. The hollow truth was finally fleshing out. This wasn't the afterlife—not yet anyway. And our thoughts had the power to produce magic and unleash terror. We were in control of our own destiny, and we had work to do to hone that power. Because right now, it was far too pliable.

One thought of negativity could bring the whole cabin down. And our insecurities had our teeth falling out. To be optimistic . . . That was going to take some training. And we were going to need to work together. As I watched everyone crowd around the dog, giving him love and affection, I wondered how I could bottle this moment and use it to spread light in all the dark places of the forest. I had some time left here in this realm, and I'd better make the best of it until I found a way out.

CHAPTER 23

I t was a crystal-clear day. The sun was high in the sky, and crowds came in from out of town to celebrate the Fourth of July at Baylor Lake. It was a special place to be on Independence Day. While the float parade wasn't anything like in the big city, it had a small-town feel that was even more festive. It was the busiest day of the year on the lake. Car doors slammed in the background, and boat motors idled on the once-placid lake. It was everybody's favorite time of year. Everybody's but mine.

The crowds made me anxious, and I was always worried something terrible would happen during the good times. Worse yet, today was the big day. I was ready to find Layla, and I now knew that I held the power to do so. I was nervous, though. I didn't know what finding her would mean, and I didn't have the time to figure it out. Walker and I had the clues that led us to this very parade on this particular day. The pressure of having only one chance to get this right had been weighing on me, and the crowds only amplified my stress. It was a mental space I needed to get out of if I wanted to pull this off.

Everybody in the cabin was getting ready to go enjoy the parade. Mason had been day-drinking, and Scarlett May was busy with her makeup and hair. Her sky-high shorts and cowgirl boots accentuated what great legs she had. Kimber chatted with her in the bathroom while Emma hid in her bedroom alone. Things between Emma and I had been awkward since she'd turned on me. But that was the least of my worries now. The entire house had been coming around since we saved the dog. We even ventured out one afternoon to show them how fast the apple tree had grown. The fact that it was right where we had left it was my saving grace. Had it not been there, I doubt they would've trusted me again, and I would've been fighting for my reputation instead of looking for Layla Barns.

As I waited for Walker to show, I checked the time repeatedly. I knew he had to be as nervous as I was, so I tried my best to relax. I knew he would feed off of my energy—the whole house would. I strived to be a beacon of confidence for them. But I had no idea what I was doing. I was just as unprepared as I could be, and I felt I was going into this mission blindly.

There was a knock on the back patio door, and by the time I turned, Walker had let himself in. He was wearing a blue and black flannel, and a dark baseball cap covered the scar on his brow, shadowing his eyes. It hadn't gone unnoticed that my stomach dropped the second my eyes landed on him. He was gorgeous. He was going to be the only reason I missed this place.

"It's a big day today," I said, wrapping my arms around him for a hug.

"It is. Are you ready?" Walker asked.

"As ready as I'll ever be," I said with a shrug.

"Shot?" Mason asked, holding up an amber-filled glass. Walker and I stared at him blankly.

"No, thanks."

Mason shrugged and knocked back the liquid, wincing as it went down. We all celebrated in our own ways. Scarlett May with her cowgirl boots. Mason with his alcohol. And me, with my suffocating anxiety. We were all a little crazy here.

Everyone was excited for the Fourth of July, and normally, I would have been too. But there was little chance of success today and a probability of failure. I'd already felt the disappointment of it before we even stepped out of the cabin. The sun beat down on my face as I placed my sunglasses on to shield the blaring sun. It was difficult to see, and I glared into the crowd.

There were people everywhere. Cars lined the windy road, driving five miles an hour trying to get good parking for the parade. Families sat in lawn chairs outside of our driveway. American flags swayed in the hands of little kids everywhere. Some people had music playing, and others had lunch spread out on their laps. Others had umbrellas, and I even saw somebody with a grill in the back of their truck. But everywhere I looked, there was a smile. And that should have made me feel good. Comforted. Reassured. Instead, it made me feel like an outsider.

It was in those smiles that I realized how different I truly was. While the thought excited them—a parade, a Fourth of July party all day and night—I was worried about survival. I was worried about my friends making it to live another day. And I was worried about my fears coming to life before me, torching the forest with flames of self-doubt. Nobody would escape that fire. Not even me.

I'd briefed the group on what to look for today. I'd shown them a picture of Layla Barns and told them she would be anywhere near a fairytale float. Anything that reminded them of their childhood. I told them we needed to capture her but not harm her. There were questions we needed her to answer. None of which I knew, of course. Other than why. Why couldn't I go home yet? Why was she so important to my survival? And I was curious about other things too—like why had she left Walker? I'd never leave him. In fact, I had conflicting feelings about that now, and he wasn't even my boyfriend, let alone my fiancé.

The parade stretched alongside the lake for a waterfront view. Rock Creek Cove, where our cabin was, was the tail-end of the festivities. The parade started in town, which was a little farther than a mile away and where most of the action was—where we were headed today. The town was lined with little mom-and-pop shops and the old historical library. We started out strong, walking into town, but it wasn't long before our team had parted.

Emma had Gunner on a leash, and his tail wagged constantly. She was stopped often by people asking to pet Gunner. She couldn't say no, and we couldn't wait for her. Walker and I continued through the crowds as Mason shouted loud and obnoxious sentiments behind us. Asher and Kimber kept to themselves, mostly. And Kai and Noah were focused on the hunt for Layla. Scarlett May had disappeared with Sampson's group the moment we'd stepped into the crowd, and I assumed she wouldn't be of help today.

I knew Kai's motive for finding Layla Barns was scientifically based. He had questions of his own; that I was sure of. But Noah? I wasn't sure why he was so interested in finding her. And I couldn't shake the feeling that maybe he was looking to get Walker out of the way.

And what better way than to find his true love? It was the very reason I *didn't* want to find Layla Barns. But when it came down to it, my gran had told me that if I could only find her, then I would have a chance at coming home. And I wanted that more than anything. I wanted to go home to my mom and dad. I didn't want to live in a world where I had so much power. Because at the end of the day, I never truly trusted myself. There was more negativity in me than I cared to admit. And we were all the victims of it. I needed to get home. To a world where my insecurities affected only me and me alone. Where my dark side hid behind my smile.

It was about an hour later when the first float was underway. We made it into town, and there were more people than I ever remembered. Asher and Kimber left the group to buy corn dogs. Mason sipped from his tainted water bottle and weaved in and out of the crowds, looking for girls. We lost Emma somewhere with the dog. Kai and Noah, as far as I knew, were hunting for Layla Barns like trusty old bloodhounds.

Walker and I stayed close together. The group had come together for one mission and one mission alone. Find Layla and survive. And even though our goals had aligned, by the time the parade started, the team had fallen apart. Self-interest trumped any chance of finding Layla. We were a team, yet we weren't acting like one. And I should have known as much on our first try. It was hard to wrangle up a group of eighteen-year-olds with motivations that differed from my own.

They hadn't seen themselves lying on the hospital bed the way I had. And they never saw the hurt in Walker's eyes when he talked about his soon-to-be fiancée. A corndog or a pretty girl was far more interesting to them. I couldn't blame them, because I realized my friends were just pieces of my mind—fragmented. I couldn't pull them together. It was *my* interest, sprawling out like the tentacles of an octopus. *I* always enjoyed pretzels and hotdogs at places like these. The funnel cake and churros were a once-a-year delicacy. *I* was sidetracked by the cute dogs and the attractive guys in the crowds. And if I couldn't even focus myself, how could I expect them to?

The parade marched down the streets of Baylor whether we were ready or not. Our beer garden float had turned out quite nicely. Pretty girls in beer maiden dresses danced on top of the float with mugs of beer in their hands. Music blared up and down the street, and flags waved back and forth in the crowd. There was a lot of movement and loud sounds. The sun was blindingly bright. There was almost too much to take in, and it made it difficult to keep my eye out for fairytale clues.

Just when it started to seem that the venture was hopeless, I saw a dwarf. Then two . . . and three. Seven dwarfs turned the corner, marching in front of a float and singing. There was a giant apple tree on the float that looked just like the one in the forest. Snow White stood beautifully, waving to the crowd. As she turned the corner, my heart lurched, and I grabbed Walker's arm. I pointed toward the float. "That's it! That's it!"

"Shit! What do we do?"

I had no idea. The float was fast approaching, and I had absolutely no idea—no plan for what to do when it arrived. My eyes scanned the scene, now hyper-focused as I looked for ideas. It wasn't until I landed on Snow White's face that I realized she was more than just a character. She was Layla Barns, herself.

"Walker!"

I looked back just as he had made the realization himself. His face drained of blood, turning pale and peaked. He looked as though he might pass out. I reached for him right as he went down. He fell to his knees in the midst of the crowd. Tears streamed down his cheeks as he stared at Layla with wide, red eyes. My heart broke right alongside his.

I looked back as the float was directly in front of us. Time was closing in. I had to act quickly, and Walker was too riddled with grief to do anything at all. I searched the crowd. None of our group was around to help. I looked back at Walker one last time, and he was in so much pain he could hardly look away.

"I'm sorry. I'm so sorry," he uttered beneath his breath in a whisper that Layla couldn't hear.

I made the split-second decision to leave him behind and do what I needed for the both of us. I ran to the back of the float and lunged to the top. I heard the crowd gasp, and I knew I had made a mistake. Behind the trunk of the tree, I hid. The float stopped, and I knew it wasn't long before security would take me away. My heart pounded and sweat beaded on my forehead. But nobody was looking at me.

Everybody was looking at . . . I stretched my eyes far into the crowd and saw Mason on top of one of the dwarfs. They were wrestling, rolling around on the ground.

"Wilde! Wilde! I got one!" he screamed at the top of his lungs.

I felt my face flush, and I knew I needed to act quickly to use this distraction to my advantage. I crept up behind Layla. Her presence alone made me uneasy. I couldn't help feeling inferior as I stood next to her. Even in her costume, she was absolutely stunning. The perfect woman.

"Layla?" I asked. She whipped her head around and her eyes struck mine. I felt her look straight into my soul, and my blood ran cold. Her eyes dropped, examining me as a threat to her. Then she laughed. She threw her head back and cackled. It wasn't the sweet Layla I imagined her to be. She was a villainess. In a blink of an eye, she was off the float, running. She leaped and landed with grace, even in the giant dress and heels.

"No! Wait!"

As I tracked her into the crowd, I caught the seven dwarfs running after Mason down the street, in the opposite direction. I glanced back at Walker but couldn't find him in the crowd, so I charged after Layla myself. I jumped off the float with little grace and followed her. She was fast. Incredibly fast. But her dress made it easy for me to spot her.

"Wait, I just need to talk to you! Please!" I screamed out, running through the crowd.

Little kids stepped in my way and a grandmother in a wheelchair nearly ran over me. I tripped and fell as I tried to dodge a lady with a baby. Layla gained some distance as I picked myself up and continued. I vaguely felt the burn in my hands and realized I'd skinned my palms on the asphalt. But I kept after her.

She looked back at me now and then, laughing when she did. Whereas I was running full speed, heart pounding and lungs burning, she was frolicking. Laughing. Playing. I'd never worked so hard in my life. I ran with every ounce of energy I could muster. My feet were heavy and it felt like I was running through a sand bank. Still, I managed to close the gap between us. I was winning. I was gaining on her.

Maybe I could do this?

I took my shot. I reached my arms out as I flew through the air. I grabbed hold of her shoulder, bringing her down to the ground with me. If she didn't want to talk to me, I was going to make her. This was *my* realm. *My* time. And I'd be damned if I let her slip through my fingers. But as we fell to the ground, it was only me who bashed into the asphalt.

The asphalt grated my elbows as I landed upon nothing. Layla had disappeared within my arms in the seconds it took for me to fall. I lay on my stomach on the boiling-hot asphalt as a crowd formed around me. My wrist was sprained, and road rash covered my forearms. I heard her cackle all around me, inside and out.

I rolled onto my back, staring up at the crowd. I knew at that moment that I hadn't caught her because I wasn't ready. I didn't know what that meant exactly—just that it wasn't my time. I wasn't worthy yet to go back to my body. And for that, I needed to stay here in Baylor for a little longer. It was a game I didn't want to play, but had to.

I'd come so far, yet I was still so far away. I'd gathered a team, but where were they now? Walker had been searching for her for twenty-plus years. And when he laid eyes on her for the first time, all he could do was crumble with guilt. It wasn't just me; it was all of us. None of us were ready.

"What are you doing?" Kimber asked through a mouthful of corndog. I focused my eyes and searched the faces above me to find Kimber and Asher watching me like a caged animal at the zoo. I extended a hand and Asher helped pick me up off the ground.

"Ouch," I said, looking at my wrists and forearms.

"Oh, that looks like it hurts," he said. I dusted the bits of gravel off my freshly grated skin, and the burn set in.

"While you guys were off snacking, Layla Barns was here, and she got away! And freaking Mason . . . charged after a dwarf! All seven of them ran after him! He's probably half-dead in some alley right now! Where were you guys?" My voice splintered. Kimber looked at me like I was stupid and then gave her corndog a shake.

I rolled my eyes, taking in a deep breath and pinching the bridge of my nose. I reminded myself it wasn't her fault but mine. "We need to find the others."

"Why? Don't we need to go after Layla?" Kimber asked.

I scanned the crowd even though I had known she'd disappeared into thin air. She was nowhere to be found.

"She's gone now. We need to find Mason," I said. We started down the street, but a little girl stopped me in my tracks when she pulled on my T-shirt.

"Excuse me. Excuse me. You dropped this," she said. I turned around to see a little redheaded girl with a fist full of my shirt. She had an envelope in her hand. I hadn't dropped an envelope, but as I started to deny ownership, I saw my name clearly written on the front.

"Thank you," I said, giving her a smile and taking the envelope from her.

Kimber and Asher thought little of it, and I slipped it

into my backpack. We continued through the crowd, looking for a dwarf or two, and I kept my eye out for Walker and Emma. I didn't know what was in that envelope, but I assumed it was my next clue. A chance to go home. Another deadline.

CHAPTER 24

The sun was high, making for a sweltering Fourth of July. The parade had ended, and the small town was crawling with families making their way back home. It took some time for the rest of our group to reconvene. We found Emma with another lady and her long-haired puppy. The leashes of the playing dogs had intertwined. She looked apologetic when she saw us, but I let her know there was nothing she could have done to change the outcome. I tried to hide the defeat on my face, but I just wanted out of here. I wanted to go home.

Home? I wasn't sure where that was anymore. A part of me wanted to go back to the cabin. It was only a mile or so down the road, and I could be there in fifteen minutes. I could kick off my shoes, get a drink, or take a cold shower. But the thought of going *home, home . . .* seemed so far away. It seemed like a lot of work—and I was tired. Too tired.

I guess I wasn't ready to get back to my reality and begin a new fight for recovery. And I could only hope when the time came, and I truly was ready, that I'd find a way to capture Layla. She'd be the one to send me back. I was sure of that now. And even though I considered this a failed mission, I was starting to understand what it would take to make a successful one.

Kai and Noah showed up with promising smiles on their faces, and hope rattled in my belly. At least the bloodhounds had done what they were supposed to. "We found the dwarfs. And guess what? They were chasing Mason!" Noah said, barely able to get the words out.

Kai stifled his laughter.

"They were what?" Emma asked.

I rolled my eyes. *What a shit show . . .*

"Apparently, he thought he was helping but must have misunderstood. He was supposed to look for anything resembling Snow White or a fairy tale. Instead, he made a mockery out of it," I said, bringing my hand to my forehead. "Does anybody know where Scarlett May is?"

"Yeah, I saw her earlier. She said Sampson's throwing a party tonight for the Fourth. He said he could see the fireworks really well from his cabin. She went with him to help set up. I think we're going to go tonight," Kimber said, looking to Asher.

"That sounds fun," Emma said, nodding.

I had other plans. Those plans were to be anywhere that Walker was. The first step was finding him. I'd left him back in the crowd, and he hadn't resurfaced since.

"I don't think I'm going to make it tonight. Look, we're missing Walker and Mason. Do you think you guys can track down Mason and get him back safely?" I asked.

I saw a subtle flash of aggravation in Noah's eyes. But ultimately, everyone agreed. Even though the parade had ended, the crowd was still going strong. Everyone had been on the move for some time, but the population hadn't thinned at all. I watched a mom scold her kid for touching something on the ground, then proceed to wipe his sticky fingers with a wet cloth. Gunner wrapped his leash around not one, not two, but three people, in one minute flat. I groaned, feeling the hopelessness wash through me. We couldn't do anything right. And I was the one in charge? *What a joke . . .*

I looked out, scanning the crowds. Hundreds of faces. All of them looking for something. I didn't see Walker, and I had no idea where he was. I tried to retrace my steps, but that didn't work. It wasn't until the group had made a collective plan and the crowds had thinned sometime later that I saw him sitting on a bench all alone —his head drooping down to his chest. Defeated. He looked like a kid who had dropped his ice cream one lick in and watched it melt on the hot sizzling cement. Or better yet, he looked like a man who had lost his only love.

I wished I could do more. But for whatever reason, when I'd locked my arms around Layla, it hadn't been enough. And if only I knew why my grasp wasn't strong enough, I would at least have some way to fix it. A direction to run toward—something to work on. But I had nothing, not even an idea. All I knew was that I had failed because I wasn't ready. I felt as terrible as Walker looked.

I took a deep breath and then made my way to him. He didn't lift his head when I sat down on the bench, but I felt his pain ease with my presence. We sat in silence for what seemed like forever, and then at some point, I reached over and grabbed his hand. I pulled it onto my lap and encased it in both of my hands. Gently, I rubbed the back of his knuckles with my thumb. He not only let me keep his hand in mine, but I think he felt comforted by it, too. There wasn't much else I could do, but I could be there for him, and I knew how to show that.

I laid my head down on his shoulder, and a moment later, I felt the weight of his head on mine. We stayed like that for quite some time, watching the people dissipate until it was a ghost town, and we were the only souls in sight.

I was wrapped up in a dream world. My mind, body, and spirit separated into three silos. Yet somehow, with Walker's hand in mine, I felt whole. I didn't understand,

and I didn't try to. I just enjoyed the moment. I took full deep breaths, and for the first time in a long time, I felt optimistic that everything was going to be all right. Despite the rocky road we had been on and the long treacherous path ahead, as long as I had him by my side, I felt . . . almost . . . good?

"Will you watch the fireworks with me tonight?" I asked. My eyes fixed on the littered road before us. The remains of the parade painted the street, and bits of trash fluttered by the curbs.

"Yeah. We can do that. But I don't really want to go to Sampson's house," he said.

"I don't either. Not really in the mood for a party. Let's watch them from the canoe. I'm sure there's a secret spot you haven't shown me yet?"

"Yeah, actually, there is." His voice perked up for the first time since seeing Snow White.

We took our time on the bench, enjoying each other's company, and then we went our separate ways. By the time I showed up at the cabin, it was alive with festive sarcasm. Everybody was there joking about Mason's extravaganza with the seven dwarfs—everybody except Mason.

"Where's Mason?" I asked, my stomach dropping in fear. If I lost another one on my watch, I'd give up right here, right now.

"We found him. He's in the drunk tank," Noah said.

I took a sigh of relief. "Figures," I said, shaking my head.

"Yeah, he has to stay there for twenty-four hours. We're allowed to pick him up tomorrow," Noah said.

"It's probably best." I thought of all the things Mason would do on a night like tonight to draw attention to himself.

"Are you sure you don't want to go to Sampson's tonight?" Emma asked. She was trying to make things as normal between us as possible. It was her way of saying, "I'm sorry for turning my back on you." But I wasn't about to hold grudges—not at a time like this. Noah's eyes and ears were open to my response, so I locked arms with Emma and led her away.

"Walker was pretty upset today. I didn't tell anybody else, but I found Layla Barns. I actually caught her. I wrapped my arms around her and then . . . then she . . . she just disintegrated like she was nothing. She left this world for another . . . I don't know," I said in a low voice. Asher mimicked Mason's wrestling match, and Kimber laughed as he jumped on the floor. We ducked into the den.

"You did?" she asked, eyebrows raised.

"Yeah. She was beautiful. She was dressed as Snow White," I began.

"Oh! Because of the apples," Emma said, piecing it together.

"She kept laughing. It was like this sinister laugh. And

even when she disappeared, I could hear it echoing in the air. It was almost like she was here, even when she wasn't. I don't know. It was unsettling, really." I sighed.

"And Walker?"

"Oh, boy. He didn't do too well. One look at her and he crumbled. Fell to his knees and started crying." I winced at his pain fresh in my memory.

"He cried?" Emma's brows arched.

"Well, his eyes were glassy and red. He kept saying he was sorry. The whole thing really damaged him. I feel terrible for him." I crossed my arms over my chest and leaned against the wall.

"Are you sure you guys don't want to go to Sampson's?" she asked. "It could be fun."

"Yeah. I don't want to see the whole scene again. You know, with Levi and all. I don't want to remember that night any more than I have to. Plus, I think Walker needs me. We're just going to have a quiet night on the lake."

"Okay." Emma leaned against the wall, deep in thought.

"Are you okay?"

"Yeah. Yeah. Just thinking about Levi," she said.

"I'm sorry. I shouldn't ha—"

"No. It's okay. Call me if you need me," she said, placing a hand on my shoulder. It felt good to have her back. She was the only friend I had in my corner.

As everyone left the cabin to go across the lake to

Sampson's house, I watched the group and remembered when there were twice as many of us. An eerie feeling trickled down my spine, knowing that so many of us had disappeared and we were only halfway through summer. I watched each one of them leave, and I prayed it wouldn't be the last time I saw them. But I tried not to dwell on it, because the more I thought about it, the more it had a chance of coming true.

I turned my focus on the night I had ahead of me. I showered and changed into some warm clothes in case the night brought a cool breeze. And after the sweltering day that we'd had, I hoped it would. I didn't know what hoops I'd have to jump through to get out of here alive, and I didn't want to think about it. All I really wanted to do in the moment was make Walker feel better. The hurt I saw in his eyes made me feel hollow inside. Like a hole had been punched through my heart. Like there was nothing I could do to ever feel better.

I imagined that was how he felt. I didn't know what it was like for him to be constantly chasing his soulmate in a realm that she couldn't be reached, but I had to guess it was miserable. Devastating, each and every day. And to spend eternity like that? What I'd seen in his eyes when his knees hit the pavement was probably a small fraction of what he felt on the inside. It was then that I realized, his guilt was the scar that sliced through his brow. It was his wound on the inside that showed in his reflection.

Sometimes it was fresh; sometimes it would bleed; and other times, it looked almost healed.

When Walker paddled the canoe into the cove, I grabbed his flannel in the crook of my arm and locked Gunner inside the cabin. I stilled on the back porch when I saw him standing at the end of the dock with his hands tucked deep into his pockets. He was too far to see the details of his face, but I knew that he wore a somber expression under the bill of his hat. As if his feelings reached out in the space between us for me to sense. I crossed the grassy hill down to the dock, and stopped to pick up a daisy. I plucked it from the grass and twirled it between my finger and thumb until I reached him.

"Here, it's for you," I said, holding the daisy out to him. It was simple enough, but it worked. A small smile spread across his lips. Instantaneously, my lungs expanded, and I could breathe again.

"Are you ready?" he asked, admiring the flower.

"Yeah. I hope you don't mind. I brought your flannel."

"I told you, it looks better on you, anyway."

My stomach dropped, and I vaguely wondered how long I would torture myself with the impossibility of him being mine.

My mind said I shouldn't have come. I shouldn't be spending my time with this lost soul. I shouldn't be wearing his flannel and picking him flowers. But I was. I wanted to. And it was going to be the death of me. Yet, I threw caution to the wind, because that's where my heart wanted to be. If it was my dream, I would live it the way I wanted to. And right now, it was the Fourth of July, and I was going to spend that night floating on the lake with this ruggedly handsome guy. And I wouldn't convince myself otherwise.

Walker pushed the canoe off the dock after I got situated. His strong hands gripped the paddle, and his muscles bulged as he rowed us into the middle of the lake. I tried not to stare. I only stole glances when it seemed I wouldn't get caught.

"So, today was a bust," he said.

"Was it, though? We saw her. Have you seen her before? I mean, after the . . ."

"No. I haven't. It's the first time in twenty years that I've seen her. It makes me wonder, has she been here the whole time? Maybe she's been avoiding me? I don't know. I . . . I just froze up. I'm sorry I didn't help you." Walker turned his head to the side and looked out to the dense forest. His profile was my favorite because I could gaze all I wanted without ever getting caught.

"Don't apologize. I was pretty close to catching her, but she was too fast," I said.

Walker chuckled as if remembering a time when he'd chased her. I didn't want to think about it. I also didn't want to tell him that I'd caught her. And that she'd laughed at my attempt. That she'd mocked me for even trying. I thought it might hurt his feelings to know that she chose not to give herself up.

"Yeah, she is fast," he said, looking behind himself at the lake. I forced a smile and looked out at the channel we were entering. Another finger of the lake I had never seen before.

"I think we're getting close, though. I mean, she didn't know who I was, and I was chasing her. Of course she ran from me. But we're going to find her again. And when she sees you, she won't be running anymore."

"Yeah, you're probably right. But we don't know where we're going to find her next. She's gone, and she didn't leave a single trace. Unless your gran has something to say? Another hint? Another book?" Walker asked with brows raised, with an inkling of hope. It reminded me of the envelope the young girl gave me after I collapsed on top of Layla's ghost.

"Actually, I have a little something. . ." I dug around in my bag, and once I found the envelope, I pulled it out.

"What's that?" Walker asked.

"I don't know. A little girl gave it to me. It had my name on it. I think it might be another clue. Do you want to open it?" I asked, holding out the envelope. Walker's eyes flickered from mine to the envelope, and then he slowly withdrew his hand from the paddle to take the envelope. The canoe drifted as he ripped the seal open. I watched his face contort with pain as I saw the back of another photograph in his hands. It took a little time for him to soak up the memory, and then, when he was ready, he handed it to me. The photograph was of him and Layla in a hot-air balloon. It was a great photo. The sun was setting behind them, and they looked perfect together. I could see that they were true soulmates, and they were meant to be together. It hurt to look at the picture, but not for the same reasons it hurt Walker.

"You guys rode in a hot-air balloon?" I asked, trying to hide my heartache.

"Yeah. That was the Baylor Balloon Festival. The summer before the accident was when we did it. We were planning to do it again. We had big plans that summer."

"Sounds like me and my friends. We had big plans this summer, too." My gaze dropped to the dirt clinging to the belly of the canoe.

"At least you're doing them," he said.

"Yeah, kind of."

"Do you think that's her clue?" Walker asked. For the first time that night, his eyes had a sparkle. Aliveness behind them I hadn't seen since before the parade.

"The balloon festival? Maybe she's going to be there . . ." I said. It was only a couple of weeks away. And if we had her next known location, there was a lot I needed to do to ensure that she remained in my arms if I caught her again.

"Yeah. Maybe," Walker said, beginning to paddle again.

We rode in silence, the balloon festival on our minds and looming in our near future. It was another chance for me to escape. And a chance for Walker to live out his life the way it should have been all along. The last thing I wanted to do was screw it up again. Because who knew if I would have another chance. I felt the stress of the balloon festival thick in the air. The stress to be successful was suffocating.

A loud blast exploded. I startled, falling off the bench and landing on my back with my feet in the air. I gripped the wet rim of the canoe as Walker let out a loud and boisterous laugh. The first of the fireworks danced across the sky in a brilliant aqua blue. I laughed, awkwardly sprawled across the bottom of the canoe, and then I lowered my eyes to Walker laughing—because he was more beautiful than a sky full of fire.

CHAPTER 25

By the time the fireworks fluttered down and fizzled out on the water's surface, I realized just how deep my feelings for Walker had grown. I started to have thoughts of abandoning my mission to survive and living out my eternity with him by my side. It was a dangerous mindset to be in. Far more worrisome than the fears that took root and grew into monsters of the deep, turbulent lake. Because the love that was spawning inside me would surely seize my heart, and I wouldn't be leaving Baylor alive.

This had all been a game. A game of the mind. A game I had no choice but to conquer. Win the game and I'd go home. But that was never certain. My gran's words played back in my head, *"And when you're good and ready, you'll come home. Hopefully . . ."*

Hopefully was the key word. And for the first time, I

realized what she had meant. If I fell in love with Walker, I may choose to never go home, and that was absolutely horrifying.

Another thunderous crack above startled me as I climbed back to the bench. Walker clutched his stomach, and his head tilted back with a rolling laugh. Then another and another. The sky lit up in yellows, greens, aqua blues, and pinks. Walker's laughter was contagious, and for no reason at all, I laughed too. We both looked up at the sky to see the embers fluttering down all around us. It was gorgeous. The sound echoed off every corner of the lake like surround sound. The sizzle of the fireworks going out as they touched down on the water was electric. It was the most beautiful thing I had ever seen, and my heart swelled. I never wanted it to end.

It encapsulated us in falling fireworks and the soft glow of the night sky. I didn't see the fireworks slowing at first, but as my laughter died down, I noticed they hung in the sky a little longer than usual. And the more peculiar it seemed, the more I realized something surreal was happening. They slowed to a complete stop. They still glimmered all around us like streamers in the night sky, but they were no longer falling. Overhead, fireworks were no longer bursting.

"What's happening?" Walker asked, looking all around him.

"I don't know!" I said, my back arched with alarm.

It was as if time had stood still for everything except us. I reached my hand out to a bright, luminescent, blue ember and cupped my hand around it. It shimmered like magic in the palm of my hand. It was warm against my hand with buzzing energy. Fascinated, I closed my hand around the ember, and when I opened it again, the ember was gone. Smothered in my tight grasp.

"Did you do this?" Walker asked.

"Did I do this?" I asked, slightly offended, as I looked for signs of the snuffed ember in my hands. But when I turned to Walker, I could see he meant no harm. His eyes were like a child filled with wonder. In fact, he meant it as a compliment. I blushed with an inkling of pride.

"It's like you stopped time . . ." he said, marveling at me instead of the sky.

And then it hit me. That's exactly what I wanted to happen. It was the moment I knew I was falling in love with him, and I never wanted it to end.

My jaw dropped, and I looked out at the millions of embers floating in the sky. I had stopped time here in Baylor. Did the clocks still tick back in reality? Did I even care?

"I did it," I said in a whisper.

Walker laughed, his dimples deeper than I'd ever seen. "Yeah, you did," he said.

"I was just thinking about how special this was. How beautiful the night sky was with the fireworks. And you laughing. I didn't want it to end," I said, feeling the warmth hit my cheeks.

Walker's gaze was intense. His eyes were smoldering, and my cheeks were burning hotter than the surrounding fire. I couldn't hold his gaze any longer, and even though I wanted to be brave and forthcoming, I looked away, embarrassed for what my heart had done without my permission.

"It's magnificent. I've never seen anything like it. You are so . . . wow," he said. My heart sang with joy but was quickly snuffed like the ember I held.

"I feel bad for you. I feel bad that you're stuck here, in my world. It's not where you belong."

"Your world?" Walker chuckled, somewhat surprised.

"Yeah, you're stuck in my dream," I said, pointing to all the glimmering streamers suspended in the air. It was a vulnerable thing, falling for someone when your feelings painted the world around you. Like I was made from glass, and everybody could see inside. No secret safe.

"That's funny because I always thought *you* were stuck in *my* world. I felt bad for *you*," he said with a smirk.

"And how do you figure I'm in your world?"

"Because, Wilde, you can see me. Nobody can see me. Or at least, they hadn't until you came around. I'm dead without you. I've been gone a long, long time. And the fact that you're here with me proves that you're in my world. You may not be a ghost, but you're in my realm," he said.

Walker let go of the paddle and rubbed his hands together.

"I don't think so." I shook my head. "I think I am in my dream realm. And you . . . you're over there, in the afterlife. Maybe we're in two separate worlds," I said, regretting the sound of it. I didn't want to be in separate worlds.

"Side by side?" he asked.

I nodded. And it hurt too much to think of the day that I might wake up without him.

"I don't know what I'm going to do without you, Wilde," he said, reaching up for a fallen ember.

"Don't say that." My throat seized like I wanted to cry.

"I remember the first time I woke up without Layla. The first time I realized I was invisible. That I had died." He snuffed the ember in his fist. "I was living out my punishment alone, and it was torture. It's been torture." He took his hat off and threw it into the boat. He ran a hand through his hair and let out the breath he'd been holding. "But pulling you out of this lake was the best night I've had in forever," he said.

"I almost drowned that night," I said with a sarcastic tone.

He chuckled. "You know what I mean. It felt like a gift had fallen from the skies. Just for me."

I found myself lost in his words. Had he really felt that way? Like I was a gift from the heavens? Like I was just for him?

"I know what you mean," I said. Thinking about how I'd never felt so comfortable with somebody before. How he completed my other half even though we were realms apart.

"God, it was so hard seeing her today. I can't tell you how much I miss her," Walker said, batting at a stream of simmering fireworks. They crumbled like dust, and my stomach turned over. He didn't feel like I came from the heavens because I was his soulmate. He just thought I was going to help him find Layla.

"Hey, Wilde? Do you think . . . do you think you could wish me away? Wish all this pain away?" he asked. His brows stitched together, both in pain and grievance.

"What do you mean? Like make you forget her?" I asked. Thinking back to the time I made Kimber and Asher get back together—or Levi and Emma. I cringed, thinking of the mistakes I'd made.

"Maybe? Do you think it would work?" He was desperate.

I felt the sickening spread of greed cross my stomach because I wanted to do it. I wanted to erase her from his heart and soul. I wanted to become his everything. And I knew I would absolutely hate myself if I did.

"I can't." I swallowed back my tears. I was standing in the way of the only love I'd ever known, but I couldn't do it. I couldn't live with a black heart.

"I didn't think so," he said, hanging his head.

"But, Walker, don't forget all of this." I motioned to the sky full of twinkling lights. It was gorgeous. They were dazzling as far as the eye could see. "Don't forget the beauty that's here, too. I might not be able to make you forget her, but there are things I *can* do," I said, not fully understanding the full depth of my talents. My power. My magic.

"Like what?" he asked. His tone was rough like gravel. Almost like he was taunting me. Pushing me. Like he wanted to play with fire. Like he had nothing left to lose. It made me nervous, like I might take his heart and relish his love, even though I knew . . . I knew it didn't belong to me.

"Well, for starters, I can make the backdrop absolutely stunning. I waved my hand, and the fireworks twinkled from reds to blues to greens. My eyes widened with surprise, as I hadn't known I could do that, but there it was right before us. I cracked a smile and looked back at Walker, but he was no longer happy. He was no longer interested in the fireworks. What he needed now was so much more. He needed to fix the hole in his heart.

"But if this is a dream and you can make things happen by just imagining them, then can you make this better? Can you make her come back to me?"

"You know, I saw my real self, lying in the hospital. When the doctor came to talk to my mom, she was crying. I held her hand. This is a dream and I know it. I know it. Here." I placed my hand over my heart. "But for whatever reason, I just lack the control to make it my own. I don't know how to do the things you ask. And all of this . . ." I waved my hand at the fireworks, "I don't know how it happened. It was just a feeling deep inside. A want. A hunger."

"You wanted to stop time that bad? Why?" he asked, considering the possibilities as he looked into my eyes.

I glanced down at my shoes and clicked my heels together nervously. He knew the reason. We both did. It didn't take a rocket scientist to see that I was falling for him. My love was gleaming all around us, and it was breathtaking.

"Because there was a feeling. Something I'd never felt before. A warmth deep in my chest. Your laugh made me happy, and I felt content." I didn't dare look at him.

"I feel that way too," he said, crossing the canoe and sitting next to me. The boat dipped, and the water rippled out. His warmth heated the side of my body, and he wrapped his arm around my shoulders. "I've never met anybody like you before, Wilde. I'm really glad we found each other," he said.

I sighed heavily. "Do you really think I could just wake up?" I asked.

"Look at what you've done here. It's nothing short of magnificent. You might not believe in yourself, but I believe in you."

"You do?" I asked, peeking up at him. He gazed into

my eyes and nodded. He was saying one thing, but I was feeling another. My heart fluttered, and I wanted to close the distance between us and kiss him.

"I think you can do anything. You just have to really want it. I don't know why, but I think you just need somebody in your corner. I know you want to get out of here, so that's not the issue. I think the problem is that you don't believe in yourself. But I believe in you." He leaned over and planted a warm kiss on my forehead. I all but melted. "And I'm going to teach you what it means to have confidence in yourself. And before you know it, this is going to be your lucid dream." He waved a hand through the air, making Baylor seem so big.

"My lucid dream?" I asked.

"Yeah. It's a dream that you control. It's a dream with awareness. You're already aware; now we just need to work on the control. You have that power. And whether or not you like it, you've got the time to build upon that strength. And I'm here to help you. Hell, if I'm stuck here for the rest of eternity, the least I can do is set you free," he said with determination.

I pondered over that. How *I* had wanted to set *him* free, just like he wanted for me. We cared about one another, that much was clear. But did I want to leave? Right when things were getting good?

"You believe in me that much?" I asked, needing to hear it just one more time.

"I do," he said. I felt his face inch lower towards mine.

A firecracker burst.

"Whoa!" he gasped, grabbing my arm.

It surprised me to see the entire lake illuminated. It was like a giant flashlight had sunk to the sandy bottom, lighting the depths from within. What once was a lake of secrets now appeared a lake of hope.

The fireworks burst overhead, and the streamers waltzed down to the glowing lake. Swans glided in and out of the sizzling firework streamers that trickled down to the water. There must've been hundreds of them. Beautiful, elegant, white swans. Their necks were sleek and their feathers pure. They glowed like floating candles in a bathtub. It stole my breath. The beauty was almost too much to take, yet I couldn't steal my eyes away.

Walker stood up, rocking the boat. "I told you! I told you, Wilde. You can do anything you set your mind to!" he said, wide-eyed and giddy.

I turned away from him, amazed to see all the swans swimming in the sacred lake. I had made all of this? It was hard to imagine that this serenity poured out of me the moment I realized I was falling in love. The moment I thought he might feel something for me in return. I wondered what else I could bring to life. What my world might be like if I had everything I ever wanted.

"Woohoo!" Walker yelled, arms outstretched and head tilted toward the fiery sky.

If Walker was right about one thing, it was that I had time to develop my strength. I watched him hoot and holler, and my dark little secret rose from the bottom of the lake to the surface. And just as the water had illuminated with my hope, it shed light on the only real problem I had here in Baylor: I might not *want* to wake up.

THANK YOU

Thank you for taking the time to read Dark Reflections. It means the world to me.

Please take a moment to write a review or give a quick star rating. It really helps me get the series out there.

Want to find out what happens next? Read Haunted Waters.

For more information, subscribe here:
    https://www.subscribepage.com/redenbooks
    Xoxo,
    Laura

ABOUT THE AUTHOR

Laura C. Reden is an emerging author of paranormal romance and dark fantasy.

Overcoming the struggles of dyslexia, Laura found that creative passion and hard work triumphs over her disadvantage.

Laura is a Southern Californian native, wife, and mother of two daughters. Her pastimes include video production, pottery, and horseback riding. While she received an education in social and behavioral science, she currently works as the chief financial officer for her family-owned law firm in San Diego.

If you are interested in staying updated on new releases, subscribe to my monthly email list. It's short and sweet with opportunities to help name characters, get advanced review copies, and even have your pet featured in upcoming scenes.

https://www.subscribepage.com/redenbooks

Xoxo,
Laura

ALSO BY

YOU'VE HEARD THE TERM «OLD SOUL» BEFORE,
BUT WHAT IF SOME SOULS NEVER REALLY DIE?

THE
TETHERED SOUL
SERIES

FOLLOW THE TRAGIC TALE OF A DYING GIRL,
AND BOY WITH AN IMMORTAL SOUL.

LAURA C. REDEN

DREAMS ARE FICKLE, EMOTIONS ARE BOLD.

THE
PHANTOM SERIES

CAUGHT BETWEEN WORLDS,
KINSLEY WILDE CAN SEE THE DEAD,
MANIFEST HER DREAMS, AND CONJURE HER FEARS.

NOTES FOR BOOK CLUB:

NOTES FOR BOOK CLUB: